PRAISE FOR VIVIAN AREND

"If you've never read a Vivian Arend book you are missing out on one of the best contemporary authors writing today."
~ *Book Reading Gals*

"The bitter cold of Alberta, Canada, is made toasty warm by the super-sexy Coleman brothers of Six Pack Ranch."
~ *Publishers Weekly*

"Brilliant, raw, imaginative, irresistible!!"
~ *Avon Romance*

"This story will keep you reading from the first page to the last one. There is never a dull moment..."
~ *Landy Jimenez*

"I definitely recommend to fans of contemporaries with hot cowboys and strong family ties.."
~ *SmexyBooks*

"This was my first Vivian Arend story, and I know I want more!"
~ *Red Hot Plus Blue Reads*

"Vivian Arend kicks off her new Heart Falls series with the emotional, heartwarming, and sensual story of a single dad hoping to make his daughter's lives better by hiring a nanny to help them as they grow and mature."
~ *Guilty Pleasures Book Reviews*

ALSO BY VIVIAN AREND

Six Pack Ranch

Rocky Mountain Heat

Rocky Mountain Haven

Rocky Mountain Desire

Rocky Mountain Rebel

Rocky Mountain Freedom

Rocky Mountain Romance

Rocky Mountain Retreat

Rocky Mountain Shelter

Rocky Mountain Devil

Rocky Mountain Home

Thompson & Sons

Ride Baby Ride

Rocky Ride

One Sexy Ride

Let It Ride

A Wild Ride

A full list of Vivian's print titles is available on her website

www.vivianarend.com

THE COWGIRL'S SECRET LOVE

THE COLEMANS OF HEART FALLS, BOOK 2

VIVIAN AREND

The Cowgirl's Secret Love
Copyright © 2020 by Arend Publishing Inc.
ISBN: 9781999495756
Edited by Anne Scott & Manuela Velasco
Cover Design © Damonza
Proofed by Angie Ramey & Linda Levy

1
____

April, five years ago. Rocky Mountain House, Alberta

After a full day attempting a job that was still well beyond her, every part of Karen Coleman's body ached. She glared at the wooden exterior of Traders Pub and debated going home.

Only there was nothing back at the ranch that would improve her mood. She brushed her hands against her jeans, cringing as the palm of her left hand connected too vigorously with the solid thigh-to-ankle cast encasing her leg.

It wasn't the reminder she needed at that moment.

Neither was the piercing whistle that rang across the parking lot. Her cousin's taunt echoed in the quiet outside the pub.

"Damn, that's pathetic. You look like something the cat dragged in."

Jesse, one of the more annoying male cousins in the horde

Karen faced almost daily, wore far too happy an expression as he jogged forward.

She was ready to cut him down to size when someone tall and muscular stepped from the shadows and intercepted Jesse.

"Watch your mouth." The dark-haired stranger folded his arms over his chest, biceps pressing against the cotton of his shirt. He eyed Jesse with disdain.

Jesse stopped in his tracks, completely thrown by the call down.

"Don't bother," the stranger said when Jesse recovered from his shock enough to open his mouth, probably to offer another wisecrack. "Keep walking."

Karen had many reasons to be cranky, not the least because her deep-seated annoyance at being below full physical strength was not going away any time soon.

But when for once in his life Jesse actually took the smart route and left with nothing more than an exaggerated eye roll, she had to admit to being slightly charmed by her well-meaning protector.

Charmed turned to something heated when her nameless defender rotated toward her.

She'd caught a glimpse of his firm jawline in profile, but the strength of his face combined very nicely with dark brown eyes that held the possibility of a dangerous smolder. He checked her over quickly, his gaze lingering on her cast and the crutches she'd finally caved and agreed to use.

It seemed only right that while he was occupied, she should return the favour.

Yes, his face was very pleasant, without any sort of fanfare. He looked the type to be silent except when he had something important to say.

She examined his mouth, amused by the solemn set of his

lips. He'd obviously thought Jesse was a lot more of a threat than the turkey truly was.

A moment's glance over the rest of her champion allowed her to admire the entire cowboy. He wasn't wearing a hat, but his boots were real, freshly polished and worn in the right pattern to be more than window dressing.

"You okay?" His voice was a soft rumble that teased her senses.

Karen's gaze shot up to meet his. Those eyes were serious, and yet a hint of a twinkle appeared momentarily. It might be fun to try and trigger other kinds of reactions in the man.

He'd come to her rescue, unneeded as it was.

"I'm good. Name's Karen." She thrust a hand forward, teetering as she fought to keep her balance and control the crutch trying to escape.

Her hero moved instantly, his firm grip sliding around her waist and bringing her back to vertical before she could tumble to the ground in an inglorious heap. "Careful. Looks as if you're still a little shaky on those colt legs of yours."

A laugh burst free. "Oh, honey, a colt is the last thing I should be compared to right now." She gave her thigh a careful pat, not hard enough to hurt. "I've seen newborns get to their feet with far more grace than I'm capable of with this contraption."

He was so close his scent wrapped around her and made interesting responses flash through her body. Ones she hadn't expected tonight, let alone while doing her best elephant limbed imitation.

Dammit, the warmth of his body teased in a million tempting ways, and Karen considered leaning in a little harder rather than moving away.

Somehow she did the right thing, finding her equilibrium

then meeting his gaze again. "Thanks for standing up for me, but Jesse didn't mean any harm."

The stranger examined her face before tilting his chin slowly. "I'm sure you could've taken care of him, but I didn't mind stepping in. It's only right."

"He's family. I guess they get to be a little more asshole-ish than your everyday stranger."

"*Chérie.*" He spoke softly. "Family should support instead of push."

That was a mouthful. In light of all the other annoying things in her world, broken leg notwithstanding, Karen didn't want to spend a lot of time thinking about family and their lack of support.

What she did want was to enjoy flirting with this intriguing man.

She offered him a smile and a bit of a raised brow. "I didn't catch your name."

His lips curled at the corners. Just enough to turn his rugged expression dangerously sexy. "Finn. Can I buy you a drink?"

Considering she'd debated going home, the idea of staying was more attractive than expected. "If you don't mind that I left my dancing shoes at home."

"We'll see about that. Drink first."

The nearest door led onto the dance floor, which was a bad idea, all things considered. The closest parking space Karen had been able to find meant she planned to walk through the noisy side of the bar and head into the quieter section to meet up with her sisters. While the Coleman clan tended to gather on Fridays at Traders Pub, there were enough of them that even though it was Tuesday, more than Lisa and Tamara were bound to be around somewhere.

Only, Finn had an agenda on this side of the pub. He

guided her to the side of the room where tall chairs were placed around high-top tables. "Let's see if I can get you comfortable."

The innuendo in his tone sent shivers along her skin. To hell with it. The only deadline she had in the morning was a meeting she wasn't looking forward to. No chores beyond the basics, so having a little fun with a stranger who would be gone by tomorrow sounded like the perfect distraction.

Finn had tucked his arm around her, their bodies close enough for them to hear each other over the music and the din of voices. Karen turned toward him, cheek brushing his. "Comfortable is not a word I'm familiar with at the moment."

He rocked slightly, heat rising. He twisted behind her, lips ghosting her earlobe as he answered, "Let's see if I can do something about that."

There was something delicious about doing this here. On her home turf, where she knew everyone except the man settling onto the chair behind her. He opened his legs wide then leaned her against his strong thigh.

"Ease back against me, *cherie*. That's it. That's got to be more comfortable than a minute ago."

He stroked her hair back over her neck. She wondered what weird magic he possessed that made her feel free to do this. Not to mention that no one from her family had come rushing forward to give her hell or ruin the moment.

Because it was a moment. She was enveloped in heat. At her back, along her side. His arm supported her, his thigh as well, and the faintest smile on his lips said he knew all too well exactly how relaxed she was.

Except for deciding how far she wanted to let this go, everything was absolutely perfect.

"What can I get you to drink?" Finn asked. A deep rumble that tickled in her ears.

"Pepsi," Karen said dryly. "With ice."

He hesitated for a moment before understanding spread across his face. "You're on painkillers."

"Bingo." She adjusted her arm to get more comfortable, which *happened* to mean sliding it around his torso. "This okay?"

"Just fine." Finn waved over one of the waitresses, ordering Karen's soda and a beer for himself.

Tiffany eyed Karen, then Finn, then Karen again.

One of the downfalls of small-town living. Everyone knew everyone.

When the girl walked off without making a comment, Karen wondered if she'd actually fallen into some sort of alternate reality. First Jesse, now Tiffany, leaving without teasing or digging for dirt?

If this was an alternate universe, how long did she get to stay?

"How bad is your leg?" Finn asked.

His hand around her waist was warm and strong and very distracting. His thumb slid back and forth along the line where her waistband ended.

Karen made a face and for once told the truth. "Pretty bad. I had a bit of a run-in with a horse trailer, which makes being hurt damn annoying as well as physical bullshit. I don't have problems with horses," she informed him briskly. Then she made a face. "Except this time. I don't blame him, it was an equipment failure, but it messed me up pretty good. I want to get back to work, but the pain's bad enough I have to take the meds."

"And then the meds mess you up more?"

"Damn annoying," she repeated.

"I get that. It's tough to not be able to do the things you're used to doing." Her T-shirt had come untucked on one side, and his thumb was now sliding against bare skin, an evilly distracting touch that made her think about other things she wasn't able to do right now.

Then again...

Their drinks appeared on the table.

Finn lifted his beer bottle in a salute, that hint of mischief dancing in the corner of his eyes. "Here's to learning new ways to have fun."

Was the man reading her mind?

Screw it. It was time to flirt and have as much fun as she decided she wanted. Or as much as her leg would allow before she had to call things off because of pain or awkwardness.

Karen offered him a wink as her glass and his bottle *clinked*. He smiled before tipping his head back, throat moving rhythmically as he drank. That hand of his stayed firmly in place on her waist. If anything, he tucked her tighter against him.

Oh, yeah, the pain in her leg was the last thing on her mind. The tingle rising *between* her legs had feature billing at the moment.

The music blaring around them changed to a soft ballad, and Finn put his glass down. "Give me that."

Her barely sipped Pepsi vanished to the high-top, and the next thing she knew, he'd tugged her a foot to the left into an open space on the dance floor.

"Oh, no, this won't work," Karen protested.

"Trust me," Finn said as he tucked her body against his.

Okay. Not at all what she'd expected tonight, but dear sweet foals in the field, this was what she'd been craving.

He held her firmly, barely swaying. Just enough motion that their bodies made contact as she balanced on her good leg. They were close in height, and her cheek rested against his, the slight scruff of his five o'clock shadow doing dangerous things to her libido.

"You're not getting much of a dance partner," Karen told him a little breathlessly.

He adjusted position, and her breasts pressed more firmly against his rock-solid chest. "Hear me complaining?"

Nope. They were so close the other changes in his body were apparent as well. It wasn't just his torso that was firm, and all things considered, the fact Finn had reacted and wasn't afraid to let her know...

It might've been the most juvenile thing ever, but knowing that in spite of the unwieldy cast someone found her attractive? It was a powerful thing.

"You in town for long, Finn?"

"Don't like to talk when I dance," he said quietly a second before his lips brushed her neck. Right where there was some sort of magical control button, because goose bumps arrived, a heat wave hit between her legs, and her nipples reacted—all at the same time.

Okay. Silence worked for her.

She wrapped her arms tighter around him, swaying to make it clear every bit of his attention was very much appreciated.

The music went on for long enough that Karen's cheeks were hot, her body was hot, and most of her annoyance had washed away in their truly delectable, somehow secretive, corner of the dance floor.

The tune changed to something far too upbeat, and she eased away reluctantly, offering what had to be a slightly stunned smile. "You're a good dancer, Finn. Even if you don't like to talk."

"I can think of better uses for my mouth." The comment fanned the flames even higher as he brought her back to the table. "You good here?"

A loud crash sounded across the room, followed by raised voices and laughter. An entire group rushed in from the opposite side of the bar, including the familiar faces of the Coleman clan. Karen's short-lived magical flirtation was about to be discovered.

But when she turned back to prepare him for the onslaught of her family, Finn was gone.

A second later her younger sisters, Lisa and Tamara, were at her table, looking her over as if she were some sort of hospital specimen.

"What're you doing over here by yourself?" Tamara demanded. "We've been waiting for you. You totally ignored our texts."

Karen had been enjoying some sort of lovely delirium and had been too busy to answer texts, which wasn't anything she was about to share.

Instead, she shrugged. "Came in the west door and didn't want to mess with manoeuvering all the way to the other side. I figured you'd show up eventually."

"I'm glad you came out for the night," Tamara said. "You need to get your mind off the fact you're out of commission for a while."

Their youngest sister, Lisa, smacked Tamara on the arm. "Brilliant way to keep her from thinking about that. You know, mentioning it and all."

"I'm only pointing out the obvious. She *needs* to be off the work list and let her leg heal." Tamara put on her medical professional face, shaking her finger at Karen. "You've got a serious break, sis. If you push it too hard, you could end up hurting yourself permanently."

"Save me the lectures," Karen told her sharply. "I'm the oldest, and not only is what you're saying old news, you don't get to boss me around."

"Nice try on that one," Lisa said with a snicker. "Birth order has nothing to do with sisters giving unwanted advice.

We all do it, me less than you two because I'm smart like that."

That comment got her pokes in the side from both Karen and Tamara, setting off giggles that had the entire area of the dance floor glancing in their direction.

No matter which way she looked, Karen spotted no signs of her mysterious knight in shining armour. Which was probably a good thing, because she hadn't planned on going much further.

The distraction had been enjoyable, though.

An hour later Tamara glanced at her watch. "I need to go. Want me to drive you home?" she asked Karen. "I have time to take you out to the ranch. Lisa can bring your car home later."

Karen hated to accept the help, but she nodded. "Don't stay up too late, or you'll regret it in the morning," she warned Lisa, who had briefly returned to their corner of the dance room after kicking up a storm with one of her buddies.

"Energy to burn," Lisa said. "Don't worry. I won't miss chores. Plus, I'll be there as support after whatever Dad throws at you."

And she would. The same way Karen knew that Tamara would do what she could. *They* were solid—three sisters who had stuck together through thick and thin, which was the only reason Karen had made it this far dealing with their father.

"It'll be okay," Tamara assured her twenty minutes later as they headed down the final long, quiet gravel road that led to Whiskey Creek. "You do need to take care of yourself for a bit, though. And I know that's hard. To think about taking some time off."

Karen chuckled, staring at the springtime fields. The first flush of growth popping up through the rich ground was barely visible in the pale moonlight. "I take off as much time as you do, Miss Work-Your-Ass-off."

"I know how to relax," Tamara insisted.

"So do I." A rush of warmth stole over her as she thought of Finn and the sensation of his strong arm around her. And a whole lot of other parts of him she wished to get to know a little better.

That kind of relaxation she could totally go for. If it were possible. If he hadn't vanished.

If she didn't have a thick cast from thigh to ankle impeding all the deliciously dirty thoughts whirling through her brain, taunting her with what she couldn't have.

Still, she didn't regret the momentary flirtation.

She said goodbye to Tamara and took off into the house where she'd grown up. The same room where she'd slept for twenty-seven years.

Throughout the house, an eerie quietness lingered, one that had been there for untold evenings since their mother had died.

Karen pushed aside the sad memories and frustrations. She ignored the thin line of light shining from under her father's door and instead concentrated on the warm fuzzies still humming in her system as she remembered the sweet interlude at the bar.

Her dreams that night were rather spectacular.

Maybe it was the painkillers as well as her fevered imagination, but the next morning it was difficult to pull herself together and head to the kitchen.

The coffee pot was cold. Karen panicked for a moment when she glanced at the old cuckoo clock on the wall. The pendulum swung slower than usual, and thankfully the time on the ancient face was nothing near the one on her watch.

Unfortunately, even her watch said she normally would have been outside thirty minutes ago.

She hurriedly pulled on a coat and a single boot. The

bottom of her cast got wrapped in a protective layer of padding followed by a garbage bag to keep out the dirt.

Swinging across the yard on her crutches at breakneck speed to where her dad always held their morning chore briefings, she took the final corner a little too fast and barely caught her balance. "Dammit."

George Coleman turned toward her, his disapproval clear. "Watch your language."

Karen held her tongue. Wasn't as if her male cousins didn't swear around the ranch all the time. But she was a *lady*. She wasn't supposed to know such words.

She stuck to apologizing for her real sin. "Sorry I'm late."

Her father grumbled something before shaking his head. "You're fine. Couple minutes early, in fact."

Which was good because after that wild dash, she needed to find a comfortable position and take the weight off her leg. Only she had to make it inconspicuous so her father had no idea exactly how much pain she was in. If he knew, no way on earth would she convince him of the line she was about to feed him.

She eased against the wall. Unbidden, the memory rose of being in a similar position the night before, leaning against a firm, masculine body.

Damn it, Finn, why'd you disappear?

Distractions shoved aside, Karen cleared her throat. "I've been thinking. I know we need some extra help around here. You mentioned getting the cousins to lend a hand. I think that's a great idea, but in the meantime, I could go to the Six Pack and Moonshine spreads and give them a hand with their horses."

George Coleman was having none of it. "Bad enough you got hurt dropping off that horse for Mike. You don't need to be messing around with new animals when you're in this condition."

Karen shrugged nonchalantly. "The accident at Uncle Mike's was a one-off. That kind of situation happens once in a blue moon, and it was less the horse's fault and more the trailer's."

Shit. Probably not a good thing to mention because she was in charge of horses, but her father was in charge of the equipment.

Sure enough, his expression folded into an even deeper frown before he shook his head vigorously. "No, I've given this a lot of thought. We need help, but none of the rest of the Coleman clan has hands to spare. So I contacted a buddy of mine."

All the air rushed from her lungs. Number one because her father had asked for assistance. But the fact he'd actually gone outside the family? "You asked someone to come and help us?"

"Yep. Richard Marlette. Met him years ago, and we've kept in touch. His spread is out in Manitoba."

Okay. The shock was beginning to ease, but Karen was still confused. Bringing in one extra man her father's age to replace *her* seemed a bit of an insult. The bigger trouble was Whiskey Creek ranch had been shorthanded for a long time, ever since Tamara left to go into nursing. *Extra* shorthanded, since her father was reluctant to let his daughters work all the tasks required for a full operation.

In the distance, a cloud of dust rose along the approach road to where they stood. A good indication someone was about to arrive at the ranch. "That him?"

Her dad turned as not one, but two, oversized crew-cab Fords pulled into the yard. "One step better. Richard said he's in transition. Doing some shift over which means letting sections of land lie fallow, so his sons are at loose ends for the summer." George Coleman glanced over his shoulder, pride in his expression as he dipped his chin firmly. "The Marlette boys will help take care of things for us."

Karen already didn't like them, these Manitoba intruders on her land. Some wet-behind-the-ears kids who, just because they were male, were already considered bigger assets than she and her sisters.

She somehow kept from growling. "I can't believe you didn't talk to me about this, Dad."

"Nothing to talk about."

Anger crashed in her gut as truck doors swung open, and well-worn boots and jeans and cowboy hats appeared. A moment later, three men—not *boys*—were walking toward them with a lazy cowboy saunter.

Karen only saw one face—

Finn.

Her flirtatious fantasy man from the previous night was front and center. He stopped before her father and held out his hand.

"Finn Marlette. Good to meet you, sir."

"George Coleman. Glad it worked for you boys to come on out."

Even as he greeted George, Finn's gaze drifted to Karen. "We'll do what we can to make this a memorable summer."

Dear God, she wasn't going to survive.

2

June. Present day, Heart Falls, Alberta

nticipation rose as Finn Marlette slipped on his boots.

"Sure you don't want backup?" His best friend, Zach Sorenson, sat in one of the only two functioning chairs they had in the dilapidated ranch house kitchen. The brown-haired man leaned back, balancing the chair on two legs like a teenage boy instead of the thirty-three-year old he was. A wide grin split his face and laughter danced in his blue eyes. "I could come along to make sure Karen doesn't kill you then hide your body somewhere in the back forty."

"Dramatic, much?" Finn drawled as he put his hat in place.

Zach swung forward, the legs of the chair hitting the unfinished wooden floor with a loud clatter. "Okay, I'll admit it. I'm curious as hell how you plan to swing this. It's been years, yet you seem to think she'll let you waltz in and start romancing her."

"Worked the first time," Finn said dryly. He pointed at his friend. "Stay."

"Promise you'll tell me everything," Zach teased before offering a wink as he rose to his feet. "Okay, I'll stop being an ass. I *am* interested to see how this plays out, but you know I only want the best for you. And for her, because with all the plans I've got in Heart Falls, if you make enemies of the Stone family or any of Karen's other relatives, you'll really screw things up for me."

Finn knew most of that last part was bullshit. Still, he appreciated Zach lightening the mood more than he was willing to admit. "I'll try not to cause anybody to come after us with pitchforks and torches."

Zach rubbed his hands together. "That's all I can ask. Go for it. Break a leg."

Dear God.

Finn ignored the snorts of amusement drifting from his friend and headed out the door.

It was a glorious day to be on the Alberta foothills. The land he'd bought north of the small town of Heart Falls had a bit of a mess when it came to buildings, but the landscape was amazing.

The rolling hills spread around him and extended to the west, rising higher and higher until they blended into the feet of the Rocky Mountains. The distant peaks were still snowclad, but the rest of the terrain was bright green with spring's rich tones. These early days of June were beautiful as the brown of winter transformed to glorious verdant summer.

He took a slightly longer path than necessary from the disreputable ranch house where he and Zach were now bunking. He wandered along a trail over the peak of the hillside, pausing to pick some of the spring wildflowers poking their heads through the tall grass.

Coming to Heart Falls was part of a plan, and the small building ahead of him was where the next part of that plan would take place.

He and Karen Coleman had unfinished business.

Finn felt a bit of regret, but also anticipation, as he made his way toward the small cottage tucked into a wind-protected dip in the landscape.

Karen had needed a place to stay, and it had made perfect sense to offer her the furnished building. Having her close would give them a chance to get reacquainted even as she spent time visiting her sisters in Heart Falls.

It'd been five years since he first laid eyes on her, and he found his feet moving quicker as the front porch came into view.

Four and half years that they hadn't spent together, some of that because he hadn't been smart enough to see there was more than one solution to their problem.

He'd gotten better at problem-solving. Thirty-five years old, and finally getting his act together in this area.

It was time to let Karen know they had options, and he would do whatever it took to make sure this summer didn't end like the last one they'd shared.

Humbled by how hard his heart pounded as he stepped onto the porch, Finn gave a firm knock and pretended he wasn't nervous.

Somewhere behind him, the grass rustled, and he twisted to make sure he wasn't about to get pounced on by one of the feral cats he'd discovered running wild all over the place.

Two glittering green eyes shined at him through the tall, dry grass. A mama cat, keeping a close eye on him, still unsure if he was trouble or not.

Then the door swung open and a familiar voice slipped around him like a caress. "Hey, what's up?"

Damn. He'd seen Karen at a distance a few times over the past months. Seen pictures of her around the Stone homestead on a friend's phone. Seen her in his dreams every night.

Nothing beat the real thing.

His gaze drifted down briefly, amusement flashing as he realized she was wearing Daisy Duke shorts that showcased her limbs. A far cry from the first time they'd met when she had that enormous cast covering one of her gorgeous legs.

All that passed in an instant because it was her face he was intent on. Her eyes, the deep brown pools he'd spent hours staring into. Her lips that were slightly open in shock but so red and delicious he could damn near taste her.

Instead of doing what he wanted, which was to kiss the living daylights out of her, he held forward the wildflowers. "Welcome to Heart Falls."

A second passed—maybe three, while shock lingered—before her eyes flashed and she stepped back.

The door slammed in his face.

Laughter threatened to burst free, but he hesitated in silence to make sure he wasn't mistaken.

The very clear sound of a window opening echoed across the quiet morning air, and that's when Finn let his grin rise.

Clever woman. Beautiful, wonderful, *clever* woman.

He trotted around to where the back porch faced to the west. The window off the dining area was open, but so was the sliding glass on the porch door. He took the easy route this time, stepping up to the doorway and easing back the screen.

Karen stood in the teeny kitchen area with her arms crossed over her chest. Dark brown hair hung over her shoulders, loose and sexy. Her chin was high, and her expression was anything but welcoming.

But she'd let him in. She'd opened a window and unlocked

the door, the same way she had all those summers ago. Finn would take that as a good sign.

He paused. "Permission to enter?"

Karen let out a muffled growl. "Should have made you climb in the window, but yes. Now that you're standing outside my door, I suppose there's no use pretending you're not around."

"Is that what you've been doing?" Finn stepped in, stopping with his boots on the welcome mat just inside the door.

He knew better than to go walking across a ranchwoman's floor with his outdoor boots on. But he wasn't sure he'd be staying for long enough to take them off.

Karen rolled her eyes and gestured toward the living space. "Come all the way in. It's not as if you're a vampire and need permission to cross my threshold."

He used the bootjack tucked against the sidewall, placing his boots carefully aside before stepping toward her, the rough bouquet outstretched again. "Nope. Not a vampire, but a real life, flesh and blood cowboy hoping to make a good impression on a certain cowgirl. That means minding my manners."

Karen rummaged through the cupboards. She found a plastic pitcher, filling it with water before taking the flowers from him. She carried the bouquet into the small living space and put it on the coffee table.

Then she deliberately sat in one of the single-seat armchairs on the far side from where he stood. All of it without saying a single word, just turning her attention on him when she was ready, her gaze firm and noncommittal.

Finn joined her, settling in the middle of the couch opposite her. He had expected it wouldn't be easy—not at first, anyway—but it would be worth it.

He just had to out-silence her to begin with.

Which gave him time to look her over, and it was time well spent. That initial flash had been like glimpsing a sweet memory. The thorough examination was about appreciating changes.

She was older, obviously, yet three years younger than him at thirty-two. Her long hair was loose for once, lying over her shoulders to midway down her chest. Her curves were pronounced, the buttons of the flannel shirt undone far enough to reveal the edge of one of the sexy camisoles she liked wearing.

Contrast. Karen had always been about the contrast. Rugged jeans and working boots with silky camisoles and brightly painted toes.

Tough as nails as she'd fought to work in the fields, even with her broken leg. Soft inside, caring too much about what other people thought.

There was a bit of tightness in her eyes, and a sense of wariness around her that was understandable, all things considered.

He leaned forward, elbows on his knees and hands clasped. "How do you like the place? Got everything you need?"

She opened her mouth to respond, but then her jaw dropped.

What followed was one of those exasperated glances. The ones that all the Whiskey Creek women were really good at delivering. "Let me guess. You own this place."

No use in denying it. "I own the cottage, the main house, the outbuildings, and about five thousand acres between Heart Falls and the edge of the wilderness reserve to the west."

"Excuse me while I make a note to kill my sister the next time I see her. Her and her conniving boyfriend, Josiah."

Finn shrugged. "Well, my buddy Zach just reminded me

we've got enough land to hide the bodies if you really think that's the best way to deal with this. I've got a backhoe as well, if that will help."

He got a snicker for that comment, and some of the tension left her as she leaned back in her chair and lifted the footrest. She eyed him as intently as he'd examined her earlier.

Karen shook her head. "I've been had, but I can't say I'm too annoyed. I wanted a place to stay for four months, and the fact that you own it is not the worst thing in the world. But I really hoped you'd gotten that out of your system. The whole bit about not telling me what your plans are or *who* you are. It was annoying enough the first time we met."

He offered a head tilt but didn't say anything.

They stared at each other for a moment, eyes connected as memories flashed through Finn's brain.

They'd had good times, but they'd also had misunderstandings, and while he'd pulled some strings to get them to where they were, here and now, maybe laying all his cards on the table was the best idea.

At least then she couldn't claim she'd been caught unaware.

"You're right. You need to know my plans. Got more than one—"

"Imagine that," Karen said with a bite.

This time he did chuckle but carried on. "First on my list was a place for you to stay. A home base so you can enjoy time with your sisters and your new nephew."

Karen dipped her chin slowly. "Not sure why that was on *your* list, but thank you. This place is exactly what I need. No matter how twisted it is that you're the one providing it, I'm not about to turn down the offer."

"The second thing on my current to-do list is to get this place up and running as soon as possible."

This time she lost it. The controlled expression vanished

into one of distrust and confusion. "This place? What's it going to be, and why aren't you out east in Manitoba running your family's spread?"

It wasn't time to talk about that issue yet, so Finn pushed down the anger that even thinking about his family home generated and focused on the most important part. "That's a long story. Levi is running the Marlette homestead, and I'll explain more later, but here and now, I bought this place to turn it into a dude ranch."

This time her mouth hung open for a good ten seconds. "Get out."

He raised a hand in the air. "Honest."

Her expression was back to slightly amused. "Really. I hope you've got good people working with you, because, buttercup? Just being honest, you don't have the charisma to pull off the 'hey, city folks, of course I'm happy to help you ride these doggies, yeehaw and yippee-ki-yay' gig without someone ending up pissed at you."

Finn raised a brow. He was, however, charmed that she'd slipped and called him by the old nickname she'd teased him with.

She adjusted position to match him, her arms crossed and elbows on her thighs as she examined Finn intently. "All right, for the sake of brevity, let's pretend I totally believe you on the running a dude ranch BS. What's the next part of your unending plan?"

"Finish what we started, only the right way."

He was jerking her around emotionally, and he knew it. Yet it was the only way to be upfront and honest.

Karen took a deep breath, focusing on the floor before she lifted her eyes to his and spoke with a great intensity. "We did finish what we started, Finn. When you came to Whiskey Creek ranch and we discovered there was something between us, we said it was a fling. Nothing else. One and done for the summer, and that's what we did. September came. You went back to Manitoba, and I stayed in Rocky Mountain House, and that was it."

"But it shouldn't have been the end," Finn insisted.

"You lived two provinces away. You had work to do. I had work to do, and that was just the way it was."

Exasperation rolled for a moment before he decided to take a different tack. "Okay, fine. It was the end—of that summer. But, *ma chérie*, this is another summer. We're here in a new place, with new plans. So, I've got a couple propositions for you."

KAREN COLEMAN WAS DOING her best human imitation of a yo-yo ever. One moment up, unable to hide her amusement because Finn knew exactly how to poke her funny bone. Then he'd turned and tossed a grenade in front of her, and damn if she didn't want to—

That was the problem. She didn't know *what* she wanted or didn't want at that point. Her thoughts whirled in confusion.

No, wait.

There was one thing that she *was* positive on. She had to keep Finn Marlette from finding out how much it had hurt when their summer fling had ended.

Because as much fun as it had been, she'd made a mistake, and her heart had gotten involved.

She focused on the man across from her, who had the ability to make her body sing with pleasure—or at least he had years ago. She doubted that was a skill set he'd let get rusty, damn him anyway.

Instead of running and hiding, though, Karen braced

herself and pushed forward. "What are these propositions, Finn? Don't beat around the bush."

"I want you to help me get things prepped for the dude ranch. The areas where you're an expert, like purchasing horses and helping hire the stock crew. I know you're here for four months before you take off for school. I doubt we'll be fully operational by the fall, so I don't expect you to have everything in place. But I'd like to hire you to do what you can."

She had not seen that one coming. "Okay. I'll have to think about it for a little bit because I already made some commitments for my time here."

"Working at the grocery store is not really your forte," Finn drawled.

"Stalking me?" Karen inquired even as she shook her head. "Forget I said that. I get it. Small town. You probably asked two questions and got all the information you needed."

"I've been living with Josiah Ryder since March," Finn confessed. "I pretty much know everything that's been going on in the Heart Falls area."

She was so killing her sister. *Sisters*, because Lisa was now living with Josiah, but there was no way Tamara wasn't in on the news as well.

The only one who would maybe get away without a tongue-lashing was their newly discovered youngest sister, Julia.

"You are a sneaky devil, aren't you?" Karen said.

"Only because I had a reason. I wanted to buy this place, and I needed time."

Right. Seemed fair enough. "Give me your number, and I'll call tomorrow about working for you, June to September."

"Number's the same as it's always been. You know that."

Yeah, she supposed she did. Had stared at it enough times over the years, to boot.

He rose and closed the short distance between them, grasping her hand and pulling her to vertical. "The other thing I want? While you're here—we pick up where we left off."

Heart pounding. Throat tightening. "*Finn.*"

He stared at her with that intense look that sent shivers over her. "We had something special, and it didn't finish the way it should've. I think we should try again, and this time we change it up just enough to give us a real shot."

Dear God, temptation was being handed to her on a silver platter.

But she was finally getting to spread her wings. Not to mention, how would she bear it if after four months of spending time with this man he turned around and walked away, and so did she?

Having him leave her a second time just might put her six feet under.

"All the reasons we had before for not being together permanently—none of that has changed, Finn. If anything, it's gotten more complicated." Karen had to explain, maybe a little to herself as well. "I'm only here for a short time to visit with my family before I head to school. I'm doing something that's important to me, plus it's the first time in my life I get to experience a world outside of Whiskey Creek and the Coleman spread."

"We spend the summer together here, and at the end of it, if you want to go to school, then you go. It doesn't mean we can't be together." His grip on her fingers was gentle enough she could pull away if she wanted to, but tight enough to make it clear he didn't want to let her go. "I'm not who I was five years ago, *chérie.* We have more options, but first we need to get on firm footing."

"And what does that look like? Do we start another fling?

Fooling around in corners of the barn again and you crawling in my bedroom window?"

His lips curled upward. "While I'm very willing to crawl in your bedroom window, the hiding part needs to change. We do this the right way. We spend the summer together, but it's not going to be secret. It will be you and me out there, giving the world hell and doing everything we want. Everything that makes you happy—because you're right. You've had a rough time of it, and you deserve to spread your wings. I'm all for helping you. But not in the dark." He lowered his tone a notch, the words coming out a deep rumble that caressed her skin. "Except when you want it dark."

Dear God. This wasn't just temptation; this was temptation wrapped in shiny paper with a Godiva chocolate on top, waiting for her to take a bite.

So she did the only thing she could. Karen pulled her hand free, planted her palms on his shoulders, and turned him on the spot. "Go home, Finn. I'll call you tomorrow."

He walked toward his boots with less complaining than she'd expected. It was only after he'd pulled them on and adjusted his hat that he looked her up and down. "Call me early. I want to get started as soon as possible."

"Cocky bastard," Karen called after him as he slipped out the porch door and disappeared without a backward glance.

She followed onto the wooden decking, watching his strong body as he paced into the distance.

What a wild, mixed-up situation.

It only took a couple minutes to grab a glass of juice and position a chair toward the rolling hills in the hopes that from somewhere out there, wisdom would come fluttering toward her.

A few butterflies did, maybe, but wisdom seemed to be

hiding, because Karen was far too tempted to accept Finn's proposition.

It would be a terrible mistake. Broken heart? She'd survived it once, but enough jagged edges remained that stabbed deep at the most inopportune moments.

Was it worth getting tangled up with the man who was her personal addiction when she had a time limit on staying here? What's more, at least at this point, unless something major had changed in Finn Marlette's life recently, she doubted he planned to stay in Heart Falls for any longer than it took to make a success of his latest venture.

She wanted her education, true, but more than that? She wanted to set roots. Deep and firm, established in family and friends. She couldn't do that with a man who had *temporary* written on the soles of his boots.

The sun moved slowly. Nothing but a few wispy clouds drifted through a blue sky toward the distant mountains. It was beautiful and peaceful and exactly what she needed to make a decision.

She raised her nearly empty glass toward the fields. "I'm here for my family. I'm here to find *me*, and that means I don't have time for a fling. This is the summer of celibacy. More importantly, it means I concentrate on the task at hand."

The first of which required getting together with her sisters, and not when there was a horde of others around. Because it was not the time for group discussion; it was time for a gathering of the Whiskey Creek Coleman women where the oldest of them—namely her—explained exactly how this worked.

Aka, Karen was going to lay down the law and make sure everyone knew exactly where her priorities were. That there would be zero tolerance of any further messing with her personal life.

She pulled out her phone and sent a couple of text messages to arrange an afternoon meeting of the minds.

3

I wasn't trying to be mysterious when we met at Traders, but honest to God, I was more distracted than I want to admit. Your attitude is sexy as hell.

Please accept this flower as a peace offering. Look forward to getting to know you better this summer.

~Note from Finn to Karen, found on her second-storey windowsill the morning after he started work at Whiskey Creek ranch~

~

His visit with Karen hadn't been long enough. While Finn was disappointed she hadn't immediately jumped to accept his plan, asking for a little time was reasonable.

He'd also figured her answer to them getting back together would be no, probably for at least a couple of weeks.

That was pretty much what had happened five years ago. Back then they'd been determined to go as slowly as possible until the fire between them had ignited and become impossible to ignore.

Still, to anyone looking on, he'd pretty much blown it. Finn was tempted to take the long route back to the ranch house. Maybe if he walked slow enough, Zach would have found something new to entertain himself and left the house.

No such luck. Not only was the bastard still hanging around, another visitor had joined him in the kitchen.

Josiah Ryder, local veterinarian and, until recently, Finn's landlord and roommate, glanced up. A mess of paperwork was spread over the surface of the roughhewn table, and he and Zach had been poking through the pile.

"I don't see any missing limbs or severed arteries," Josiah offered cheerily.

"Did you really assume a positive feminine response from the lack of mutilated appendages?" Zach asked dryly. "If I didn't know you managed to land a woman, I'd be worried about your dating techniques."

"Hey, I'm just being hopeful here for our man Finn."

Finn sauntered to the table and glanced at the papers, discovering blueprints, timelines, and shopping lists all mixed together. "We need to get going on the accommodations sooner than later. Plus, someone needs to overhaul this main house layout because the kitchen and dining area need to feel homey yet still meet health and safety standards. Right now it's a pit."

Zach folded his arms over his chest and nodded slowly as if taking in every single word. Then he dashed Finn's hopes that they had moved on to the next topic. "Struck out, didn't you?"

Josiah checked his watch. "How long was he there?"

"Twenty minutes, max."

A soft whistle escaped Josiah. "Struck out, magnificently."

"Jackasses," Finn muttered. "She's thinking about it."

Two identical expressions stared back. One brow raised in speculation, lips twisted into a smirk. Then Josiah and Zach turned toward each other and completely ignored Finn as they carried on their conversation.

"Thinking about it isn't a no," Josiah pointed out.

"How long does she get to think before it's a no? Is this an open-ended thing where she gets to hit *start* anytime she wants?" Zach asked.

Josiah considered for a moment. "That's kind of how women work, Zach. The last time I looked, I wasn't calling the shots in my relationship with Lisa. Not when it came to where we go, *when* we go, or what we do."

"If you two are finished, I do have an update." Finn waited until his friends turned back to face him, smirks and all. "One thing I'm sure Karen will say yes to in the morning will be helping to prep this place. Horse purchases and livestock staffing."

Zach swore softly. "You offered her a *job*? I mean, not that she won't be brilliant at it, but when she says no to dating you, won't that make things a little complicated?"

"If she says yes to dating you, that's gonna make things even more complicated," Josiah pointed out.

"Not really. Zach, you're foreman on the project, so you'd be her boss. Contract work. Means she'll have a lot of autonomy. You plan to second-guess any of the purchases she makes for this place?"

"Of course not." His friend shrugged. "Would've been nice to have talked about this before, but it's a good twist. I approve."

"Thanks." The word dripped with sarcasm.

Then Zach lit up. He smacked a hand on Finn's shoulder. "In other news, I tracked down contacts at those restoration sites you mentioned. Got leads on at least a dozen old barns within the radius you were hoping for. You'll have to work your magic to purchase them for a decent price, but when you do, I know exactly who to bring in to make them into the best guesthouses any dude ranch ever had."

Which is why at the end of the day, when the bullshitting was done, Finn appreciated Zach so much.

They both brought skills to the business they'd been building ever since Finn officially left the homestead where he grew up. Zach had the magic touch when it came to tracking down one-of-a-kind items and the eye to choose the perfect spot for new businesses. He also had freaky good timing.

Finn knew how to work the numbers.

While they'd both had some good luck at key moments, like falling in with their mentor, Bruce Travers, they'd worked damn hard as well, and that's what had made them successful in the end.

Finn gave Zach an approving nod. "Knew I could count on you."

"Of course you can, because I'm so count-on-able." Zach turned to the other man in the room. "So, the spaces I pointed out for the horses. Approval from the veterinarian, or do we need to make changes?"

"Looks good on paper. I want to see a few more measurements for your main barn. Also, if you can double the size of the arena now, you'll appreciate it down the road." Josiah pulled some of the papers forward, and he and Zach fell into a discussion that Finn only partially listened to.

He'd come to Heart Falls with one real goal—to get back together with Karen.

Making a success of the dude ranch was important in a totally different way. Business achievements were a way of keeping track of the progress in one's life. It was too easy to get stuck in one spot. To watch life pass by as you did the same old thing, time and again.

Finn's mentor, Bruce Travers, had been all about attempting the new and reaching beyond what was possible before. It was part of the reason he'd taken Finn and Zach on as apprentices.

He'd changed their lives in ways they could never have imagined.

Being in Heart Falls with enough money in his pocket to make dreams come true was very much a legacy Finn had received from the man. But the true gift wasn't the cash. It was the sense of adventure and the striving for freshness. Those were newer attitudes Finn never wanted to lose.

He pulled out his phone, intending to check his emails, but his screensaver distracted him, pulling him into the stash of photos he'd gathered of Karen.

The ones Karen had posed for five years ago once they'd agreed to let the passion between them flare.

He found himself staring at her face again, a confident woman on horseback. Her hands rested easily on the saddle horn as she stared at him with a bright smile on her face, cool self-assurance shining through in the way she sat.

If he remembered correctly, that horse had been a hellion, yet for her the beast had all but purred. That was one of the many things he admired about her.

"Finn."

He glanced up, tucking his phone into his back pocket. "What?"

Once again, the two men before him exchanged amused glances before Zach shrugged. "It's so much fun to see you besotted. I wanted to remind you we've got a meeting at the bank in an hour. If you want to go now, we can grab lunch beforehand."

Finn had no idea what his friend was talking about. "Who the fuck uses a word like besotted these days? And why are we meeting at the bank?"

A long-suffering sigh drifted from Zach. "Because I'm purchasing the old Brewster building on Main Street."

Finn thought it over. Still made no sense. "Why do we need to go to a bank for that?"

"Because *I'm* buying it. You're my backup collateral to organize the loan."

"Well, that's a waste of time. There's more than enough money in the corporation. Buy it out of there," Finn said distractedly.

"Nope. I'm buying this one with my own money."

"I'm with Zach on this one," Josiah offered.

Okay, that was weird. "Since when did you start to develop opinions about how we spend our money?" Finn demanded of the veterinarian.

Josiah shrugged. "Since we got drunk the other night and had a deep heart-to-heart about how having all the money in the world doesn't mean a thing without the women we love. And since Zach is still looking for his one and only, we should at least let him enjoy the daily struggles of paying a mortgage without the backing of a fat bankroll."

This conversation got weirder and weirder. Finn gave Josiah a dirty look. "Number one, we did not get drunk the other night, and we didn't have a deep heart-to-heart. Fairly certain I've never used the words 'woman I love' in any recent conversation. But if Zach wants to offer up his classic cruiser as collateral for that rotting eyesore in the middle of town, I'm okay with it."

"Hey. I never said a word about Delilah being involved in this deal," Zach protested.

"The 1955, powder-blue corvette convertible he rebuilt,"

Finn told a curious Josiah. "Zero to sixty in eleven point two, and I've only been allowed to drive her once."

"And you tricked me into that time," Zach informed him staunchly. "She is *not* my collateral."

This might actually be fun. Zach had provided the perfect distraction for Finn in the way only best friends who'd been together forever could. "Good luck at the bank without me."

A furl creased between Zach's brows. "You're a bastard, and you don't actually get to drive her unless I fail on my loan."

"I'm a one-woman man," Finn said in all seriousness. "Delilah is safe unless you screw up. Although, if you do screw up, I'll let Josiah have her."

Shock raced across Josiah's face. "What? Don't get me involved in this."

"I couldn't take his car and then drive it. That would be too much like gloating. This way, like a true best friend, I will sit with him and feed him whiskey while he curses your name."

A burst of laughter broke free from Zach, followed quickly by one from Josiah.

The vet shook his head. "You two are impossible. You're also both invited to dinner on Saturday night. Lisa wants to do something with a bunch of her friends and needs guys to balance the numbers. Show up. Six o'clock. And dear Lord—I can't believe I'm saying this—you are instructed to wear sandals."

After a day filled with interesting twists, Finn wasn't sure where that one came from. "Thank God it's June. I would guess we're having a pool party, but you don't have a pool."

"We're having a spa day?" Zach guessed. "I don't think that's gonna fly."

"I have no idea, and that's the truth." Josiah made a horrified face. "I never should've introduced her to drama and my acting past, because Lisa gets these ideas in her head that are pretty banana cakes."

It was entertaining, but Finn could reassure his friend on this one. "Trust me, it wasn't you who led her astray. She's always been creative. The summer we lived at Whiskey Creek, she and my youngest brother got up to all sorts of wild shit."

A solid thump echoed—Zach's fist meeting Finn's chest. "Dude. Do not talk about the young lady's past to her current squeeze."

Shit. "Nothing like that. The two of them were like twelve-year-olds overdosed on orange crush and Twizzlers. We caught them painting a mural on the side of the barn with paintball guns once. That girl has got more imagination than is healthy."

"She's got just the right amount of imagination, and she's all mine." Josiah looked decidedly content after sharing that definitive statement. "I'll see you two on Saturday. Give me a shout if you need anything sooner."

Zach managed to restrain himself until the door closed before turning to Finn, his concern written on his expression. "Are you okay? Are you sure you know what you're doing with Karen? Do we really have to wear sandals to a party, and is that even legal on a ranch in Alberta?"

"I'm fine. Karen is fine. And I have no idea what the hell Lisa's up to, but it will be entertaining to find out."

WITH BEAUTIFUL JUNE weather pouring through the open window of her truck, Karen had herself in a far better mood than she'd expected by the time she arrived at her sister Tamara's house.

The yard outside the Silver Stone ranch house held a collection of vehicles, as usual. Some from the coming and going of the active ranch, but the three she was particularly interested in sat side by side, wildly different.

Tamara was now driving the mom mobile. With two adopted daughters, one nine and one eleven, and her newborn son who was all of two months old, the sister closest in age to Karen had given up her truck and chosen convenience for hauling her family around.

Her younger sister, Lisa, was still driving her beat-up old truck, an ancient hand-me-down that went through a mess of cousins before she got it. Karen was surprised Lisa's boyfriend hadn't insisted on her getting an upgrade. But then again, at twenty-seven now, Lisa was nearly as obstinate as Karen, so convincing her to do anything she didn't want was an unlikely scenario.

The third vehicle was the one that made Karen still for a moment and take stock of her new reality. She didn't have two younger sisters, she had *three*.

Julia Blushing might have come into their lives out of the blue only a few months ago, but she was most definitely a Whiskey Creek Coleman at heart. At least where it came to the stubbornness—the twenty-five-year-old EMT was now driving a teeny hybrid vehicle that didn't look as if it could handle the highways around Heart Falls, let alone the back roads.

Karen parked her own well-used Chevy in an open space then headed for the back porch.

Music and laughter greeted her as she pulled open the door. A moment later, three heads pivoted, identical dark brown eyes set in similar faces. Only Tamara's glasses—pink today—and their hairstyles set the three of them apart. Tamara had her hair pulled back in a ponytail. Lisa wore hers in two braids as if she were sixteen.

Julia's deeper reddish-toned hair lay around her shoulders in a riot of curls that hadn't been there a couple days ago.

Karen took her boots off in the mud room and hung up her coat even as she joined in the conversation. "Hey, guys. Julia, your hair is amazing."

"Thanks." Julia swooped the mass up to the top of her head and offered a sultry look with an exaggerated pout. A second later she burst out laughing and let it fall. "I'm afraid that's as dramatic as I get."

"It does look good," Tamara said. "It also means we aren't identical quadruplets anymore. That should make it a little easier for the poor people in town who insist they've seen me out and about without Tyler and ask when I got back into the medical profession."

Lisa looked thoughtful. "It's funny. In Rocky Mountain House, the cousins used to always complain how everyone thought they were interchangeable. If you spotted one Coleman, it didn't matter what you called him, he'd answer. And then be expected to pass on a message to whichever of them you really did want."

"One of the curses of a big family," Tamara said. "It didn't happen to us because even though we look similar, Karen would've had to have been dead to be spotted in the hospital."

It was too easy to roll her eyes. Karen slipped onto the high stool next to Julia. "You remember what I said? About only believing half the bullshit they tell you?"

"Hey," Lisa complained.

"Don't worry. I was leaning toward twenty percent, max." Julia winked then picked up her coffee cup. "I will admit it's been mostly fun figuring out this family thing. A little scary, but you guys make it moderately easy." She hesitated. "So, thanks."

A chorus of *awwwws* rose from the rest of them. Karen tucked an arm around Julia and gave her a squeeze. "I'm glad you feel that way. Although you might want to cover your ears for the next little bit, because another part of being family is giving each other hell when it's deserved."

Julia's eyes widened, her lips squeezing tight.

She wasn't the one Karen focused on, though. She turned her gaze on the other two troublemakers.

Tamara looked inquisitive. Lisa looked bored.

Which was all the hint Karen needed. She stared Lisa down. "Bingo. I know exactly who to shout at."

A firm *woof* sounded from the floor, and everybody's attention dropped to the small terrier hovering at Lisa's feet. The cream-coloured dog seemed more like a rat to Karen than an actual canine, but Ollie was one hundred percent dedicated to Lisa.

At the moment, the beast seemed intent on warning Karen off from doing anything to *her* people.

Oh, hell no. Karen spoke firmly to the dog. "You. *Hush.* Sit."

Ollie instantly settled on her butt but kept her gaze fixed on Karen, head slowly tilting to one side as if trying to distract the big, bad human from her mission.

Good grief. "I have no idea how you trained that creature, but puppy-dog eyes or not, you're still in trouble." Karen pointed at Lisa. "Finn Marlette. Start talking."

Tamara snickered then wiped a hand over her mouth as she patted Tyler's butt with the other. He wiggled in her chest carrier.

Karen shifted her finger to point in a new direction. "You're next on the hit list. Both of you knew he was in town. Why didn't you say something?"

"Because there was no reason to tell you at first," Lisa said. She lifted one brow high. "Are you seriously telling me you never heard a word about him being around?"

Tamara leaned forward toward Julia, who was obviously at

a loss. "Finn and his two brothers came to Whiskey Creek ranch a number of years ago to help out. Something intriguing went on between Finn and Karen during that time that they managed to keep all of us from finding out about until recently." She glanced at Lisa.

"Could have knocked me over with a feather." Lisa laid a hand over her chest with dramatic flair. Then she leaned forward as well, speaking softer as if Karen weren't right there listening to the whole thing. "Obviously secret shenanigans were taking place. And so, when one part of the shenanigarians decided he wanted to move to our fair town and then began asking questions about the other part of the shenanigarian duo, it piqued our interest."

Julia frowned. She turned to Karen. "We'll just push aside the fact that Lisa makes up strange words way too easily. Is this Finn guy creeping on you? Because if he is, I will put a stop to it like, yesterday."

A rush of emotion shot upward, and Karen threw caution to the wind. She wrapped her arms around her newfound sister and squeezed tight. "I like you. You're good people."

Julia patted her on the back. "Thanks. But I mean it."

Karen let her go and stared at Lisa and Tamara, who were watching closely. "You guys are turkeys. And you're both kind of assholes for not warning me, but no" —Karen faced Julia— "he's not a stalker. It's just really complicated, and as much as I love my sisters, they like to meddle."

"We learned from the best." Lisa leaned against the counter and folded her arms over her chest. "I'm sorry if Finn being around makes things tough. That wasn't our intention."

"What was your intention?" Karen asked. "Because right now I'm living in his house, and he offered me a job, *and* he says he wants to get back together. A whole bunch of decisions and situations I was not expecting when I made the move here. This was supposed to be four months to spend time with you guys and with Tyler and my nieces. And maybe go for horseback rides and daydream about the future."

"You're living in his house?" Julia blinked. "Huh."

"He offered you a job? That's unexpected." Lisa glanced at Ollie, who offered a sympathetic *woof*.

But it was Tamara who caught Karen's eye, her sister who had discovered how deep some of Karen's frustrations had gone and had always found time to listen. "He wants to get back together?"

It was the part Karen didn't want to discuss, even while she was longing to.

Quiet hovered for a moment before Lisa spoke. "What do you want?"

A snort escaped. "About which part?"

"I don't think living in his house is a big deal. You've got the place to yourself, and it's private. That's why I didn't say anything when Lisa and Josiah brought it up. But if it bothers you, we have room here, or you can move into one of the bunkhouses," Tamara offered. "I do want you to be comfortable. More than that, I want you to have a good time while you're visiting."

"It's not a big deal," Karen admitted. She offered Lisa a glare. "I still don't appreciate you pulling a fast one. 'We know someone who needs a body in their cottage. They'd really appreciate it...' Bah, humbug."

Lisa held her hand in the air. "I solemnly swear to think a little harder before I do anything tricky to you in the future."

"Or to me," Julia popped in, laying a hand on Karen's arm for a moment. "Sorry for butting in, but I thought this might be a good opportunity to strike while the iron was hot. No messing in my life, either. This sister thing is new, and parts of it are cool, but..." She pointed a finger back and forth between Karen and Lisa. "Meddling isn't what I signed on for, okay?"

Baby Tyler woke, his cry ringing across the kitchen. Tamara moved easily to untangle him and start nursing. "There you go, Lisa. Julia's already got your number."

"You guys spoil all my fun," Lisa said with a mock pout. She nodded agreement. "I promise to be nice, even though this is the first time in my life I've ever had a little sister to tease."

"What about the job?" Julia turned the question to Karen. "Did you want to work while you were here?"

"What does he want you to do?" Tamara asked.

"Help him prep his dude ranch. The animal side of things, that is," Karen confessed.

Julia's eyes lit up.

"Say yes." She popped a hand over her mouth briefly before apologizing. "Oops. It's just that I grew up on a dude ranch, and they are all kinds of wonderful if they're done right. That's really where I would love to work someday."

"I'd forgotten you said that's where you and your mom lived." Karen hesitated before admitting the rest. "It's not a bad gig, to be honest. I'd get to buy horses and hire good staff. I don't know if it's a good idea to spend that much time around Finn, though. Not if I don't want to get involved."

"So that's the real question." Lisa raised a brow. "You don't have to tell us why, but if you don't want to get involved, then we will back your play. It's up to you."

"And if you don't want to talk in front of me, I'm okay with that," Julia said. "You don't have to run your life by committee. Not even if you do have sisters."

"Why, thank you. Although you will find having sisters means parts of your life run by committee whether you want them to or not," Karen drawled.

She took a deep breath and closed her eyes, palms pressed

flat to the solid surface of the kitchen island as she tried to articulate what was going through her head.

"I'd like to take the job. After spending so many years not in charge even though I had the skills, it's like being offered the keys to a candy store."

She opened her eyes. They all stayed quiet, which was a minor miracle when it came to sisterhood. Curiosity and concern weighed heavy in their eyes. Even Lisa's usually lighthearted expression seemed restrained.

Karen went for it again. "I like that little cottage. It already feels a lot like home, so I *will* stay there. But thank you for the offer, Tamara."

Tamara adjusted her glasses. When she spoke, her voice came out clear and soft, but cautious. As if she knew this was stepping into dangerous territory. "From everything I've heard, Finn is a good man."

That wasn't the problem. The real issue was how hard would Karen fall if she gave in to the longings inside her? Was this something that might lead to forever or another interlude on the way to further heartbreak?

The door tore open, and another familiar face appeared. Kelli Stone, sister-in-law on Tamara's side, stood in the opening, breathing hard. The petite woman glanced around the room before her gaze fixed on Lisa and Karen. "I need your help. That damn wild stallion broke one of the fences, and he's taken off with a bunch of our mares. It's all hands on deck."

Karen shot to her feet, love affairs and questions shoved aside. She and Lisa hurried out the door, Julia hard on their heels.

4

The bank took less time than Finn expected.

He eyed his friend, honest admiration sneaking out. "I don't know why you took me along. You had that thing sewn up within five minutes of entering the office."

Zach grinned as he downshifted and took the corner hard enough to send gravel spraying. "You noticed."

"You just wanted an audience. Damn extrovert."

"Not at all," Zach protested. "I wanted you to see how much I've learned from the master."

Finn gagged as he was obviously expected to.

When Zach offered a scathing curse in response, Finn hesitated. "What?"

Zach slowed his truck to something close to the legal speed limit then pointed to the vehicles waiting outside their current home base, a derelict ranch house.

One vehicle was familiar. Every time he came around, something interesting happened, so the arrival of the representative from Burly, Evans, and Ives merely raised Finn's curiosity.

The other one, though. It wasn't the car that caught his attention and started his blood boiling but the man leaning against it, arms folded over his chest, glaring as they approached.

"Goddamn fucking bastard."

"That about sums it up," Zach said in agreement. He shifted into a slower gear as if trying to prolong the moment so it would be safer for Finn to open the door. "Remember, if you lay a hand on him, he's more than willing to sue your ass. Keep your temper."

"I don't remember inviting him here. Maybe I can sue his ass for trespassing," Finn growled as he eyed Brandon Travers with disgust.

He reached for the door, ready to get out there and shred arms from a certain asshole if required.

The door lock clicked shut, trapping him in place.

"Keep. Your. Temper." The words were said softly, but it wasn't much of a deterrent considering how little Finn liked Brandon and how much he would enjoy putting a hurt on the man.

Still, points to Zach for trying.

Then the bastard uttered the only words that could convince Finn to get his head on straight.

"What's your endgame?" Zach asked quietly.

Not getting thrown in jail was a good place to start. Finn took a deep breath and let it out slowly before offering Zach a chin dip. "Appreciate it. Let's go encourage our visitor to leave."

"One visitor is leaving. The other one is bound to stick around for a while." Zach glanced with curiosity at the older man sitting patiently inside his vehicle, seemingly ignoring everything going on outside.

The truck doors shut behind them with solid slams.

Brandon straightened from where he'd been leaning, shaking his hands as if preparing for battle.

"We're not open for business yet," Zach offered cheerily as if greeting some lost cowboy-wannabe. "Happy to add you to our mailing list."

His sarcasm hit. Brandon glared harder. "Still spending my money, I see. Or should I say tossing it in the shitter?"

"What do you want?" Finn snapped. He was trying to be nice. Honestly, he was. He stopped a good foot away from Brandon then casually folded his arms across his chest.

See? Totally no aggressive posturing.

Brandon stepped back slightly as if even Finn's words were powerful enough to knock him off balance. "Same thing as always. I want my inheritance. I don't know what the hell you guys did to my dad, but it's just not right."

"We're not going through this again. You've taken it up with lawyers, and you've been told that your father was of sound mind when he rearranged his finances." Zach stepped beside Finn. "You want to do another round in the law courts, it's your pocketbook that will end up hurting. *Again.*"

The other man wore a sour expression, as if assessing the value of everything in front of him and finding it lacking. "What a pile of shit."

Finn wasn't about to argue. He didn't give a damn what Brandon thought. If he couldn't disregard the broken-down buildings and see the value in the land, that was his problem, not Finn's.

Bruce Travers's biggest complaint about his son had been that Brandon refused to see beyond the surface to the true possibilities.

Well, that and the fact Brandon had pissed away the money his father provided him for years. Instead of using it for investments and to get ahead, he'd blown it on frivolous or borderline legal activities, yet still kept running back to the family coffers to try again.

The well had dried up. Bruce Travers had gone looking for new protégés to train. He'd found Finn. He'd found Zach. Both of them willing to learn and work damn hard, and in the end, they'd profited a hundredfold.

Brandon had not been thrilled when he discovered he'd been cut out of the will. Or more specifically, Bruce Travers had brought on Finn and Zach as partners. Shortly after discovering he had terminal cancer, Bruce had removed himself from the corporation entirely and left it under their control.

Finn had paid all of Bruce's living expenses for the last year of his life, spending time with the man as he slowly lost his battle. Brandon had never been in the picture. Not more than a couple quick visits during the four years Finn and Zach had spent with Bruce, during which Brandon managed to insult everyone and make himself obnoxious.

Yet he had still thought he should collect his daddy's money.

"You need to leave." Finn got the words out without snarling. He was pretty proud of himself for that. "If you want to talk, use a lawyer."

"Hey, this is all because of him. As soon as he tells me I can leave, I'll be happy to wipe the shit off my shoes and get the hell out of here."

Brandon pointed to the vehicle where the representative from the law firm Bruce had used was finally opening the door and rising to join them.

Alan Cwedwick looked every part the legislator in a made-for-TV movie with the faint tracing of silver at his temples and his well-shined leather shoes and high-class suit.

He stepped forward, black leather case held firmly in one

hand even as he shook his head, lips twisted in amusement. "Okay, boys. Head to your separate corners."

"Alan," Finn said in acknowledgement. "It's good to see you, but I don't remember giving you permission to bring trash onto my property."

"You shut your goddamn mouth," Brandon said once he reached a safe position one step behind the lawyer's back. "I didn't come here to be insulted—"

"Brandon, perhaps you should wait in your vehicle until Mr. Marlette, Mr. Sorenson, and I finish discussing business."

"How about I just go and wait at the hotel? I've seen everything I need to see here." Brandon stomped away before getting an answer. He lifted a hand as he walked, jabbing a finger at Finn as if he were poking a voodoo doll. "You're hiding something. I will find out, and in the end, you'll pay."

"Always pleasant to see you, Brandon," Zach called after him before lowering his voice. "Watch out for that pile of dog shit you're about to—well, damn. Too late."

Finn pinched the bridge of his nose, but in spite of his frustration, he couldn't stop his snort of amusement. "Is it possible for you to not be *you* for just a few moments?"

Alan wrapped an arm around Finn's shoulders and squeezed. "Good to see you guys again. Although I do apologize for having to haul Brandon along. He really is a rat bastard, isn't he?"

"If you know that, why did you inflict him on us?" Finn asked.

They headed up the porch stairs and into the main house. Alan looked around, his assessing glance a lot more like the one Finn was sure had been on *his* face when he'd first seen the disaster.

Then the lawyer refocused his attention and answered the question. "It wasn't my idea. Bruce put a number of stipulations in his will that triggered a couple weeks ago, and unfortunately, bringing Brandon here was one of them."

"Since Bruce had no idea before he died that we would buy property in Alberta, that seems a bit of a stretch," Zach said dryly. He offered Alan a chair, taking over one of the stumps they'd been using as a footrest.

The three of them settled. Alan opened his briefcase and brought out a set of papers for both of them.

"You know Bruce had a tendency to do things outside the norm, and in this case I hope it won't be too detrimental." Alan adjusted his reading glasses. "I like you two. Always have. I think you're decent, outstanding young men worth way more than that jackass pouting his way back to town. However, since it's not my money but Bruce's that we're talking about, we need to follow his orders."

"He made us partners. Then he removed himself from the company. How does he have any say in what we do anymore?" Finn was ready to brace himself.

Alan waved a hand, tilting it from side to side. "He still had some controlling power. Silent partner, if you want to call it that. And until now, it's made no difference. But at this point, knowing Bruce as we did, I would assume this is a final lesson or a kick in the pants for you two."

Zach groaned as he dropped his head into his hands. "Dear God. I can see him now, cackling as he dreamed up some horrible challenge to drop on us."

"You're not far off, I'm afraid." Alan glanced through the paperwork in his lap.

"Just tell us," Finn demanded. "I'm up for one of Bruce's challenges. If it involves working with Brandon, though, it becomes a lot less entertaining."

The lawyer went into action. "Couple questions to clarify what I've discovered then I will lay it all out for you. Finn. Last financial investment you made through the corporation? I assume it's this land?"

"Yes, sir."

"Zachary? How about you? What are you spending money on these days?"

"I just purchased a building in downtown Heart Falls, but the money didn't come from the corporation," Zach informed him. "I don't usually deal with the money side. Finn does that part. I deal with other areas."

"But this property belongs to you both? Fifty-fifty?"

A bad feeling was growing in the pit of Finn's stomach. "It was purchased by the corporation, yes. And since we share that fifty-fifty, *this* is also both of ours."

Alan nodded as he scrawled notes across a piece of paper. "Okay. Well, this makes things a little simpler. Before I go on, I want to note that your private bank accounts are exempt. I know you both have regular dividends that go from the corporation into personal savings. Those are protected and not a part of this challenge."

Finn and Zach exchanged glances. "I suspect Bruce was feeling very creative one day and that we're going to hate the hell out of this." Zach made a face. "Damn if I don't miss the bastard."

"I hear you," Finn agreed.

Alan laid down his pen and pulled off his glasses, looking Finn and Zach over solemnly. "Bruce was a wily old bastard, but he was a good man, so let's hope he planned a way for you to win the challenge. What's the idea for this place?"

No use in lying because it was impossible to know what was the best answer to give. And if he'd had learned anything from Bruce, straight-up and straightforward would serve Finn better in the long run. "It's a dude ranch. Catering to tourists, especially from Calgary, but from around the world, to come and have a western experience. Small cabins, high-caliber service, with a small town and family vibe."

He'd never seen the lawyer light up like that before. Alan didn't try to hide his grin or his headshake of amazement. "Damn. You boys get this going, and I will bring out my family, guaranteed. I've always wanted to do it."

"Live in a cabin? Ride a horse?" Zach asked.

"Be a cowboy," Alan offered before getting back on track. "What's your timeline? When did you plan to have her up and running?"

That sneaky suspicion was back. "At this point I'd like to say about five years from now," Finn drawled.

Alan laughed. "Yeah, you figured it out. Or part of it, anyway. I will have to back up your estimate with a few others in the industry, so give me your best guess."

Zach sighed. "Dear God, not again?"

It'd been one of Bruce's favourite tricks to teach them to think smarter and move faster. Deadlines that shifted unexpectedly. Budgets that got drastically cut but the project still had to be finished.

They hadn't been fun lessons, but they'd been effective.

"Realistically, we would get things set up this year and begin bookings for next spring. That would be the smart way to do it if you had the funds to put operations on hold that long. Which we do."

"And people who didn't have the funds? Who had to start making money as quickly as possible?" Alan asked.

"Hell, you would do the whole thing in stages, and start something in a month' s time, but that wouldn't be the kind of experience we're looking to establish," Zach said firmly. "And in this day and age, it's damn near impossible to break a reputation of being a low-caliber operation because social media sticks around forever."

Alan nodded. "Understood. Okay, here's the deal. You have made a financial decision and set a goal. It is now Bruce's intention to encourage you to up your game. With the timing to be clarified, you do not have until next spring to open your doors. Your deadline will be sometime prior to Christmas of this year. If you are successful, and reviews for the first month of people who come to your doors are high-caliber, five-star results, there is a second arm of the corporation that has, up until now, been operating silently. Meet the challenge, and you'll find your net worth doubled."

Blood rushed to Finn's head. The amount of money Bruce had left them in the company was already jaw-dropping. There were a hell of a lot of zeros behind the digits at the start, more than Finn needed.

He glanced at Alan. The solution couldn't be this simple. "It sounds like an interesting challenge, and I'm always game to try and do things smarter and better, but to be honest, I don't think I need more money."

Perched upon his log, his best friend grinned broadly. "Yeah, I'm not feeling the pinch," Zach said. "I agree. Alan, if we can hit your deadline, great. But if we can't because we want to make this project a success without burning the candle at both ends, I'm not looking to be a multibillionaire."

Alan offered a wry smile. "I knew you'd say that. Hate to do this to you, so I'll make Bruce do it himself. I'll read this verbatim from the message he left."

He cleared his throat.

My ever-cautious lawyer has asked what the alternative is if you turn down the challenge because you don't want to be that rich. Which you young pups will probably do, and good for you.

But having strong moral fiber and your head on straight is not what the challenge is about. So as much as I hate to do this, I figure it might be the only way to light a fire under your asses to meet the deadline, boys.

Make me proud, because if you don't succeed, it's not only the money you won't get. If you fail to meet your deadline, then this project becomes the inheritance I leave to my worthless son, Brandon. I figure he's probably giving you hell about not getting my money. While I know he can't do a better job of whatever project you're attempting, maybe winning it off you will be enough to get him off your back.

Although, I really hope you stick it to him one more time. Get off your asses and meet that challenge.

Bruce.
P.S. Wish to hell I was there to see it.

5

At the head of the pack marching across to the barn, Kelli glanced over her shoulder briefly to shout a warning. "Don't come if you can't jump fences," she said sternly. "Last time, the stallion took us up into the foothills."

"If you're looking at me, I'll be fine." Julia followed them into the arena and began saddling one of the horses with confidence. Karen watched her for a moment before concentrating on her own mount. She caught Kelli making the same sly assessments, and in spite of the urgency, had to grin.

She liked the young woman who was her sister by marriage, once removed. She liked Kelli's easy way around horses and sensed a kindred spirit beyond what she'd had in this area with even Lisa.

Quicker than Karen expected, they were in the saddle and following Kelli as she led them past Big Sky Lake and to the north.

They moved at a trot, the wide-open path allowing them to travel in a tight group as Kelli caught them up.

"Luke took a group of the hands, and Ashton—that's our

foreman," she reminded Julia briefly, "took off with another group. But they both headed in different directions, and that's when I spotted Thor running the north fence line. Thor, because Luke forbid me to call him Black Beauty."

"I still can't believe you've got wild horses this far south." Lisa held her reins confidently in one hand, jamming her hat down a little more firmly. "There're a couple of herds in the Sundre district, and they occasionally come up toward Rocky Mountain House, but I didn't think their territory extended this far south."

"It didn't until a year or two ago," Kelli informed them. "Close as we can figure it, one of the stallions got chased off when he was still young, but if the wildies make it to adulthood, they get smart. They get devious."

"And they get looking for ladies?" Julia patted the flank of the mare she was riding, moving comfortably in the saddle.

Kelli snorted. "Thor pulled a few horses at a time into his own herd, including a younger gelding who isn't a challenge but seems damn loyal to Thor."

"So now there's a group of them in our foothills?" Lisa asked. "Which means he's trying to expand his harem."

"Which he is not allowed to do. Not with our ladies," Kelli said firmly.

Karen had been out numerous times to deal with the wild horses when they'd come close to Whiskey Creek land. Her goal had always been to keep their borders intact and let the wild horses return to government land, but she knew that wasn't always the chosen method.

The gun lashed to the side of Kelli's saddle had to be discussed.

"What's the plan?" Karen asked.

They were nearing a clearing, and Kelli slowed, the horses shuffling forward, hooves quiet on the new grass. She spoke in hushed tone. "Some of the locals want to cull the wildies before they can grow any bigger or get more aggressive. I think it's worth trying to rescue most of the ones he's taken then encouraging Thor to be satisfied with a smaller following while he stays on Crown land."

Kelli's goals were right in line with how Karen felt about the situation. The wild horses had every right to live, but that didn't mean they got to poach new blood from the local ranchers.

Kelli continued, "The stallion will stand out when we see them. He's at least eighteen hands at the shoulder and shaggy instead of sleek. Then there's a grey gelding with him that came from a local ranch. Thor's got Silver Stone mares, but the rest of the females belong to people scattered between here and Highway 1. If we find the herd, cut off as many as possible and drive them toward the nearest fenced area you can find. We'll deal with whoever owns the land later." She glanced over at Karen. "How are your roping skills?"

"I'm good."

"If you get a chance, nab the gelding. Don't try for the stallion. If we find them, my job is to drive Thor off while you deal with the others."

It was a quick and dirty plan, but pretty much what would've been offered in any situation Karen had dealt with before.

They spread out, moving slowly through the trees toward the waterfall. The source of water for the town namesake rushed from higher in the foothills until it gathered on the heights at the very edge of Silver Stone ranch. The pool at the base was a lopsided oval with an indent at the top.

Thus, heart-shaped.

The water cascading down the jagged granite cliffs on the

far side crashed into the pool with a spectacular rush because of high spring runoff.

The near side of the pool was where the exit creek lay, sliding to the east before meandering its way across the Silver Stone property with stops at Big Sky and Little Sky lakes.

The mouth of the creek was shallow enough that water bubbled over the smooth river rocks.

A herd of horses was gathered, their heads down and drinking, ears pricked up even as others kept watch.

At the far edge stood the biggest, shaggiest stallion Karen had seen in a long time. She pulled her horse to a halt well within the tree line, glancing to the side to see her sisters had done the same.

By some chance she was closest to the wild stallion. Kelli was at the far end of the lineup, impossibly close to what had to be the gelding that was tempted away from his home ranch.

Karen's gaze met Kelli's. The other woman lifted her hand to slowly point at herself then at the gelding.

Karen silently nodded her agreement. She repeated the motion, pointing at herself then the stallion. The roles were now reversed. It only made sense, and she was comfortable taking on the challenge.

A soft snicker rose from the herd, and movement started. A shuffle of hips and a swaying. Heads rose as one of their sentries sensed the newcomers in the trees. Karen wrapped her fingers tighter around her reins, sitting motionless until it was time—

The stallion nickered loudly then charged toward the trees as if about to attack.

Kelli was already in forward motion, rope twirling as she headed straight at the gelding. Lisa and Julia moved as well, but that was the last Karen saw as she focused on her task.

It was time to cut Prince Charming off from his ladies.

She urged her horse forward, shifting to the right as soon as possible to intersect the stallion's path.

He saw her coming and whirled, storming toward the river ford hard on the heels of his stolen mares. Karen went straight into the river as well, water rising up in arcs on either side of Starlight's pounding hooves.

On the other side, the chase began in earnest.

The stallion no longer watched behind him. All his attention was on forcing his mares farther from civilization. They moved quickly, rushing down one gorge and up the other side. Karen held tight, gripping the saddle with her thighs and trusting Starlight to keep them upright.

It was humbling to have the riderless horses slowly pull farther away from her. Karen did her best to keep up, but though she could go over and around obstacles with the best of them, the wild stallion began cutting through low hanging trees and under widow-makers.

She had to keep adjusting her path to avoid being swept off Starlight's back.

By the time they broke into the open, the stallion and his reduced herd of females were far enough ahead that Karen didn't have any hope of catching them.

Still, she stayed on their heels, driving them farther to the west as they returned to their home territory and away from Silver Stone.

No longer at a hard run, Karen followed until she'd travelled for an hour before pulling out her phone and touching base with Lisa. "Hey, I'm good but definitely do not have any horses to bring back. How did you guys do?"

"Kelli's got the gelding. Damn, he's a mean one. We got back the Silver Stone mares—they came easily once you chased off the pretty boy tempting them with wild nights of passion. What about you?"

Karen glanced around, amused to discover she was nearly back to her temporary home. "I chased them farther into the foothills, so it seems I might've turned them into Finn's problem instead of Silver Stone's."

A snort sounded from the other end of the line. "Way to go, sis. Although I think that is closer to the stallion's new regular territory."

An unfamiliar vehicle was parked in front of Finn and Zach's temporary house. Another expensive white car was just pulling out of the driveway, turn indicator on even without another soul around.

Karen stifled her grin as she turned Starlight's head toward the shelter behind her cottage. "Well, I'm home, so I may as well stay here. It wasn't exactly how I thought I'd get my horse moved, but it works. You want to drive my truck out and join me for dinner?"

"Drat. I can't. Josiah and I are getting together with Sonora at the animal shelter. I can bring your truck in the morning," Lisa offered.

Karen could also ride back and then use the horse trailer to get Starlight home. Or...

Finn and Zach were visible on the platform behind the house. Some kind of serious conversation was taking place.

While she still wasn't sure exactly how the summer would go, her sisters were right about one thing. It would be silly to not take the job Finn had offered.

"Don't worry about it," Karen told Lisa. "I'll find another way to grab it. Have a good evening."

"Don't forget you're coming over Saturday night," Lisa said.

"I won't forget," she promised.

Getting Starlight settled in his new temporary digs felt comfortable and right. The lean-to had recently been repaired, and there was a sturdy, protective area to hang all her gear.

She'd bet anything that Finn had prepared the place for her. It was no less than she'd expected, though, once he'd said he'd bought the place with purpose. Finn Marlette was a thorough man.

It was something to put on the positive side of the ledger: his attention to detail and stubborn determination. Attention to detail had all sorts of wonderful consequences as it came to comfort for her animal.

That thoroughness in the bedroom? It had to be said. Karen had never had a man like Finn before or after.

She took her time caring for her horse, letting the warm wind rush over her with comfort and invigorating freshness. Then she slid into the cottage and got freshened up. It only took a moment before she was crossing the distance between her place and the beat-up ranch house.

She had a place to stay, and she was about to have a job to do.

If only she could decide how to deal with her third dilemma.

ALAN LEFT SHORTLY after dropping his bomb with a promise to get the paperwork and the actual deadline decided before the end of the week.

Zach glared after the departing car, pivoted on his heel, then stomped into the house.

Finn followed a little slower, attempting to put this twist into perspective. While he appreciated what his mentor had intended with the inspiration from beyond the grave, the all-or-nothing situation was complicating matters beyond the cut-and-dried setup he'd hoped for in Heart Falls.

So be it. It wouldn't be the first time they'd buckled down to get a task done.

Zach dropped into one of the beat-up Adirondack chairs on the deck and stared forlornly at the foothills.

"Well, that was entertaining," Finn offered dryly as he settled beside his friend.

An enormous sigh bubbled from Zach, and he spoke without meeting Finn's eyes. "I'm so sorry."

"Not your damn fault."

Zach made a face. "If I'd bought the Brewster building with corporation money like you told me to, *that* would've been the project we had a deadline on."

Of all the mixed-up, irrational leaps of logic…

Finn leaned forward and examined his friend intently. "You think I'm mad at you for that? Hell, if anything, I think we're in a better position having to deal with the dude ranch than convincing a bunch of beer-drinking fanatics we've come up with the be-all and end-all of small craft brew."

"It's something that might be accomplished in a short period of time. And it's also something that doesn't require good weather to bring in clients." Zach shook his head. "You always tease that I've got magic timing, but I wish this time I hadn't."

"Drop it," Finn ordered. "I'm the one who needs to apologize because you have to put your idea on the slow track until we get *this* place operational."

"Up and running before Christmas?" Zach looked doubtful. "You really think we can do it?"

"We're damn well going to do it. No way in hell is that bastard Brandon invading Heart Falls. He's the last thing I'd inflict on her friends and family."

"Who's invading?"

Finn and Zach jerked upright, glancing over their shoulders

to discover Karen at the foot of the rickety stairs from the ground level to the deck.

Finn hit his feet, holding out a hand to stop her before she took another step. "Hold on. I haven't checked those yet."

Karen paused with one foot on the bottom riser. She moved back and glanced underneath before pointing toward the house. "If you don't mind, I'll take the stable route."

"Front door's open," Zach said. He waited until Karen strode out of sight before turning to Finn. "Quick. Are we taking this challenge?"

"Absolutely. I mean it, I don't want Brandon anywhere near our friends." Only Finn didn't want to complicate matters any more than they already were. "No mention of the deadline or consequences unless we need to. Agreed?"

"Agreed." Zach raised his voice and waved a hand. "Karen. Nice to meet you. I'm Zach Sorenson."

"I've heard about you," Karen said with a smile as she stepped through the sliding door onto the deck.

"Only good things, I hope."

She arched a brow. "I hear you've got a poker face that my brother-in-law can't read. That's a good trait in a man."

Finn stepped closer. She was dressed in casual cowboy, and he wanted to pick her up and eat her in one bite. "Didn't expect to see you so soon. Hope it's for a good reason."

"Might be," she said before her head tilted to one side and she stared him down intently. "Whose plans to invade had you sounding so thrilled?"

Damn. He'd hoped she would let that one slide. Finn opened his mouth to come up with a story that was the truth without spilling all the beans, but Zach interrupted.

"You saw the car that just left? Had to deal with some legal stuff for getting the ranch up and running. There's somebody who wants to be involved we don't like very much.

We were just chatting about making sure he won't be in the picture."

Her gaze danced between the two of them before she nodded. "Sounds like a good thing."

Zach gestured to the chairs on the deck. "Want to sit for a while? I can grab some drinks."

She eyed the chairs, and the railless platform. "Is this part structurally sound?"

"Mostly. We think," Zach admitted.

A snort escaped her, and her gaze met Finn's. Their eyes stayed locked for a moment before she dipped her chin again. "If you've got a beer, I'll take one. We should talk."

Zach took off into the house. Finn pulled the chairs so they were close enough to have a discussion while still looking over the land.

Karen rested a hand on his forearm to get his attention. "How much does Zach know about us?"

She spoke softly, with a quick glance toward the house as if checking his friend was still out of earshot.

Finn straightened. "I would guess he knows about as much as your sisters do."

He got an epic eye roll for that one before she shook her head and settled in the chair on the far right. "Didn't take you for the type to kiss and tell."

"Trust me. Or more to the point, trust Zach. He's not going to say a word out of line, and he's already your biggest supporter."

That one made her start with surprise.

It was his turn to glance toward the house, thankful that Zach was taking the longest time ever to grab and open three beers.

"Karen?" He waited until she glanced up. He maintained eye contact as he settled in the farthest chair from her. "Zach is like family, but he is first and foremost a hell of a good guy. You need *anything*, you trust him."

She took a moment as if letting that soak in. Her expression softened. "Thanks for that. I appreciate it, and I'll remember it."

"Do I need to bring a notepad?" Zach poked his head out the door.

"Just get out here with the damn drinks," Finn muttered.

Karen snickered, pulling her expression back into a warm smile as she accepted a longneck with thanks. "Now it feels as if I'm on holiday. Day drinking and all."

Zach lowered a bag to the ground beside his chair then examined his beer label briefly before raising the bottle in a toast. "To our last time day drinking in a long while."

They all lifted their bottles.

Finn got down two and a half swallows before he stuttered to a stop, coughing while beer dribbled from his mouth to splash over the deck. "Dear God, what the *hell* is that?"

Karen was eyeing her bottle with disgust.

Zach alternated between sniffing the contents while swilling liquid around in his mouth. He lifted a finger, got to his feet, and walked to the edge of the deck to spit the liquid out of sight.

He turned back as he wiped his mouth. "Sorry about that. I take it yours were no better than mine?"

"Is this from that microbrewery outside Fort Macleod?" Karen made a horrified face. "I wondered what their beer was like."

"And now we know," Finn said dryly. He glared at his friend. "Zach, I thought we agreed you would warn people before you use them as guinea pigs."

Zach reached into the mystery bag he'd dropped beside his chair and pulled out three new longnecks. A familiar, national brand. He popped the tops like a pro, handing them over immediately with a wink. "I forgot."

They drank deeply. Finn was hoping to wash the god-awful taste out of his mouth, but he was amused.

Laughter danced in Karen's eyes as well. She leaned forward in her chair. "So. You mentioned a contract job here at your nameless dude ranch. Want to tell me more?"

Hallelujah. She was going to do it.

What before had been an offer so she could use her talents had now become a very serious asset to winning the challenge.

Finn pointed toward Zach. "He'll be your boss. We'd be working together to brainstorm and figure out exactly what we need, by when. Some of the dates are still up in the air, but we'll nail them down as soon as possible."

"You need trail ride guides? Horses? Barn staff or anything else?"

Zach coughed apologetically. "All of it. We've got leads on some, but once Finn mentioned your name as a possible coordinator, I figured we'd wait to see how you wanted to deal with it. If you knew people who are good to work with. That sort of thing."

She looked thoughtful. "Depending on when you open, I might have a couple of very experienced guides available. I don't know if you remember, Finn, but the summer you were out at Whiskey Creek, I was setting up a side gig. Wilderness trail rides in the Willmore area outside of Jasper."

It had been one of the things she'd been so proud of. "I checked out your most recent website update. You're doing great."

Her smile lit her face. "The camp leaders, Dani and James, have a lot to do with that, but Willmore is definitely a seasonal camp. They've been wintering at a different ranch, but I might be able to talk them into coming here if there's a salary involved."

Zach actually rubbed his hands together. "That's what I like. Problem-solving before problems even present themselves." He glanced at Finn. "I think Karen would work great as a member of this team, and if you're okay with it, I'll set up a job description and compensation package then go over it with her."

Sounded brilliant to Finn. He tossed the question to Karen. "Does that sound like something you'd like to do while you're here? I know you want to spend time with your family, and we'll make sure that happens, but this will be a real job."

She glanced over the fallen buildings and unkempt fields. "It looks like enough work to be a real job, but you know, that's okay." She nodded slowly as she brought her gaze back to meet both of theirs in turn. "I don't think I really get the concept of this holiday thing. I like to work, and I like to spend time with horses, so it sounds a lot like a working vacation."

In spite of his uncertainty about the twisted challenge presented to him and Zach earlier that day, the knot of tension inside Finn eased.

She'd said yes to part of it. It meant she was staying, which meant he had longer to make his case.

They belonged together. Now he had time to prove it.

Zach rose to his feet, holding out his hand to Karen, who gave it a firm pump. "Welcome to Nameless Dude-town. Glad to have you."

"From me as well. You're going to be a huge help," Finn assured her.

Karen accepted Finn's outstretched hand. Her handshake was firm, but the expression in her eyes was soft and slightly teasing. "Let's see what we can do to make this a memorable summer."

6

———

I'm not sure if I'm even madder after reading your note or if it worked a little. A flower and an apology—awesome.

Left on my windowsill? That's a little stalkerish, dude.

I blame the painkillers because I'm slightly charmed by your handsome face and cocky attitude.

What are we doing to make this a memorable summer? Does it involve dancing? Naked dancing? Because being in your arms was not a hardship.

(Maybe blame that last bit on the painkillers as well, k?)

~Note from Karen to Finn, summer at Whiskey Creek
ranch~

*S*he didn't know what had come over her. She was still not sure she wanted to dive into the deep end with Finn, but the temptation was strong.

Repeating his words from so long ago—ones she knew he remembered because they'd become a part of their mantra that summer—was her mouth making promises she wasn't sure she wanted to keep.

Thankfully, the distraction factor kicked into high gear.

Distraction otherwise known as Zach Sorenson.

He hauled her off the deck and into the living room and proceeded to nail down a job description. Then he offered up a compensation package that made her blink and started a to-do list that would keep her busy for the next three weeks.

In spite of the excitement all the work-related details caused, it was Finn's expression that returned to her mind over and over again.

A flash of remembrance, a whole lot of hopefulness, and then that sexy smolder had arrived. The one she couldn't get enough of.

Somehow she left without doing anything foolish like throwing herself at him. She had a temporary contract in her pocket and a whole lot of questions bubbling in her brain as to the best way to get started.

Karen was already walking in the door of her cottage before she realized she hadn't solved her transportation issue.

An answer arrived a moment later in the form of a phone call.

"Hey. I was leaving Silver Stone when I noticed your truck is still here. Want me to swing by and grab you so you can get it home?" Julia paused then added, "I'm also free for dinner if you'd like some company."

Exactly what Karen needed. A little ongoing distraction so

she didn't up and race back to the ranch house to tell Finn she wanted to sign on for the rest of his offer.

"Perfect, on both counts. Come get me, then we can take both vehicles out. I'll splurge for a steak if you want to go to Longhorn's."

"Deal."

Twenty minutes later Julia's out-of-place-looking neon-blue Lotus pulled up in front of the cottage. Karen grabbed a jacket and her purse then wedged herself into the tiny vehicle.

"Is there an expansion button if somebody over six feet wants to get in?" she teased.

"You have fun last time you parallel parked on Main Street?" Julia returned dryly.

Karen laughed. "Point taken. It means I get my exercise, parking a street over then walking to where I'm going. Thank goodness Longhorn's parking lot is the size of a football field."

"I haven't been yet," Julia confessed. "We can go Dutch, because I intend to get the biggest steak possible and all the sides. Despite how hard I work as an EMT, chasing after the horses gave me an appetite like I haven't had since the *last* time I went chasing horses."

"It was good to have you join us," Karen admitted. She eyed her new sister who had only been found for all of two months. They'd been slowly getting to know each other better, but there were a lot of years to catch up. "And to make it clear, I *am* buying. You go ahead and get anything you want, but this is a celebration. I have a new job."

"You took it. It sounded as if you wanted to," Julia said. She glanced sideways briefly. "Did you make a decision on the other matter? Because I meant it. If you need backup, I'm there for you. Nothing worse than a guy who won't accept no."

A comment which brought up a whole lot more questions Karen wanted answers to.

She answered quickly, not wanting Julia to get the wrong idea. "Finn is a good guy, and I mean that. And yes, he's kind of possessive and a *this is the way I want things* type guy at times, but he's not an asshole. If I tell him I'm not interested, he'll drop it."

"Some guys interpret *no* as one step away from *maybe* which to them is practically *yes*." Julia nodded firmly. "Your call. If anything changes, you give me a shout. Anytime, day or night."

"I will," Karen promised.

They talked about the wild horses until Julia pulled in next to Karen's truck.

"I need to gas up," Karen said. "Meet you at Longhorn's?"

"No problem. I'll grab us a table."

Only by the time Karen got there, not having a reservation had turned out to be a problem. Julia was standing outside the door—

Chatting with Zach.

Karen glanced around to see where Finn was because she was pretty sure the two men were like bookends. Find one, you'd find the other.

Julia spotted her. "Hey. We've got about forty minutes before they can sneak us in."

Zach flashed her a bright grin. "I hear you're celebrating getting this really fantastic job. Oh, and I hear your supervising boss is one hell of a guy."

"I didn't say anything about that." Julia sounded confused.

"*He's* my boss," Karen offered dryly.

Julia nodded slowly. "*Ahh.* Let's hope the man isn't delusional."

A sharp snort sounded behind her, and Finn appeared. "She's already got your number, Zach."

The powerfully built man in front of them laid a hand over

his chest with as much dramatic flair as Karen's little sister would have. "Not a word of it was a lie."

Finn lifted his chin toward the restaurant doors. "You ladies want to join us?"

Confusion hit first, then cautious curiosity. "You just happened to have a reservation for four?"

"Sort of?" Zach hesitated, glancing at Finn as if looking for direction.

Julia offered Karen some serious wide-eyed 'you need to call the shots on this one' signals.

She took a deep breath. This was about enjoying a good steak. She didn't have to make a decision about forever. "We would love to join you."

"Back in a minute." Zach disappeared through the front door.

Finn turned to Karen. "I know this is your sister, but we've never been introduced."

Julia thrust forward her hand. "Julia Blushing. EMT trainee, former dude ranch resident, and youngest Whiskeymouse."

A laugh bubbled up before Karen could stop it. "Dear God, we need to deal with Lisa."

But Finn grinned. "Well, there're lots of lovely things to unwrap in that introduction. I think I like your version of the nickname better than the one I heard before."

Julia looked confused for a moment as if going over what she'd said.

She smacked a hand against her forehead. "Whiskey*teer*. I mean it's a cute name, but damn if it's not a mouthful."

The door opened and Zach poked his head out, gesturing inside. "Come on. They're adding a couple of place settings for us."

Longhorn Steakhouse was one of the best places to go for a

meal if you had a little money to spend. Karen had been there a couple of times since Tamara moved to the Heart Falls region.

She'd never been up the tall staircase at the far end of the room.

Never knew the private room at the top of the stairs existed. A decent-sized table rested in front of a massive picture window that faced west toward the Rockies.

Four place settings waited, one at either end and two along one side. Zach pulled out the chair for Julia at one end then made his way to the far side, which left Karen next to Finn.

"You obviously have an inside track with management," Julia said as she looked around with appreciation. "Thanks for the invite. This is amazing."

"We know a few people," Zach admitted. "Same menu as downstairs. Since the kitchen at the ranch house isn't operational right now, I'll admit to eating here more often than I should."

"He doesn't like my mac and cheese," Finn said.

"You don't use blue box," Zach complained.

A mocking gasp rose from Julia. "No. Does he also use no-name ketchup?"

Zach straightened and gestured firmly at Finn. "See? *See?* This is exactly what I'm talking about. Everyone knows from the first moment I mention it what a travesty your cooking habits are."

It was all too amusing. Karen found herself grinning as she relaxed back in her seat. Zach kept teasing, and Finn dryly took it, a lot of grace and amusement in his tone with every response.

By the time their appetizers were devoured and she'd nearly finished a glass of wine, Karen was feeling pretty damn mellow.

Finn topped up her glass. "The day go differently than you expected?"

Jeez. "This day has been about five days long, considering everything that's gone on." Karen sipped the wine, watching as the sun slowly dipped toward the distant mountains.

Zach and Julia continued to talk across the length of the table. Zach was picking her brain for all the details she could remember from the ranch where she'd grown up.

In the middle, Karen and Finn sat in a bubble of quiet. It was a familiar feeling, reminiscent of the time she'd spent years ago with him. In the room with others around, yet feeling that sensation of being utterly alone and completely connected.

His leg bumped hers. An innocent act as he reached across the table. Karen took a steadying breath then faced him with a smile. "Sometimes surprises work out. Thanks for the job. I would've gone out of my mind with boredom working at the grocery store," she admitted.

"Thanks for accepting it. I really am glad you're helping us with this." Utter truth in the sentence. His gaze fixed on hers as he lifted his glass in a salute.

Crystal clinked together softly.

"I'm not sure about the other matter," she said quickly.

He dipped his chin. "It's not tomorrow yet."

Laughter rose again. "You're right. Remember my previous comment about how this day has gone on forever."

"Sleep on it," he encouraged. "I find a good night's sleep answers all sorts of questions. Sometimes in my dreams I come up with solutions. Thinking over old memories, good times from the past. That sort of thing."

He was bad.

And good, because sweet dreams *were* a part of their past. Good memories had been rushing in all day between the other busy parts of her adventure.

The steaks arrived and the conversation went wide again. Between the delicious food and the company, Karen got to put a hold on the last question she needed to answer.

Her dreams that night were far too dirty.

FINN MADE himself scarce for the next couple of days and let Zach take Karen around the place. He figured it was the best way to make it clear he really did want her opinions.

It was also the easiest way to stop from fawning over her or groveling to be put out of his misery.

He had enough to keep himself busy. The to-do list had blown up by epic proportions. His previous casual contacts with people for work down the road required updates. A kind of "put me on your list *now* because I need you as soon as humanly possible" update.

But he caught enough glimpses of Karen to mean she was constantly on his mind. She'd pulled her hair back into a familiar ponytail, and her grin flashed sharply whenever Zach was his usual amusing self.

She moved differently. Not only because she was no longer hampered by her full-length cast, but she seemed more at ease in her own skin.

Finn was pretty sure she'd put up with a lot of grief at the Whiskey Creek ranch over the years. Hell, he'd worked that long-ago summer with George Coleman and knew exactly the type of man Karen's father was.

Old-school. Clueless and unintentionally unkind.

Karen had stayed soft.

Not as in strength, because damn, the woman might outwork him at the rate she was going. No, it was that she hadn't grown bitter in spite of all the barriers tossed in front of her.

He reflected on the changes in himself and wasn't able to make the same claim. Yes, he'd learned a lot from Bruce Travers, and he counted all of that as good.

His bitterness—fallout from family disappointments—was the part Finn didn't quite know how to deal with.

After three days of keeping his distance, it was time to remind Karen he expected an answer. He headed into town after lunch, coming back to meet up with Zach, who had left Karen and Josiah chatting in what would be the main horse barn.

Zach flashed Finn a thumbs-up. "You're brilliant. She's got exactly the right ideas *and* the contacts we need to get this done. Between her and some of the comments Julia made the other night, I feel a lot more optimistic about meeting the challenge."

"She's the brilliant one." Finn glanced at his watch. "What time did you tell her to knock it off?"

His friend frowned. "I didn't. She's a private contractor, so she can work whatever hours she wants to."

Perfect. "Meet you at Josiah's at six."

Zach paused. "Okay. We're not going together? I just had Delilah shipped in. Thought I'd take her for a spin beforehand."

Finn thought about the shopping he'd just done, and a small smile snuck out. "Tell you what. I'll call you if I need a backup plan."

That got him a confused look for a second before Zach clued in. His friend grinned. "Break a leg."

"You need to stop saying that," Finn muttered even as he chuckled under his breath.

He waited until four-thirty, then with his afternoon purchases in hand, made his way to Karen's cottage.

His brisk knock on the front door was answered with a yell. "On the back deck."

A five-second stroll brought him around the edge of the small building. Karen reclined in the comfortable lawn furniture he'd made sure to purchase. Stuff that was a hell of a lot nicer than what was currently up at the main house.

She eyed him with confusion and a sweet hint of approval in her eyes. "Why are you all dressed up and ready to roll? Party's not until six," she pointed out.

"Brought you a present," he said. He placed the basket in her lap then stepped back to admire her trim body. He didn't care one bit that her T-shirt and jeans were dirty after tramping around the ranch all day.

"*Finn*. You shouldn't have done that." Indignation drifted in her tone until she started poking through the bottles and tubes he'd shoved into the wicker container. She gasped and held one up. "Oh my God, this is wintergreen foot cream."

"You got the word about tonight's footwear?"

Karen made a face. "I tried to get Lisa to tell me why we have to wear sandals, but sometimes my sister is just plain mean."

Finn sat on the footstool in front of her and lifted her bare foot into his lap.

She tensed.

He sat there, motionless. Well, mostly motionless. Her skin was so damn soft he had to trace circles with his thumb against the inside of her arch.

"You want to grab a shower? Or get a massage first?"

The expressions dancing across her face just might kill him. She clearly wanted him to touch her, but indecision was there as well.

Finn squeezed her foot. "Just a rub, I swear. Let me take care of you."

Karen swallowed hard. "Give me a minute."

She leapt up and damn near ran into the house.

Finn sat back on the stool and concentrated on taking long, slow breaths, lowering his heart rate and shoving aside the need drilling through his system.

If it took a while for her to make up her mind, so be it. He was not some Neanderthal who couldn't control himself.

But dear God, he needed to touch her. He needed it as much as he needed his next breath.

Less than ten minutes passed before she was back. Her hair lay tousled over her shoulders, the strands wet and somewhat tangled from where she'd rubbed at them with a towel.

She wore sweatpants and an oversized T-shirt, and she was so gorgeous he couldn't take his eyes off her.

"You bring your brush?" His voice rasped past vocal cords tight with desire. Probably sounded like the grumpy asshole she expected, though, because all she did was reach into her pocket and haul out a brush.

He grabbed it and gestured to the chair. "Lean forward."

Karen settled, placing her hands on her knees. Finn stood and slipped behind her to hide the erection pressing the front of his jeans in silent demand.

Then he tormented himself by running his fingers through her hair and untangling the knots. Working the brush through from her scalp to the ends of the long layers until her hair lay in smooth strands over the pale blue of her T-shirt.

If there were any justice in the world, he'd be able to finish this by pressing a kiss to where her pulse pounded in her neck. He'd be able to lick her earlobe and suck it into his mouth. He'd follow that by kissing his way along her jaw before taking her mouth as hungrily as he wanted.

To consume her and taste her all over for the first time in almost five years.

Instead, he laid the brush aside and moved back into position at her feet. After lifting them into his lap, he covered his hands with wintergreen and rubbed the thick cream against the pads of her toes and heels then pressed his thumb against the arch of her foot.

He gritted his teeth when she moaned in pleasure. Only a sick bastard would ask for this kind of punishment, but hell if he wanted to stop.

Finn pushed the elastic at the base of her sweats past her knees to work the muscles in her calves. One foot, then the other, as she leaned back against the thick cushions. Her eyes closed and her mouth slid open, except for the moments he hit a sweet spot. Then her lips would purse slightly as if in preparation for his kiss.

"You have the hands of a god," Karen whispered. "You always have."

"I like touching you," he confessed.

Then he shut up, because this wasn't about browbeating her but waiting for the confession of her need.

They fell quiet for a while, or as quiet as it could be outdoors at five o'clock on a June day in Alberta. In the distance a tractor motor rumbled. Birds sang enthusiastically, and somewhere over the nearest rise, a whole bunch of dogs were barking their fool heads off. Even the trees in the nearby coulee added to the music as the wind rubbed their branches together.

A wilderness symphony.

"I've been thinking about what you said." Karen's eyes were still closed, but she tensed slightly at the confession.

Finn dug his fingers into the back of her legs more firmly, and whatever she was about to say vanished into a moan that just about took the top of his head off.

Somehow, he held his tongue.

"I have a lot of good memories from our summer together. And we've got chemistry—or we did." She popped one eye open and glanced at him from under the arm she'd laid across her face. "I somehow think we still do."

So far, she wasn't saying anything he hadn't been thinking.

She took a deep breath. "I still need more time."

"It's just a foot rub," he repeated.

She made a face. "You're driving me wild, and you know it."

"I blasted in here a couple of days ago and threw a lot at you." Finn worked her toes for a while. "*Chérie*, as much as I want you, if you asked me to jump you right now, I'd say no."

That got a response. She sat upright, eyes no longer clouded, the cutest crease between her brows. "Really?"

He slipped his finger between her toes and teased, getting her squirming. "Didn't jump your bones right off the bat all those years ago. Even when you begged me to. Sometimes you've got to work up to it so it's even more worthwhile."

She cursed softly, but her lips twisted into a smile. "You're an asshole."

He gave her foot a final squeeze but hesitated. "Got any nail polish?"

Karen raised a brow, but she was smiling again. "Maybe I should do *your* nails. You want green? Blue?"

"Not a chance." He tilted his head toward the house. "Hurry up before I rescind the offer."

When she got back with the polish, she'd slipped into jeans and soft blue shirt, ready for the party except for her bare feet.

Things remained surprisingly chill. It was as if doing the out-of-the-blue activity allowed her to stop worrying about the sexual tension flaring between them. Instead, while he painted her toes, she chatted about the ideas she and Zach had discussed. All the plans she would put into action over the coming weeks.

She even mentioned a couple of tasks she and Finn could work on together.

By the time they were ready to leave, Karen offered him a smile with honest-to-God openness.

"Thank you. That was…" She shrugged. "Just thanks."

He extended an arm. "Come on. Let's go see what your sister has dreamed up this time."

7

The house Lisa had moved into with Josiah sat at the top of a long rise, with views that would rival the place Finn and Zach were working on.

The biggest difference, though, was while Finn's place was a classic long, low rancher, at some point in the past, an abandoned silo had been attached to Josiah's, as if the house had castle delusions.

It was unique, which Karen had to admit suited both her sister Lisa and the bighearted veterinarian. With two massive barns within easy walking distance and a parking area that rivaled the one at Silver Stone ranch, the whole place was practical and yet pretty.

It was also full of people.

"Did Lisa invite the entire town?" Karen peeked in the window before tilting her head and tugging Finn around the side. She didn't want to step into the living room before figuring out what was going on.

With Lisa, it was better to be forewarned than to assume.

Finn stayed close, peering in the windows as they passed. A

soft chuckle escaped him. "For someone who has only been in town for a short time, she's definitely made herself at home."

Which again sounded very much like her little sister—the life of the party. A momentary jab of discomfort was followed immediately by a rush of guilt for the jealousy.

She forced as much enthusiasm and pride into her voice as possible. "You can toss Lisa into just about any situation, and she'll come out smelling like roses."

Karen stopped at the edge of the back deck. Finn crowded against her back. A solid, safe, very warm, presence.

His cheek briefly brushed hers as he whispered in her ear. "Good thing it takes all types to make this world. Life of the party *and* those of us who are quiet or grumpy."

Karen pivoted on the spot, outraged on his behalf. "You're not grumpy." She paused. "Not usually." Honesty prevailed. "Okay, you're somewhat grumpy, but it suits you."

The corners of his lips twitched. "Like I said, it takes all types."

He was right. Besides, she had long ago come to grips with her position in their trio of sisters—now quartet. She was not the fun one, but that was okay. Lisa created enough fun for the rest of them with ease and charm, just like she would tonight.

"Okay, everybody. I think we're all here. It's time to get the evening rolling." Lisa rattled the dinner bell, clanging the long metal rod enthusiastically off the triangle hanging by the back door.

People settled in chairs on the massive deck, others poking their head out from the house before joining in.

Karen counted at least twenty people, including herself and Finn. Maybe two dozen.

"First up, we've got food and lots of it. Before you grab a plate and load up, there are three baskets on the table. Pull one slip of paper from each and keep them hidden. I'll explain the game as soon as we're all eating. The only rule at this point is you can't pull your own name."

The rich scent of barbecue and what looked to be a massive tray of macaroni and cheese hauled Karen out of the shadows eagerly. She grabbed her slips of paper and shoved them in her pocket without even looking, then accepted the empty plate Finn handed her and stepped into line at his side.

They had settled in chairs next to each other before she realized how comfortable it was to keep doing things with him.

The rich creamy taste of her sister's homemade mac and cheese exploded in her mouth, and she moaned happily. "This"—she jabbed her fork toward the pile she'd heaped on her plate—"this is what it's supposed to taste like."

Finn shrugged. "If you say so. It's good to know you have a few flaws."

Karen gasped. She glanced at his plate to discover he hadn't taken any of the pasta. "You're not even trying it?"

"Didn't want to take any and leave less for you," he said magnanimously.

"You don't know what you're missing. Here." She scooped up a mouthful—a small one, mind you—then held out her fork. "Try it."

Finn leaned forward obediently, one hand settling on her thigh to stabilize himself. His lips closed around the tines of the fork, but his gaze fixed on her face. He pulled back slowly, the palm of his hand scalding hot on her leg.

They stared at each other.

Karen somehow remembered how to breathe.

Then he dipped his chin. "Not bad. The seasoning is good."

She was about to tell him...something, except he was still staring at her mouth, and she was about to self-combust.

"Okay, everybody, listen up. Here's the rules for the game."

Thank goodness for little sisters. Lisa stood on a milk crate so she was tall enough to be seen.

"The three slips of paper you have are the name of somebody here, a location, and an easily found household item. Between now and ten p.m., your goal is to give your chosen person that item, in that location. If you manage it, they're dead. You take over their three papers and keep playing."

Karen thought it through. "It's like the game Clue, only with real people."

Lisa snickered. "And we're doing the killing, instead of the solving. Last person standing wins."

There was a flurry as people checked their slips of paper, and a whole lot of laughing ensued.

"You sure you wrote down *common* household items?" Mack, one of the local firefighters, looked skeptical.

Josiah nodded. "Common around this place. It'll make sense when we start dropping like flies. Once you're told you're out, go ahead and have fun with your death scene."

"Because discovering that Mr. Greene did it on the garden swing with the castrator isn't hysterical enough?" Zach's quip got more laughs from the gathering.

"That game is ongoing," Lisa said. "For now, enjoy the food. There will be other activities to try later. If you want to know why, it's because I'm in charge of the kids' games at the Canada Day party, and you're test driving them for me tonight."

Which turned the evening into something resembling one massive birthday party setting with twenty and thirty-year-olds fully getting into Lisa's brand of mischief.

Karen peeked at her papers as she wandered through the house, but she was more interested in enjoying the good food and the buzz of happiness filling her soul. Lisa was in all her glory, laughing like a kid one minute and the next, snuggling against Josiah. Her thirty-seven year old partner looked at her as if she hung the moon.

Tamara and Caleb were there as well, baby Tyler held easily in Caleb's muscular arm. Or more realistically, Caleb had control of his son when the kid wasn't being passed through the ranks like a ball in a rugby scrimmage.

Even Finn took a turn. He had settled in Josiah's massive easy chair when someone placed Tyler in his lap. For a moment Karen thought she would have to rescue him, but instead he shocked the hell out of her. Finn comfortably rotated the baby, holding him competently with one hand as he looked Tyler in the eye. He tapped his finger on Tyler's nose, chuckling when the little tyke's arms flailed outward, grasping for Finn's hand.

Something inside her flared, and it wasn't sexual this time, but still centered low in her gut. Avoidance seemed the easiest way to deal with the rush of emotions striking out of nowhere.

She turned and spotted Julia making her way over, mischief in her eyes. "Why do you look like a cat who found the cream?" Karen asked.

"I just saw the setup for the next game Lisa's running. Look." Julia leaned in conspiratorially and held forward the strangest rubber duck Karen had ever seen.

"What the heck?" She took it from Julia to examine it more closely. It was a rubber duck all right, but this one had a little cowboy hat and a holster and a mighty fine moustache. Laughter bubbled up and Karen glanced at her sister. "That's cute."

Julia grinned. "It also means that I got you. Karen, in the living room, with a rubber duck. Go ahead and hand over your targets before you die."

Well, drat. Karen pulled out her clues and slapped them into Julia's hand. "That was far too cheesy. And I should've known better than to take anything from you."

"It is true, though. We are having duck races," Julia said consolingly. Then she wiggled her fingers. "Have a nice death."

She turned and walked off, head down as she examined Karen's slips of paper.

Karen wasn't much for the dramatic, but she owed it to Lisa to give it some effort. She pulled out her phone and set an alarm, choosing the classic duck ringtone.

Then she sat on the couch next to Josiah. "I'm so glad you're in charge of that one now, because she is more trouble than a barrel of monkeys."

Josiah blinked. "Come again?"

"Lisa. She's your problem, sweetie, and it couldn't have happened to a nicer guy."

Karen leaned back on the couch, placed the duck on her chest, then set off the alarm. She closed her eyes and gave her best gasping, gurgling, death knell as an insistent quacking echoed through the room.

FINN WANDERED, watching with interest the various games that had been pulled out of nowhere.

On one corner of the deck, a group was bouncing ping-pong balls into cups. But unlike the classic pong version, no beer was involved. The red cups were lined up on the back of a Roomba that was constantly changing position, and the shrieks of laughter rising from the group rivaled any drunken revelry.

"You're not joining in." Zach stepped beside him. "There's a wicked game of pin the tentacles on the octopus going on in the kitchen."

Dear God. "I'm saving my strength for whatever twisted masterpiece Lisa has for the grand finale." He glanced over his shoulder and unerringly found Karen.

She hadn't been out of his thoughts all evening. And damn it if she hadn't been within eyesight the entire time. He was trying to give her space, but it was as if after all those years of being apart, they instinctively kept rotating into each other's gravitational force.

When she glanced up and looked directly at him, he hummed contentedly. She was as bad as him.

Her cheeks flushed, and she returned to the conversation she was having with the Fields sisters, Tansy and Rose. They were joint owners of a coffee and knickknack shop in Heart Falls that was doing well enough it had caught Zach's attention.

Although Finn wasn't one hundred percent certain it wasn't the dark-haired beauty, Rose, that Zach was keen on studying.

Finn tilted his head toward where the women stood chatting. "Saw you had a meeting on the books with Ms. Fields. What tangled webs are you weaving?"

Zach managed to look surprised and shockingly innocent at the same time. "I was playing with ideas for future adventures of the brewhouse, but that's on hold for now. After tonight, it's full-on concentration until the ranch is ready."

"No need for you to swear off all entertainment while we're working. Bruce would never have approved of you acting the saint." Their mentor had enjoyed an amiable divorce from his first wife followed by a stream of women who all left his company contented. The man had been a miracle worker in more than just the business field.

Zach glanced around at the partygoers, but his gaze kept returning to where Karen stood, now with Rose, Tansy, and Julia. "You just go on with your bad self and let me worry about my sources of entertainment."

"Hey, Zach." It was Julia, calling across the distance.

Zach glanced at Finn and spoke softly. "She's murdered at

least seven people I know of. This has got to be a setup." He raised his voice and offered a cocky grin. "What's up?"

"Toss me that ball beside you?" she asked sweetly.

Zach folded his arms across his chest and gave her his patented poker grin. "Sorry. I don't play with my balls in public."

Finn pinched the bridge of his nose and attempted to not die laughing. "Bad wording, man."

Feminine laughter agreed with him, drifting on the air and becoming louder as Karen and Julia closed in on them.

A small hiccup escaped Julia, and she covered her mouth briefly before eyeing Zach boldly. "That suspicious nature doesn't look good on you, baby."

"You *have* proven to be a load of trouble," Karen pointed out.

Julia released a hefty sigh. "I'm so misunderstood." She tipped her head in farewell and went to step around Zach. She staggered, stumbling toward him, her nearly full glass teetering precariously.

Zach caught her and her drink before they all crashed to the floor. "Watch it. You might want to go lighter on the liquor, darling."

She popped to her feet and grinned, completely sober and obviously pleased as punch. "And you might want to practice your death throes, because I got you. Zach, by a table, with a glass."

Zach stood motionless for a second before rolling his eyes. "Well, *damn.*"

The expression on his friend's face was priceless, and Finn twisted away slightly to hide his smile. Karen was beside him, and the two of them ended up grinning at each other.

"Pass over your clues," Julia mock whispered.

"Eager to make your next kill?" Zach dug into the threadbare pocket of his jeans, Julia watching intently.

She accepted the strips of paper, a brilliant smile crossing her face. "It's safe to play with your balls if you want."

Finn had always been proud of his ability to keep a straight face, but that line was too much for him to bear. He twisted even farther away. Karen leaned her forehead against his chest, and the two of them shook as they attempted to contain their laughter.

Behind them, Zach groaned dramatically. "Yeah, yeah, I fell into that one. I'm drowning my sorrows. Either of you want anything? Karen? Finn?"

Karen snickered helplessly, so Finn answered for both of them. "We're good."

He wrapped his arms around her, gently guiding her toward the railing. They both rested their elbows on the sturdy wood beam and concentrated on their breathing. The view was beautiful, and the woman beside him was as full of life and energy as he remembered. And even though there was a hell of a challenge ahead of him, Finn was completely content.

They stared over the spring green landscape, enjoying a quiet moment of companionship.

When she did speak, it was in her usual tone of voice. Back in control and sweetly intense. "Well, that was fun."

"Zach will complain about this for the rest of the summer." Finn twisted position and placed his elbows on the railing as he gazed at her face. "It's good to see you with your sisters. Julia fits in so damn well it's like watching a case study for nature versus nurture."

"It has been interesting to see what character traits might be genetic and what sprang up from the way we were raised. I think we've still got a lot to learn about each other, though." She looked thoughtful at that. She shook it off and met his gaze.

"Hey, I wanted to ask. When did you get so comfortable around babies?"

Finn had known at some point he would have to share some sensitive information. He'd been racking his brain for the best way to do it. Everything that had shaken down over the past five years wasn't the stuff to shove at a person all at once.

Thank goodness fate had been on his side because this was about the most perfect opening he could've asked for.

"Remember Levi?"

"Your youngest brother and Lisa's cohort for raising hell that summer you all invaded? It would've taken therapy to forget," Karen offered dryly.

Finn stifled his amusement. "He had such a crush on you. Hero worship, really."

"And that was the other part I've been working hard on forgetting." But she said it with a smile. "Don't tell me that boy's got babies in his life."

"Three of them." His announcement received a satisfyingly enthusiastic gasp. "The first one was a bit of a surprise—we got home at the end of that summer, and the girl he'd been seeing before we left had a profound announcement to share."

Karen whistled softly. "Is it terrible to say I'm glad he and Lisa never hooked up?"

"Levi was completely gone on Chelsea. Still is. We got home, they got married. Baby number one, Andrew, arrived before Christmas. My nieces showed up over the next two years." They were amazing kids. His brother and sister-in-law were absolutely content with their family and their home situation. Even though it had taken shaking the Marlette family apart at the roots to make sure the right parts would survive.

"Good for them." Karen examined him closer. "Why do you tell me this as if there's something wrong with the news?"

"Because I figured you'd think it a little strange." He

shrugged. "They're running the ranch instead of me. They're doing the job I left you to go home to."

"Ahhh." She dipped her head slowly, still watching him carefully. "There's more to the story, isn't there?"

Should've known he couldn't pull a fast one on her. "There is, but it's not something to share in the middle of a party. And it's settled. I'm happy for Levi and Chelsea, and they're in the right place. It's exactly what I want for them, and really, the ranch can only support one family. I'm glad it's them."

She looked as if she would ask something else, but then the damn dinner bell went off again, and Josiah was calling them all down the stairway to where a series of kiddie pools were connected by what looked like miniature creeks.

It was enough. Finn had broken the ice on one secret in his world. It would have to do for now.

He held out a hand. "Come on. It looks as if the reason you needed pretty pink toenails has arrived."

She went with him willingly enough, and they made their way down the stairs hand in hand.

Zach stood amongst those gathered below, his gaze making note of the connection between them. His friend tilted his head slightly and gave Finn an approving wink.

"I hope you're all ready for this." Josiah glanced around the gathering. "And don't worry, there was only one death by duck in the game today. You're safe while you're playing."

"Who is even still alive?" Tansy asked.

A whole group pointed at Julia. Another group pointed at Lisa. Both of them had made some fairly spectacular and sneaky moves. There were only four people still playing, the other two being the big local Fire Chief, Brad Ford, and his fiancée, Hanna.

Petite Hanna blushed at the cheers she got.

Finn leaned in against Karen. "Don't buy that innocent

look from her. The little minx took me out of the game by pretending to be terrified by a spider. She was pinned to the wall in the hallway, gasping as if she would faint right away. Turns out she carried the spider with her and held on to it until I came around the corner."

Karen burst out laughing and gave Hanna a high five. "You go, girl."

Lisa and Josiah exchanged glances, a soft smile on her lips. He shuddered violently.

Then they buckled down to explain the rules, which were one step short of ultimate chaos.

What followed involved a great deal of splashing as everyone was assigned numbers and a trio of rubber ducks. Soon there were grown adults frolicking in the water, creating waves to guide their miniature flocks from the start to the finish line without touching them.

The straightaways were fine, but the kiddie pools were like vast black holes. Finn couldn't get his plastic targets to head in the same direction for the life of him.

He was racing Lisa, and she was a good five feet ahead of him when a circular Frisbee sailed through the air and hooked around the neck of one of Lisa's ducks.

She caught hold of the ring to remove it, jerked to a stop far too late, and tripped over her own feet. She crashed into the pool and a wave of water arched skyward.

A loud hoot and holler rose from the crowd as she crawled out of the water, soaked but grinning happily.

She glanced around to discover Hanna coming forward. "Tricky woman. I should've known better—I'm the one who wrote Frisbee on the murder weapon list."

Hanna held out a towel. "It will be hard to finish this considering there's only three of us left and we all know who to watch for."

Lisa stepped from the pool and rubbed the towel over her hair and clothes. "That's fine. We'll make it work."

She dug in her pocket and handed over three soggy strips of paper.

Hanna read them and laughed, eyeing her fiancé as if making evil plans.

Brad raised his hands in protest. "You are dangerous."

The petite woman pressed a hand to her chest. "Me? I'm innocent. You can totally trust me."

Julia snickered.

It was only a minute later, after the next set of ducks were being dealt with in the kiddie pools, that Julia sent up a loud cry. "*Nooooooo. I've* been fatally done in by a piece of strawberry pie."

Finn was mostly dry by this time, once again standing at Karen's side as she pressed closer in an attempt to see what was going on at the edge of the deck.

He slid his hand around her waist and tugged her in front of him so she had a better view. Having her in his arms, leaning back on him as if that was exactly where she was supposed to be? Perfection.

Julia was shaking her finger at Hanna, but she handed over her clues with a wink. "Good luck. We all know who you're gunning for."

Brad stepped forward and swept Hanna into his arms. "She's already knocked me off my feet and stole my heart," he informed the gathering. "She's welcome to win the game by knocking me off, period."

A chorus of *awwwww* rose from the crowd.

Sweet Hanna caught him around the neck and kissed him, right then and there, triggering more laughter.

A slow clap started. Julia turned to all of them and beamed as she made an announcement. "We have a winner. I declare

Hanna the last one standing now that she's caught *Brad* with a *kiss, outside the house.*"

Hanna blushed. People cheered. Brad threw back his head and laughed the loudest.

In the circle of Finn's arms, Karen sighed happily.

It was comfortable, and contentment at being in Heart Falls, in this community, grew in a way that Finn hadn't expected. Not here.

Really, not anywhere.

For most of his life, home had meant one location... Now the word conjured up not a place but people.

More specifically, a *person*. Karen had come to represent home, so this other sensation was interesting.

But it wasn't something he needed to spend a lot of time dwelling on. His priorities were clear. Do what it took to be with Karen, and make sure Brandon never got to have a piece of this pie.

8

How are you getting your tasks done for my father and still finding time to pick me flowers? It's not working, by the way. Not making me soften up and forgive you for tricking me into that kiss behind the barn the other day.

That's a total lie. There's nothing to forgive because I was a full participant in that kiss, and we both know it.

Painkillers talking right now, but I'm having dirty dreams about kissing you. Maybe more. Trying to figure out where and when is taking up way too much brain time, damn you, Finn Marlette.

Don't you dare follow me into the chicken coop later today. I swear I won't have any inclination to kiss you again.

~Note from Karen to Finn, summer at Whiskey Creek ranch~

The next week passed in a blur. It was pretty much sunup when Karen got out of bed, and then the day would explode into activity.

She went for regular rides on Starlight. Some with Zach, some with her sisters. All the while looking for routes that would satisfy everyone from the rawest beginner to the most experienced riders.

She made phone call after phone call, not only to her contacts at Willmore Wilderness camp, but also to people she'd talked to over the years while working at Whiskey Creek.

Mealtimes when she stopped for a break, there'd be a knock on her door, and someone would show up with blueprints that needed her opinion or her ideas. Her phone buzzed with messages from her sisters and regular pictures at crazy intervals as Tamara gushed over her baby boy.

It was the busiest Karen remembered being in a long time, and it was good.

The only part missing was Finn.

After his talk about wanting to get back together and wanting to be with her, it seemed he had absolutely meant the bit about leaving the timing up to her. He was scarce. Or more correctly, he was always around, but never close enough to chat with. It became impossible to get her fix in a casual way like she had at Lisa's party.

She'd admit it. She liked spending time with Finn, and the urge to say yes continued to grow.

He left wildflowers on her back porch every morning.

While her body was very willing, she still didn't know if it was the best idea. She wished she could stop being wishy-washy, yet taking this time felt right. Felt necessary.

It's not as if she had a ton of time to get lonely. Not with popping over to Tamara's, or over to Lisa's, or even to Julia's teeny studio apartment. Spending time with her sisters was a great distraction.

They'd finished another dinner at Julia's when Lisa spoke up from her place at the sink. "Hey, Karen. Okay if I come spend the day with you at the soon-to-be dude ranch?" She placed a clean plate in the drying rack and reached for another dirty dish. She gestured with her head toward Julia, who was putting away the rest of the leftovers into her tiny refrigerator. "Jules is on day shift, Josiah's got a full workday, and I'm at loose ends."

"I don't mind, but I'm putting you to work," Karen warned. "There's a heck of a lot of buildings to go through and see if there's anything we can salvage."

"I thought you were in charge of the horse side of things, not construction." Julia started putting away the dry items Karen had stacked to the side.

"My job description got expanded. I don't mind," Karen said. "I have a lot of people I'm waiting to hear back from, so I may as well give Zach a hand."

Lisa and Julia exchanged glances. "Giving *Zach* a hand. Sure you're not giving Finn a hand?" Lisa asked.

"Haven't seen him for days." The words came out sharp and annoyed.

Silence shouted back at her.

Yeah, she had kind of stepped into that one. "Okay, yes, I'm a little grumbly I haven't seen him for a while. I thought he was interested in me."

"Did you *tell* him you want to see him again? Because I think he might need a written invitation." Lisa wrinkled her nose. "Which is not what I expected when you first mentioned this, so you're right. I get why you're snappy. When a dude makes a play, he should keep on it."

"Disagree with you on that one," Julia said bluntly. "He's

waiting for her answer. Keeping in her face would be an asshole move. This is not being an asshole."

Lisa paused then dipped her head. "I hear what you're saying."

"I mean, if he vanished completely, that would be one thing. But you said he's still around. Sort of." Julia eyeballed the flowers Karen had brought because her still-expanding bouquets had filled the teeny cottage to the brim.

Karen pressed her palms against her temples and let out a tired breath. "I don't know what's wrong with me. I need to make a decision and not keep dragging this out. You're right, Julia. He's not being a jerk. I am."

"Maybe you need to make this not so enormous in your head. I mean, start dating and see what happens. It's not as if beginning something means you're making a lifetime commitment." Julia shrugged.

The topic got dropped until the next morning when Lisa showed up on Karen's doorstep bright and early. The cream-coloured terrier, Ollie, danced around her sister's feet, but more importantly, Lisa had cups of coffee from Buns and Roses and two enormous boxes to boot.

Karen accepted the coffee, ignored the fact a dog was in her house, and took an appreciative sniff of Lisa's burden. "Don't tell me those are cinnamon buns."

The box was opened a moment later, and Lisa dug in, gooey white icing dripping down the side of the baseball-sized treat. "Okay, I won't tell you."

Mouthwatering goodness was inhaled in a flash. Karen licked her fingers and gazed at her sister happily. "I brought you up right. Even though you forgot the rule about dogs belonging outside."

Lisa snorted. She gestured to the glass on the counter that held a single crocus flower. "Finn?"

He was being persistent in a very sweet way. "Do you think I'm terrible for not giving him a straight answer yet?"

Lisa shrugged, eyeing the remaining cinnamon buns as if the weight of the world hung in the balance. "I think you have good reason to not leap. But I also think Julia was right last night. Maybe it's time to stop worrying about how much it might hurt if it doesn't work out and put a little more hope toward things going right."

A flutter of something wild and untamable went off in Karen's gut. "You have a point."

Lisa grabbed another cinnamon bun and arched a brow. "Share?"

"Forget it. I want another whole one to myself."

Cinnamon buns devoured and sticky hands washed, they headed out the door and into the workday.

Another reason why being in Heart Falls was right—

Lisa had only been gone from Whiskey Creek since December, helping Tamara while she had trouble with her pregnancy. But that meant it had been over six months since she and Karen worked together on a regular basis. Yet they fell back into it with a smooth rhythm, and it was good.

Finn had hired a group of guys to help with demolition and salvage. Brawny fellows with loud laughs and a few with gazes that lingered a little too long. Nothing out of the ordinary. Nothing either of them hadn't faced before.

Lisa just rolled her eyes, smiling sweetly as she dropped things on the toes of anyone who got too close. After she'd *accidentally* canned a second guy while rapidly swinging floorboards, the group of them backed off slightly.

"You ladies want to come see what you think of the boards we found? Finn had some idea of using them to do feature walls in the cabins." Zach gestured them toward one of the taller buildings near the barn.

"Kind of a rustic feel. Is that what you're going for?" Lisa asked.

"Pretty much." This from Finn, to Karen's utter amazement. He finished signing something then handed the clipboard back to the construction foreman who was dealing with final barn renovations. "You got room for another on that tour?"

Ollie stepped in front of him, braced her legs, and barked enthusiastically.

Karen was just about to excuse the dog when Finn dropped to a crouch and slipped a hand over the pup's head. "Yeah, you're invited too."

Lisa's eyes widened, and she made one of those faces. The ones where she was trying to get a whole message across without words, but Karen wasn't sure if what she was saying was "dude likes dogs, so he's got to be okay," or if she was acknowledging the man knew exactly how to score points.

What was unfolding made Karen happy, though, and that was a convincing factor. She had enjoyed her time with Finn immensely. It had been the hurt later that had soured the experience, and that hadn't been either of their faults but a matter of time and circumstance.

Like Julia had said, dating Finn was not a commitment to forever. It was something for here and now.

Outside a narrow, two-storey building, Zach paused. The door opened in front of them with a tormented creaking sound. "We're not sure what this building will be used for. Anything you think that's worth salvaging, make a note or stick a pin in it."

"What was this place?" Karen asked as they paced through the rooms. "Definitely not a house. Not a barn."

A soft cough of amusement rose from Lisa as she riffled

through some papers in the corner. "It looks as if somebody might have lived here."

Karen slipped over to join her and glanced down at a bunch of flyers and ancient newspapers. One announced baths for an astonishingly low price.

It was the one that showed a dance hall poster that made her hesitate. And the one under that.

"Dance hall? Ladies for hire?" She turned to the others, amusement rising. "Finn Marlette, you bought yourself a house of ill repute."

FINN HAD BEEN TRYING his best to give her space, but with Karen's eyes laughing at him, he gave in to temptation.

He stepped forward, closing the gap between them. "You've no idea how bad Zach has been teasing me about saving wood from this place."

Something close to a donkey bray escaped his best friend, but it really was too funny. In the midst of a shit ton of work they had to get done, it was good to have some things to lighten the mood.

Zach clapped his hands to get their attention and force them back to work. "Let's keep moving. Those papers are in the pile of things we're saving, because yes, I think it's hysterical we managed to grab the one place in the area that has a very —*ahem*—rich history."

They headed down the hallway, peeking into what must've been individual rooms. Not much was left except the structure itself, but Karen ran a hand down the dark walnut paneling with approval. "These would be beautiful reused."

They'd made it through about a half dozen rooms, picking

out things that were worth saving, when Ollie took off. She barked loudly as she headed up the stairs to the second floor.

Lisa apologized quickly, slipping after her pet. "Sorry. Don't know what's gotten into her."

Karen stepped toward the next room, sliding past Finn close enough that their bodies touched. Warm and soft and sneakily intimate. The hallway was narrow enough to explain having bumped together, but that didn't answer why she had that look in her eyes. Her hips swayed just enough to brush against him a second time.

He stared, hunger aching in his gut.

Reality returned in a rush when Zach nudged his side. His friend's concern shone clearly as he pointed upward. "I don't know that anyone should be running around on the second level."

Shit. "Lisa, hold up. It might not be stable up there."

That got everybody's attention.

Karen was on the move as well, calling after her sister. "Lisa. Slow down and call Ollie back."

"It's okay. The stairs are solid, and she's right here." Lisa stopped at the top of the landing then bent and wiggled her fingers. "Come on, sweetie. Come show me what you found."

Finn slipped up the stairs and past Lisa, assessing the boards between him and the dog. "I'll grab her."

He moved slowly, trying to guess where the support beams were beneath the floorboards.

Ollie was sitting now, nose pointed intently at a small hole in the corner of the room. Finn got down on his hands and knees and peered inside to discover a pair of diamond-shaped eyes staring back at him.

The teeniest *meow* triggered a series of barks from Ollie, and suddenly the kitten was gone, back into the wall.

"I'll grab this one for you, then I've got someone else to deal with." Finn had Ollie by the scruff a second later, transporting the squirming beast back to her owner.

Lisa tucked Ollie under her arm and slipped down the stairs.

"Need a hand?" Zach asked.

"Careful," Karen said. The two of them stood at the top of the stairs. Karen's gaze snapped over the floorboards with growing horror. "Finn? I think you'd better get back here."

The meow sounded again.

To hell with it. Finn dropped to his knees, reaching into the hole and hoping nobody had set rat traps in the building in the past.

A swear burst from Zach. "Finn. Leave it. Something's coming apart. That section of the floor is going to—"

"Get out. Now," Finn ordered as his hand brushed fur. It was enough to allow him to hook a finger around a limb and haul the creature forward.

As he lifted the kitten in the air, a cloud of sawdust exploded in his face. The wall in front of him deconstructed like a mummy being hit with a cyclone wind. A loud crash echoed in his ears.

He fell.

Finn scrambled at the floorboards with his free hand, but the wooden slats pulled apart like toothpicks, flying from his grasp as he plummeted downwards. He hoped like hell Karen and the others had retreated down the stairs far enough—

He hoped his feet would touch first so he could roll with the momentum, but something swung into him from the side, pushing his legs to the right and propelling him into a solid object.

The space above him dropped, and he landed hard as something stabbed through his lower leg.

His teeth jammed together, trapping a shout inside even as his body screamed silently in protest.

Searing pain shot through his right leg, and something soft but extremely pokey jabbed his left hand. Finn pushed through the waves of pain radiating from his shin and sucked in a breath. Adrenaline rushed his system.

Clouds of dust were settling around him, and shouts sounded from a distance. Zach and Karen. Familiar voices that made him tense for a moment until he realized they were calling his name.

Good. They were safe.

He held it together long enough to lift his hand in front of his face to discover he held a snow-white kitten. The little thing had its claws sunk in deep, and it was quivering but not trying to escape.

He saw stars. Then nothing.

9

Karen finally knew what that phrase *heart in your throat* actually felt like.

It wasn't something she'd been hoping to experience.

After they rushed down the stairs, the deafening noise that exploded behind them had ripped her apart in so many ways.

All she could picture was that second before escaping, where Finn had stared back at her, concern in his eyes as he ordered her to safety. Then everything had crumpled like a house of cards collapsing in on itself.

"Finn. Dammit, answer me," Zach shouted, scrambling forward before the timbers had finished settling.

Karen caught the back of his collar with both hands, jerking him to a stop so he didn't rush into danger. "Finn won't thank you if you get hurt going after him. Wait."

Although, she was quivering on the spot as well. Everything in her wanted to push past Zach that second and find out what had happened.

Thankfully, the crashing soon died down, and the instant the air quieted, both she and Zach were on the move, shouting

Finn's name. The air was full of dust, sunlight turning the motes into cloudy spotlights.

A muted groan sounded, and both she and Zach veered to the right. They stepped over fallen debris, moving toward the spot where a pile of timbers crisscrossed over Finn's body.

Fear coated her tongue. She hurried as quickly as possible to his side.

"I called 9-1-1," Lisa shouted from somewhere behind them. "And a bunch of the crew members are on their way over."

Which was a good thing because Finn was buried under heavy beams, his tanned face shockingly pale in the shadowy corner where he lay.

Karen held her breath as she pressed her fingers to his neck. A second later she exhaled sharply. "He's got a strong pulse. Hey, Finn. You're going to be okay."

He had to be okay. That was all there was to it.

"Dammit, Finn. What the hell were you thinking?" Zach shifted a piece of wood away then cursed. "Lisa. We need some help in here."

The next timeframe passed in an eerie combination of slow-motion and high-speed chaos. Half a dozen guys were in the space, lifting things off Finn. A tiny kitten opened its mouth, its little pink tongue drawing Karen's attention. She scooped it up from where it had nestled in the crook of Finn's arm and settled it inside her outer shirt.

Zach had his hands clamped around Finn's leg, rich red smearing his fingers. Karen held Finn's hand, and as a log beam was lifted off, his eyes fluttered open, and he groaned loudly.

"Hang in there, buddy," Zach said. "Don't try to move."

"You guys good?" Finn's stunned gaze danced over Karen's face. "You get hurt?"

"Dumbass." Zach responded before Karen. "You're the one

who went surfing. The rest of us took the stairs like normal human beings."

"Wasn't my idea." Finn's face contorted for a moment. "Hurts like hell."

Karen squeezed his fingers, leaning in a little closer so he didn't have to strain to see her. "We'll take care of you."

In spite of the pain on his face, hopefulness flashed in his eyes. "Promise?"

It was good to be able to answer honestly and instantly. "Promise."

As if her answer was as good as a shot of morphine, the tension drained out of him. Finn's eyes closed, but the grip of his hand in hers increased as he held on tightly.

His thumb started that back-and-forth motion again. The one that was so familiar and so right.

"Do we get him out?" asked one of the crew, staring in horrid fascination.

Zach met Karen's gaze. "Everything else seems solid enough. I think it's safer to keep him here."

"Then we won't move him," she agreed. She looked up and offered a few orders. "Grab some blankets. And send someone to the gate so the emergency crew knows where to come."

"What can I do?" Lisa asked.

Karen reached into her shirt for the kitten that had been kneading its claws against her stomach. "Take this. Wait—first, we need something to help Zach apply pressure."

Zach motioned Lisa over. "Take off my belt. I need to get the bleeding slowed, but I'm not about to go near that bone."

The one that was poking through sturdy jean fabric, and God, Karen knew Finn had to be in a ton of pain, but he just lay there, breath ragged, his fingers linked iron-tight with hers.

They stabilized him as best they could. Lisa helped Zach tighten the belt around Finn's upper thigh then took control of the kitten. Karen ignored the blood on Zach's hands and soaking through Finn's jeans. Instead, she offered Finn a steady stream of reassuring words.

The local emergency crew arrived before the ambulance did, which meant Julia was there, sliding in next to Karen, while Brad Ford took his place on the other side.

"You with us, Finn?" Julia asked, all business after giving Karen a quick shoulder squeeze.

"Don't want to be." The words came out rumbling and low. "Hurts."

"We'll get you fixed up, then you're taking a trip to Black Diamond." Brad motioned to Julia, and they worked quickly, stabilizing him even more and offering a painkiller to help until the ambulance arrived.

"Much better," Finn said, his grip on Karen's hand loosening slightly. Then he opened his eyes, heavy-lidded, and unerringly met her gaze. "Come with me."

"You got it." He wasn't going anywhere without her.

In the end, Zach drove and Karen rode with him, following the ambulance to the hospital where Finn was taken into surgery almost immediately.

Karen's skin crawled as she sat there in the white-walled emergency waiting room, hands clenched, staring at the clock as they waited for news.

God, she hated hospitals.

Beside her, Zach seemed just as miserable. He alternated between sitting forward, head supported in his hands, and bouncing to his feet and pacing. His boots scuffed heavily on the linoleum floor.

He dropped into the seat next to her for what had to be the twentieth time before he finally spoke. "So damn stupid. We checked all the buildings. Somehow I fucked up."

"It's not your fault," Karen began.

"It's got to be my fault. I'm the one who okayed the building. I could've *sworn* it was structurally sound enough to be in. I never would've taken any of you in if it was close to collapsing."

Karen laid a hand on his arm. "Of course you wouldn't have. There must've been some flaw that showed up in the past while. The big rainstorm we had the other day—maybe it messed with the footing."

Zach threw himself back in the chair, legs stretched out in front of him, utter dejection on his face. "Doesn't make sense."

"Doesn't help anything for you to beat yourself up over something we can't change," Karen said dryly. "And you tell me. You think Finn will give you hell for this?"

He hesitated. "Probably not, but we've already established that he's kind of a dumbass."

A snort of amusement escaped her before she could stop it. The next thing to arrive was a wave of emotion that overwhelmed her. Tears rushed upward, and the next thing she knew, Zach pulled her against his chest and patted her back as she cried her eyes out.

"Hey. It's okay. It's going to be okay. That stubborn bastard will be bossing us around in no time. Hell, he's probably telling the doctor how to fix his leg right now. Opinions? He's always got a few."

It had to be partly from memories as well as the current tension, because Karen wasn't the type to lose it like this. Hospitals were not somewhere she enjoyed, and she would admit that to anybody who asked.

But her loss of control was humbling, nevertheless. Slowly letting the tension go, her breathing evened out. Zach patted her back the same way Tamara would've. His hug was comforting, like having family to hold.

Finn's words came back to mind. How he trusted Zach implicitly.

While Karen wasn't certain what exactly she was signing on for, she knew her future involved being with Finn, at least for the summer.

She gave Zach a final squeeze then pulled herself together, accepting the tissues he handed her to wipe her face dry.

The smile she put on was a little on the watery side, but it was an attempt. "Thanks. It *will* be okay, but you know he's stubborn."

"As the day is long," Zach offered.

Karen ran through options quickly. "I don't know what they're fixing, but I know how it felt when I broke my leg. What can we do to make the time when he gets out of here easier?"

Zach considered. "Depending on what type of cast he gets, he might not be able to drive."

"Skip that part for now," Karen suggested. "How are you guys set up at the house? Will he be able to get around safely?"

"We can set up a bed in the living room. There's no way he'll be able to do stairs." Zach hesitated. "Or put it this way, he'd probably insist on doing the stairs, but we should try to set it up so that he avoids them."

She refused to beat around the bush. "There's a second bedroom in the cottage. I think he should move in with me."

Her determined announcement seemed to knock the wind out of Zach's sails for a moment. Then he examined her carefully. "You don't have to do that."

Ride or die.

"I want to," she admitted. She met his gaze straight on. "I've been waffling for too long. Finn says you know about our past, so you'll get that me having to help him with anything personal won't be an issue."

She didn't expect the soft chuckle in response. He reached down and tucked his fingers under her chin. "Sugar, Finn wanting to be in a relationship with you again wasn't him looking for a nurse."

"Yeah, but we don't always get what we want, do we?" She waved a hand. "Look, first off, I meant it about the two bedrooms. This is about him having a place to sleep that's comfortable and safe. Secondly, you know Finn. The amount of nursing I'll get to do will be slim to none after he gets his feet under him, so to speak. I'm just saying..." She hesitated, because it was still so fresh and new, this idea of taking the chance. "I need to be there for him. Does that make sense?"

A slow smile spread over Zach's face. "It makes sense. And if you need anything, like help holding the bastard down because he's doing something he shouldn't, you call me. You got that?"

"It's a deal. We're a team."

The entry door opened, and Karen's sisters piled into the room.

"What's the latest word?" Tamara demanded.

"How are you doing?" Lisa echoed in the same tone.

Julia tilted her head toward the nurse's station and went to run interference. "I'll grab an update."

It was like having a whirlwind join them, and it was perfect. It was family wrapping themselves around her and Zach in the way her sisters always had.

Which made waiting that much easier. She wasn't alone.

She didn't have to be alone.

Bright light stabbed through the window. A pulse set off at the back of his skull, the same tempo as the blood drilling through his veins. Finn closed his eyes briefly then tried opening them again, but everything refused to focus.

"Slow down, pal. You've got nowhere to go and a long time to get there."

Finn swiveled toward the voice, and a sharp pain struck. "Shit."

Raising a hand to rub his neck ended with his arm jerking to a stop after not even an inch.

"Finn. *Chill.*" A hand settled on his arm, and Zach's familiar voice buzzed on, a low lilt of laughter in the tone. "Figured you'd wake up swinging. You're okay. You're in a hospital bed, and you probably feel like you got hit by a Mack truck. Stop jerking yourself around and ease into it."

It sounded like good advice, so as tough as it was, Finn took a deep breath and let it out slowly. Relaxing even as he did a quick assessment of what hurt and what didn't.

The first list was a hell of a lot longer than the second one.

When he finally opened his eyes and blinked the world into focus, Zach was sitting beside him, his cocky grin noticeably missing.

"Who died?" Finn asked, his throat raspy and dry.

Zach's lips twisted for an instant. "Bastard."

"Can't get rid of me that easily." Finn glanced down to take a closer stock of the situation. "Hell, that's going to make it difficult to finish my dance lessons."

The bed was bent into a vee, pillows behind Finn propping him until he was almost upright. His left leg stretched under the blankets, but his right one was raised in the air, a half dozen pulleys and ropes propping it into a convoluted position.

His left arm was strapped to the guard rail, IV tubes disappearing to the left of the bed.

A curtain to his right, a window to the left, and a clock on the wall that said nine. "It's a little bright out for that to be nine p.m."

"You lost a night," Zach told him. "You were awake earlier but pretty doped up from the surgery. I'm sure the nurses will be in here to explain stuff, but other than head-to-toe bruising, most of you survived a building collapse really well."

Finn reached up and ran a hand over his thigh. "And the part of me that didn't hold up well? Looks like crap."

"I have been up close and personal with more of your bones in the last twenty-four hours than I ever want to see again." Zach undid the strap holding Finn's arm in place then leaned back in his chair and folded his arms over his chest. "There was some fancy medical term for it, but basically you smashed your tibia hard enough that it decided to try and crawl out of your body. Congratulations. You will now set off TSA security. They installed two metal rods while putting you back together."

Finn examined his leg again. "Hell of a thing."

He was obviously doped up enough the pain was a low-level buzz, but the sight of the cast made it pretty clear this was nothing he could walk off.

He glanced back at Zach to find his friend staring morosely at the cast. "Everybody else okay? Karen?"

"The rest of us were fine. So is the kitten you rescued."

"Kitten?" It had to be the drugs. Finn worried for a moment until the memory trickled back in. "Ollie. She found a kitten trapped in the wall."

"Karen's got the creature back at her cottage. It's too little to be alone yet. She said she'd take care of it."

The mention of Karen's name washed the lingering question of how the hell did a kitten get trapped in the wall and replaced it with an image of her face. "How is she? This probably set off some bad memories."

Finally, his friend smiled. "Maybe, but you can ask her yourself. She was here last night until it became clear you weren't alert enough to remember a thing. I took her back to the ranch for some shut-eye, and the only reason she agreed was I promised to bring her back for visiting hours."

"She's here?"

"Got waylaid doing a task for her sister. She'll be here in a few minutes." Zach leaned forward, his gaze intent. "You don't worry about anything, okay? I'll keep things rolling at the ranch, but if it comes down to it, screw the challenge. We both know Brandon doesn't really want to have anything to do with the dude ranch. He just wants money. I bet we can work out some deal to convince him to take funds and leave everything to us."

There weren't enough drugs in Finn's system to make that an okay idea. "You know something I don't? Like, am I stuck in this bed for the next six months or something? Because I don't see how me breaking my leg means we can't meet the challenge."

"Alan called with a deadline. He didn't know you'd been hurt, but that doesn't change things." Zach shook his head. "You're still not hearing my point. The most important thing is for you to heal, not for you to hurt yourself more trying to stick it to Brandon."

Finn snorted. "Trust me. I am a fantastic multitasker. I can heal *and* stick it to the bastard."

"Just saying. We keep our priorities straight."

"They are straight. I'll heal, we'll get the ranch running, Brandon will go and cry." He managed to get a laugh out of his friend, but the effort made Finn happy to relax back against the pillow. "Stop holding out. What's the deadline?"

"Alan insists he did his research, but I'm suspicious he's also planning to enjoy this. First guests arrive Thanksgiving weekend." Zach rolled his eyes like a teenager. "I'll give you one guess who the first guests are. Go on, you'll never guess it's a hotshot lawyer who told us he's a cowboy wannabe. Him and his entire family."

Finn laughed, choking it off quickly when he realized his ribs hurt too much to follow through. "Fine. Third week of October. That's not impossible."

Zach inclined his head. "You're right, it's not. But back to that priority thing, we're adjusting lists. You'll be pleased to know you're now stuck on the computer. Plus, you can deal with contract calls and phone orders. I'll work the front line."

It was instinct to protest. "Fine. But as soon as I'm up and mobile, we'll talk about this again."

His friend rose to his feet, reaching behind him to grab his hat. "Oh, and just to warn you, that whole priority thing means you'll take the time to heal and to be with important people."

What the hell was he talking about? "You headed back to the ranch already?"

"Grabbing a coffee." Zach strode to the door and pulled it open, greeting someone just out of Finn's sight. "He's awake and in his right mind. Or at least as close as he gets."

Karen slipped into the room, and some of Zach's teasing messages suddenly made sense. Somewhere in there his friend left, but Finn's attention was focused on the dark-haired woman stepping hesitantly to the side of his bed.

She stopped too far away for him to catch hold of her the way he wanted. She barely glanced at his leg before fixing her gaze on his face.

He crooked a finger, gesturing her closer. "Go on. Check me out. You know you want to."

Something close to a hiccup escaped as she closed the gap, brushing her fingers over his cheek. "You look like hell."

"Say something else sweet to me," he answered softly.

That hiccup happened again, and she swallowed hard. She laid her fingers on top of his and held on. "This is a trip down memory lane I really didn't want to take."

"I have a new appreciation of what you went through," Finn told her. "I'll be fine. You showed me how."

Her gaze drifted along his leg, and when she met his eyes again, it was as if she were preparing for battle. "Since you know I'm experienced in these things, you won't be foolish and fight with me over some little suggestions I have."

"Zach's already told me he's babysitting me at work," he informed her.

"Knew I liked him for a reason."

Finn stayed quiet because laughing would hurt.

That determination in her expression showed up again. "The doctor talked to you yet?"

"Nobody but you and Zach that I remember at this point."

Her chin dipped. "They'll give you the details, but it looks as if you're here for a few days. Once they release you, you're moving into the cottage with me."

That phrase should have triggered a rush of satisfaction. Instead, he eyed his leg then her. "You damn well better not be planning on babysitting me as well."

Finally, *finally*, the Karen he'd been looking for stepped forward and showed herself.

She picked up his hand and lifted it to her mouth. Pressing a kiss to his knuckles, she frowned slightly at the bruises and scratches she found there. But even though she took a deep breath as if bracing herself for battle, when she spoke, it was soft and sweet. "I want to be with you. While I have no idea how that will look, and I have no idea how long it will last, I want to give it a shot."

It wasn't everything he'd hoped for, but he was smart

enough to take it. Smart enough to relieve the tension shaping her shoulders, making them sit high and rigid.

He lifted one brow. "This isn't a pity fuck, is it?"

A sharp burst of laughter escaped her before she covered her mouth, glancing toward the hallway to make sure the door was still closed. She twisted back to offer him a classic Whiskey Creek expression. The one halfway between serious and *what the hell?*

"Who said anything about fucking?" she deadpanned.

He still had hold of her hand and used it to tug her closer, sliding his free hand up her arm to wrap his fingers around the back of her neck.

She came forward willingly, thank God, because an instant later her lips were inches away from his.

He stared into her deep brown eyes. "We'll take our time. There's no rush, but I will be there for you. Going to make you remember every little thing that was so fucking fantastic about us. Need to taste every inch of you, talk with you for hours, stare into your eyes as I drive you wild with my fingers and my tongue. And when the time is right, when you tell me that it's time, that's when I'll sink my cock deep into your body where I belong. Where *we* belong, *ma chérie*. Exactly how we belong. Connected. Together."

She barely blinked. Hadn't swallowed.

Finn lowered his voice and growled out his final point. "And we won't be fucking."

He closed the distance between their lips. Or maybe she did, because his hand wasn't around her neck anymore but cupping her cheek. Lips moving together, tongues exploring gently as if for the first time.

Dear God, every inch of his body ached, but he was still one step shy of heaven. That's what being with her was. What it meant.

Karen trembled slightly, but her mouth was on his, a willing and eager participant. Soft murmurs of pleasure teased his ears as her taste swirled into his system.

When they pulled apart, she was panting heavily. Her eyes glowed with heat and something else.

Hope.

10

With an unknown amount of hospital time ahead of Finn, everyone agreed it made more sense to save the visiting for the end of the day and keep work on track as best as possible.

Karen rose early and got into her tasks. When her meetings with contractors and potential employees were done, she joined the work crew, swinging a hammer to put up stalls and finish tasks in the barn.

She rode Starlight and found a new trail, and all of that was as perfect as a workday could be.

Then she and Zach made the hour-plus trip to Black Diamond. That part wasn't as perfect, because seeing Finn in pain and clearly struggling to stay alert wasn't good for anyone. Karen held his hand because he demanded it, but other than that, it was a wearying evening.

Zach was the one to suggest a change after the second trip out. "Would you think I was an asshole if we skipped the visits for the next couple of days? If us being there lifted his spirits, I'd be all for it. But I think we're wearing him out."

Karen thought back to the first days after her injury and how sometimes company had been more of a pain than pleasure. "We should let him rest and get better. If he wants company, though, I want to go."

The following morning, Zach followed up, and an official pause was called. Confirmed by a call from Finn to Karen only a few minutes later.

"Hey, you."

Karen stared over the windswept field beside her, the kitten rubbing past her ankles. "Hey. How's your day?"

His voice rumbled over the phone, softer than usual and slightly strained. "I might have a second nap after I finish waking up from my first nap. My to-do list is hell right now."

The ache inside her was rock-hard. "You're also healing, Finn. That's on your to-do list in three-foot-tall letters, got it?"

"Got it. Hey, chatted with Zach. I think it's smart for you to skip the trip out for the next couple of days. I'm still loopy most of the time from the drugs. I have no idea when I'll be coherent. I'd prefer you spend time with your sisters than my comatose body."

"I don't want you to be alone." Admitting it was hard but good.

Then he knocked her knees out from under her, his voice gone soft. Laced with pain but even more with kindness. "*Chérie*, I know how much you hate hospitals. I don't want you hurting yourself coming to see me. I mean it. Stay home."

She spoke around a throat gone tight. "Okay. But when you're coherent and bored, call. Or text. You're *not* alone, okay?" The need for him to know that was vital.

"I hear you." Finn's words faded toward the end. "Now go get in Zach's way since I'm not there to bother him."

Not having Finn around placed Karen in a strange sort of

limbo, and strangely, it was the time at home that seemed the most off.

What had started as such a treat—a place to call her own and to do whatever she wanted without anyone else's dictates—wasn't a treat anymore.

It was lonely.

The kitten Finn had rescued helped fill some of that space. Karen named the little creature Dandelion, and the fluffball slowly took control of his territory. This seemed to involve lots of pouncing, especially on Karen and any parts of her anatomy that happened to be moving.

Her toes. Her feet. Her finger on the table. Her head, first thing in the morning when the hellion decided her nose needed biting.

"He hasn't had any problems after being trapped in that wall," Julia pointed out while visiting a couple days after the accident.

"Ollie thinks Dandy is the cutest thing she's ever seen." Lisa glanced over her shoulder to where the two animals were circling each other. Or more precisely, Ollie was moving slowly, her tail wagging enthusiastically while the kitten stalked, preparing to pounce. "I have never seen Ollie like this. She chases away all of the ranch cats."

"By the way, Kelli told me there's a new batch of kittens in the loft," Tamara mentioned. "I can take Dandelion back with me whenever you want. I'm sure the mother cat will take him in. I know you're not keen on animals in the house."

"He's okay here for now," Karen said quickly.

That was the other reason Karen wasn't completely lonely. Her sisters kept invading, in ones or twos. Or all three. Today Tamara was along as well, having brought supper for the four of them to Karen's.

"You hear any more information about school in the fall?" Tamara asked.

She and Karen were still at the table as Lisa and Julia worked at the sink, cleaning up from their meal.

Karen thought about the envelope sitting unopened on her desk. "I did, but I'm not worried about it right now. Until Finn's back, we're all buckling down extra hard. I've been trying to step it up a little to make sure I'm doing my share."

"I doubt that's a problem," Tamara said dryly. "You doing anything for fun? I mean, not that I expect you to go out dancing or anything, because I get that you're still kind of shocked from the accident and all."

Currently she was more shocked about what she'd proposed in terms of Finn's living arrangements—a small detail she hadn't yet shared with her sisters.

Karen redirected the question. "I went riding a few times. Spotted that wild stallion in the area. He's definitely set up base in the foothills to the west of here. We'll have to make sure he's contained before we bring in a lot of more horses, or he'll constantly try to steal them away."

Tamara looked concerned. "That is a problem. I'll mention it to Caleb and see if Silver Stone can work with the ranch here to deal with them. Also, did you know that Kelli's been working with that gelding she cut out of the pack? The owners didn't want him back—said he was too wild to begin with and they don't want him teaching the rest of their herd any bad habits."

Karen would never cast off an animal like that. The gelding wasn't doing anything except what came naturally.

She shook her head. "Good for Kelli. Once things settle down around here, I'd love to come and give her hand."

"She'd love to see you." Tamara grinned. "It's been kind of fun having Kelli hero-worship you every time she comes around."

Karen was shocked. "She does not."

"It's like listening to my daughter go on and on about, 'Kelli says this' and 'Kelli says that.' Only now it's Kelli talking and she's all, 'Karen says the best way to deal with that is...' All the Silver Stone ranch hands think it's hysterical."

Obviously, Lisa wasn't the only one of her sisters with an overabundant imagination. Karen reached for Tyler and put him into burping position. "In other news, what's happening the next couple of weeks? I kind of lost track of time."

"Canada Day on Saturday. There're the events down at the park during the day, including the potluck supper and the bachelor auction." Tamara finished adjusting herself after nursing and glanced up with concern in her eyes. "When is Finn home from the hospital?"

"Hoping for two days from now. That's Wednesday, right?"

Tamara made a face. "I wonder if whoever is coordinating the bachelor auction heard that Finn's out of commission."

Karen's spine stiffened. "Bachelor auction?"

Her sister frowned. "Remember, I told you about Ivy buying Walker a couple years ago? Zach and Finn got signed up this year because they made a bet with Lisa, and they lost."

"Finn needs to cancel."

"Oh, hell no." Tamara paused. "Let me rephrase that. The one thing I learned when you were busted up was to not assume. Yes, it makes sense for him to cancel, but think how pissed you would've been if we had cancelled plans without consulting you first."

"You did cancel my plans, and I just about—"

Shit. The memory rushed in. Five years ago, in the situation of being broken and bent, she'd blown up hard at her sisters for taking over her calendar even though they'd meant well.

Because having another thing ripped out of her control had only exacerbated the problem.

Karen hated having a hard truth handed to her so neatly. "You're right. I'll remind Zach at our morning meeting that it's coming up, and they can decide what they want to do."

She didn't go out to the hospital that night either, staying home and chatting quietly with Julia and Lisa even after Tamara had taken Tyler home to be with her family.

The only message that day from Finn had been a short update.

Doing okay. They took me out of traction and gave me a cast. It's hugely awkward, but at least I'm not tied to the bed anymore. Hope you're enjoying the sunshine. Sorry I missed getting your flowers these past days.

Midmorning Tuesday, Karen went riding on one of the back paths at the very edge of Finn's property. A soft nicker caught her attention, and she slowed, pulling Starlight to a standstill.

The wild herd moved slowly through the trees. They angled toward a gully that led up a nearby ravine. Karen followed cautiously, not wanting to spook the horses into a panic.

By some chance she hit the very edge of the cliff as they moved into a clearing. Counting quickly, she observed the herd covertly.

The stallion was clear. Hands taller than the rest of them, he moved like the cocky bastard he was, adjusting position to crowd parts of his herd and ensure none of his followers loitered behind.

One of the mares in the group was heavily pregnant. She popped in and out of view at the outskirts of the group as they grazed on the fresh grasses of the clearing.

The mare moved slower than expected, and Karen examined her gait closely, wondering why.

It was her hind leg. She barely used it when she moved. With the added weight of the baby, the mare was having a hard time keeping up.

The escape from Silver Stone the other day probably hadn't helped matters, and guilt rushed in.

Wild animals always had difficult challenges to face. If Karen hadn't chased them, cougars or a pack of coyotes looking for dinner were always in the area. Injured beasts were culled by others in the animal kingdom all the time.

Karen tugged the reins to the side and slowly led Starlight far enough away to avoid spooking the herd before she increased tempo and returned to the cottage by a different route.

She kept herself busy because waiting for Finn was easier while distracted.

Tuesday night there was a thing down at the elementary school with her nieces, although listening to grade threes play recorders was more like torture than distraction.

Still, it meant that when Wednesday came around, it'd been more than a couple of days since she'd seen Finn.

Zach stopped by the house before she'd finished her first cup of coffee. "Finn sent a text. The doctor's in after lunch, so Finn won't get parole this morning. I'm headed to Calgary to do some shopping until he calls to say he's ready. Don't count on his arrival until maybe suppertime."

"Not a problem," she said. "Why don't you stay when you drop him off?" She offered him a wry grin. "Maybe he'll be on his best behaviour if we gang up on him."

"Are you ever delusional." Still, he gave her a wink. "You know he's probably going to be a bear to deal with."

She paused, wrapping one arm around herself as she

cradled her coffee mug in the palm of her other hand. "You ever break a limb, Zach?"

"Nope."

Karen tilted her head at him. "He gets to growl all he wants. At least at first. Later we'll get him to behave, but speaking from experience? I bet he'll get here and pretend like everything is hunky-dory. Heck, I bet he asks for a coffee at some point, when what he really wants is to go lay down and not move for a good twenty-four hours. I love my sisters to pieces, but nurses are assholes. Every single time I'd fall asleep, someone would come by to take my temperature or draw blood. Or they'd take my blood pressure and then tell me I needed to relax."

She got a full-on laugh out of Zach at that one. "I bet you're right. Okay, how about this? I'll be in town anyway. Why don't I grab whatever we need for supper before I pick up Mister Bear?"

"Sounds like a plan." They tossed a couple of menu ideas back and forth before Zach took off and Karen headed to work.

If she spent some of the day distracted by thoughts of Finn Marlette lying in the bedroom next to her that night, she'd write it off to the overactive imagination gene that obviously ran rampant in the Coleman family.

Finn was itching to leave by the time he'd gotten the doctor's approval.

Conditional approval. She stared him down, this teeny thing who didn't look old enough to have finished high school let alone gotten her residency.

Dr. Sydney Jerimiah stood behind her clipboard and gifted him with a high-voltage stare. "No pressure on the leg whatsoever. That means no *accidentally* walking on it for the next six weeks. You understand that's not a suggestion?"

He shook one of his crutches at her. "Pretty sure that's why you gave me two of these. Also, with the angle you set my leg, I have zero chance of walking."

"Imagine that." Her firm expression slid into the barest hint of a smile. "While it's the correct angle to fix your particular kind of break, you'll thank me later that your foot is that far off the ground. I figure I have zero chance of keeping you out of barns, and casts don't shake off manure quite as easily as cowboy boots."

"Thank you." The words came out gruff, but he meant them. He extended his hand and offered a firm handshake.

It was almost another forty minutes before Zach got there, which barely gave Finn enough time to get dressed, considering the damn cast.

He'd forgotten that even though he'd mutilated a pair of his jeans by cutting them off at the thigh, he still had to get the waistband over his foot in the first place. With the immovable cast in place, he was barely flexible enough to bend that far. Some fairly complicated wrangling ensued, and by the time he did up his zipper, he was sweating. Not to mention pain had flared hard enough that he didn't plan to do any more moving than necessary.

"Ready to blow this Popsicle stand?" Zach slid into the room, pushing a wheelchair. He eyed the abandoned jean fabric sticking out of the garbage can. "Looks like you're ready to roll. Literally."

"You'd never make it on the comedy circuit," Finn informed him bluntly.

Zach tossed Finn's bag over his shoulder, gesturing him toward the wheelchair. "Don't argue. I swear you can abandon the wheels at the exit door."

"Not arguing," Finn snapped.

His friend tossed him a sympathetic glance then shrugged. "I'm guessing you're in a lot more pain than you'll ever admit. Tell me to shut up if I start getting on your nerves."

Finn sighed. Great way to show his appreciation by biting Zach's head off over nothing. "You haven't done a thing. I'm just..."

"I get it. Honest. No reason to apologize."

There was a reason the man was his best friend.

Somehow Zach got him up on the truck seat and into a position that didn't make Finn feel as if there were ice daggers driving into his skull or his leg. When Zach turned the music on quietly then didn't say a word for a good half hour, Finn closed his eyes and let the painkillers wash through his system.

His phone went off.

Zach spoke up quickly. "It's your brother. You're set to Bluetooth through the truck, if you don't mind me listening in."

"Answer it. You'll get all the dirt later anyway."

A moment later, Finn's middle brother was on the line. "Sounds as if you picked a bad time to go kitten hunting."

"The ferocious beast is doing fine from what I've heard," Finn said. "Hey, Duncan. I've got you on speaker. Zach's here as well."

"Hey, Zach. You need me to send you a box of duct tape to slow my brother down for the next while?"

Zach laughed. "I think we'll be okay. The doctor has him wrapped up plenty tight."

"Full-length cast," Finn offered. "I'm not riding anything but shotgun for a long time."

"Like what Karen Coleman had that summer we were at Whiskey Creek?" Duncan offered a soft whistle. "Damn. Sorry to hear that."

"I'll be fine." Finn glanced at his friend in the driver seat. "How'd you hear I got hurt?"

"Not from you the way I should've, dumbass."

"That's what I told him," Zach informed Duncan as an aside.

Duncan snorted. "Yeah, he probably didn't want me to worry. But I am worried. You take care of yourself, Finn. Let people take care of you. I know it goes against our stubborn nature to be anything less than self-sufficient, but when you need it, help's the best thing in the world."

Tangled emotions whirled in Finn's gut. It was good to hear his brother talking about help as a positive thing, but the fact Duncan had dealt with enough bullshit in his life to need help still infuriated Finn. "I'll do my manly best to accept help when it's offered."

"I'll hold you to that. I hear differently and I'll be pissed." A rumbling sound echoed in the background. "Heading into a weigh station, so I'd better make this short. Next time don't leave it up to Levi to let me know when something happens. And I mean it about taking care of yourself."

"I hear you," Finn told him.

"Good. And Zach, always nice to hear your voice. If my brother's a dumbass again in the future, I expect you'll let me know."

Zach outright chuckled. "I'll put you on speed dial. Keep your wheels turning."

"Ten-four that," Duncan signed off.

Finn stared at the ceiling of the truck and attempted to recalibrate his world. This wasn't what he'd hoped to be dealing with at the moment, but there'd been a lot of unexpected things over the years.

In the big scheme, breaking his leg was only a temporary glitch.

He glanced at Zach. "Don't you go gossiping to my brothers without asking first."

"Are you kidding me? Of course I told them. Duncan's the size of a brick shithouse, and Levi's kids are so adorable they can sweet-talk me into anything. You're only my best friend. You carry way less clout."

Finn snorted, the noise grinding into a groan. "Don't make me laugh. It hurts."

"Speaking of which." Zach tossed a bag on the dash. "I filled your prescription. Keep ahead of the pain or you'll regret it."

Something other than pain snuck in. "You think I made a mistake agreeing to move into Karen's cottage?"

"You worried about that? Nah, it makes perfect sense." Zach shrugged. "I know you have a goal in mind when it comes to this thing with her, but for right now, take your brother's advice to worry about yourself and healing. That's all this is about, really. Moving into the cottage will make things easier for you."

"Going to make it harder for Karen," Finn grumbled.

"Only if you're a grumpy bastard," Zach retorted. "Look, I know you'll want to go full speed ahead as soon as you can. I'm okay with you helping with whatever tasks fit in between taking time to heal. And if you need me to come over to help pull on your pants every morning and take them off at night, I'm there. Zero obligation on Karen's part."

"Don't be too sure I won't take you up on that. It's a bloody nightmare trying to get dressed."

"I wondered about that. Skip the jeans and wear sweats— we'll buy some big enough to fit over the cast. Also, there's this grabbing tool I saw when I did a search online, so I ordered you one. Should be here tomorrow." Zach flashed him a grin. "Just because I offered to help you get dressed doesn't mean I actually want to see your ugly mug that early every morning."

Whether it was the painkillers or the whole experience, Finn found himself a little shaky as the truth escaped. "Glad you're my friend."

Zach coughed into his hand. "Damn. I need to try some of your drugs."

"Asshole."

Beside him, his friend was all but chuckling. "Love you too. Now, shut up."

They passed the final part of the ride in companionable silence.

Zach parked with the passenger door as close as possible to the cottage path. He let Finn handle his crutches and getting out of the truck on his own, instead storming up the walkway, bags in hand as he rapped his knuckles on the front door. "Uber Eats."

The face of an angel appeared as Karen slid the door open and gestured them in. "Thank goodness. I was about to eat dessert first."

Finn made it through the door and into the living room without falling flat on his face, which was a pretty damn good first accomplishment. "I see nothing wrong with starting with sweets. You going to kiss me hello?"

Zach snorted but kept walking into the kitchen area.

Karen blocked Finn's path, fists balanced on her hips and her brow raised. "You're either loopy or you're feeling better than expected."

"Let's go with I'd feel even better if I got a kiss."

Yeah, he was pushing it, but—

Shit. He was pushing it.

He met her gaze. "Probably should blame that one on the drugs."

But she stepped closer, their bodies right in contact, and lifted her lips to his. "Welcome home."

The connection was over too fast and not nearly as intimate as he craved, but it was sweet. Both the kiss and the sentiment, and he'd be happy to take it for now.

She stepped aside and gestured him forward. "Come on. We'll get some food into you, and then you can crash. If you'll forgive the expression."

A kitten dashed across the floor, ducking under a chair to stare at him. He smiled but left the creature alone for now.

Finn settled at the table when he realized the cottage wasn't the same as it had been the last time he'd seen it. Even as Zach put the take-out bags on the table, Finn glanced around the room to categorize the changes.

He turned back to Karen. "You took out furniture."

She nodded. "And an area rug. It was extra stuff that wasn't really needed. I remember it being a pain in the butt to manoeuvre in our crowded living room when I had my cast. Kept banging into things, and not only is that hell on the furniture, it doesn't feel so good."

But her living room had stayed exactly the same the entire time she'd worn the cast because none of them had thought to fix the situation for her.

Regret rose, but he pushed the emotion aside because the only way to make it up to her was here and now. "Thanks."

The food didn't taste like much. He did the best he could, but after pushing things around on his plate, Finn was two steps away from nodding off right there at the table.

"Head to bed for a while," Zach suggested.

Finn attempted to snap himself awake. "I'm fine. Maybe a cup of coffee."

It didn't seem the kind of comment that should've set Zach and Karen off laughing the way it did.

She came close enough to place a hand on his shoulder. "Just like I know it will be easier without the extra furniture, I know what you need right now is not a cup of coffee." Her voice got softer, her gaze gentle yet still insistent. "Stop fighting, buttercup, and do the right thing. Come lie down."

For a fiercely independent individual like Finn, accepting help to rise out of the chair and head down the hallway kicked hard in the ego.

When Karen went to lead him into the master bedroom, he paused, some weird mixture of hope and confusion working through his brain.

"That's your bed." Which was exactly where he wanted to be, but not in his current condition.

"Not now, it isn't," she said. "His stuff is on the chair in the corner, Zach. Give me a shout if you need a hand."

"Will do." His friend's cheerful answer ricocheted through Finn's brain like an out-of-control ping-pong ball. "Come on, man. You look like the walking dead. Give it up, and I'll help you get ready for bed."

Between hitting the bathroom and ending up flat on the mattress, a whole lot of details vanished. He heard Zach and Karen talking, but it was much easier to close his eyes and listen to the *whoosh* of blood rushing past his ears.

He felt like crap, and he hated that he was messing up Karen's clean sheets, but getting any kind of words out was a fail.

The edge of the bed dipped slightly, and Karen's sweet scent surrounded him. He breathed deep to take in as much of her as possible, because if this was a dream, it was a pretty good place to begin.

"No idea..." He forced the words, fighting to stay awake.

Fingers against his face. "Relax. We'll talk tomorrow."

It seemed vital to get this out. "No idea what you dealt

with. Thought I knew. Hell if I did. Going to make it up to you, *chérie*. Every little bit."

"Shhhhh. Go to sleep."

Another soft stroke along his jaw then down his neck. Her hand landed on his chest. He caught her fingers in his and gave a gentle squeeze, just holding on.

Keeping her close, right where he needed her.

11

Finn: *How are you feeling this morning? Hated to leave you last night.*

Karen: *I'm amazingly well-rested. Someone worked me over hard, and I slept like a log.*

Finn: *It was my pleasure.*

Karen: *Oh, I totally meant the other guy who crawled in my window after you left.*

Finn: *Careful...next time I'll refuse to leave your bed.*

Karen: *You getting caught in my room would make it tough to keep this fling a secret. I don't need sleepovers. I'm just glad you didn't give up because of my stupid broken leg.*

Finn: *You have no idea. Having tasted you, touched you—fucked you—you think a damn cast can stop me from enjoying every minute we can find?*

Karen: *That's dirty. And hot. And you dealt just fine. I wish you didn't have to deal, that's all.*

Finn: *Ma chérie, for the privilege of unwrapping you, I will do more than deal with a simple cast.*

~late summer, Whiskey Creek ranch~

~

*S*he had an appointment the next morning. It was probably a good thing, though, because being babied was the last thing Finn would want.

Although, she did stand in the doorway of the master bedroom for too long, staring at his scruff-covered jaw. His body was relaxed, one arm thrown over his head. The sheets were tangled over the mass of his cast, his naked chest partially exposed.

He didn't look completely comfortable, but that was to be expected.

She snuck in and straightened the blankets as best she could without disturbing him then headed out.

The three interviews she'd arranged for that morning were barely done when her phone went off with an alert.

Julia: *you have time for lunch?*

Karen: *I'm already in town.*

Julia: *buns and roses?*

Karen: *can be there in ten minutes*

She didn't bother moving her truck, walking from the library where she'd been using their video conferencing equipment to the cozy coffee shop.

Karen gave a quick wave to Tansy, who was behind the counter working, then settled next to Julia at one of the small tables.

"You finish an early shift or getting ready to start a late one?" Karen asked.

Julia looked intrigued. "It's rather fascinating you know to ask that question. I'm headed into a night shift. I woke up earlier than I wanted."

"Then we'd better get you some coffee. Breakfast for you, lunch for me."

"Since pizza is the perfect food for any time of day, we won't quibble about what we call it." Julia tilted her head toward the board listing the daily special. "My treat. Whatever you want. I'm having a pizza bagel."

"Let me order. I need to talk to Tansy for a minute."

They were early enough the lunch crowd hadn't arrived yet, which gave Karen time to put in their order then make a special request. "Girls' night out next month. How do you think everybody would react to the idea of doing a moonlight trail ride?"

Tansy's eyes widened before she pressed a finger over her lips. "Keep it quiet, or we'll have Rose squealing for the next month."

That sounded positive. "I take it you don't think it's a terrible idea."

"Hell no. It's a fantastic idea. Even though some of you spend a lot of time in the saddle, I don't think you'll hear anyone complain."

Karen nodded. "It'll take me some time to get the details into place, but we can test run a route we might use at Finn's ranch."

"Let's talk about it this coming month—which is a week from Monday, by the way. I don't think anyone will have a problem with it." Tansy started on their coffees. "How are things going at the ranch? Is Finn back and overdoing it yet?"

"Just back. He hasn't had time to start overdoing it."

"He will," Tansy said confidently. "Bet you Zach has to sit on him to slow him down."

That wasn't a bet any of them would be willing to take. "You've been hanging around Lisa too much," Karen told her.

She waited until the coffees were ready, carrying them back to the table where they'd been joined by Julia's boss, Brad.

"I won't interrupt for long," he said.

Karen waved the comment off. "It's okay. No use standing by the door and pretending you don't know us while you wait for your order to be done."

A big sheepish grin crossed his face. "Well, I don't know that I'd be pretending. I mean, you haven't been in town that long. And Julia and I've only been working together since April. We hadn't seen each other for a year before that."

Julia rolled her eyes, and she leaned forward and spoke in a conspiratorial tone. "We do so know each other. I'll prove it. That little game of Clue we played the other day. Remember that?"

Brad stiffened.

Karen's sister forged ahead in spite of his uncomfortable body language. "You remember where your sweet fiancée killed you with a kiss?"

He didn't say anything, and for a moment Karen worried this might head in some weird direction, but Julia was smiling too hard for it to be anything terrible. "Tell us, Brad. How many people did you actually take out before you ended up with Hanna as your target?"

It took a moment for Karen to figure out what Julia was suggesting. "Wait. I don't remember *anybody* saying Brad knocked them out. That means—"

"Exactly. It means Brad had Hanna's name from the first minute of the game and never even tried to get her gone." Julia leaned back and crossed her arms over her chest. "And that's exactly what I would've expected from you, Mister Knight in Shining Armour."

He looked uncomfortable, glancing around to make sure nobody was listening to their conversation. "It's not that I didn't want to win the game, but I was having a good time being with my friends and kind of lost track of time. Besides, it was seriously entertaining to watch Hanna sneak around and surprise everybody."

Karen might die from the sickening sweetness of that comment. "You're terrible," she informed Brad.

"I'm in love," he tossed back. "Makes you do all sorts of things."

The sincerity with which he said it rattled her down to her toes. Watching Julia gloat over being right helped keep Karen's thoughts from sliding down a dangerous path.

Brad visited for a few more minutes before Tansy called out that his order was ready. He glanced between the two of them. "Julia, I'll see you at the start of your shift. Karen, hope you have a great day."

He took off to grab two large bags from Tansy, pushing the door open with a shoulder and heading into the beautiful sunny day.

Julia watched him go, a curious expression on her face.

Karen paused. "What's that about?"

Her sister shook her head as if tossing away thoughts. "Oh,

nothing. Just shoving away a few memories that need to behave."

Which was more intriguing than an answer.

They enjoyed their meal together, then Karen headed back to the ranch as Julia took off in the direction of the fire hall to prepare for work.

During the month Karen had been around the ranch, huge changes had already taken place. All of the outbuildings that were beyond saving had been taken apart. The usable pieces had been salvaged and stockpiled in an area behind the main barn. The rest were stacked in heaps, ready to be burned.

A group was gathered near where the house of ill repute stood. Karen made her way across the yard to find not only Finn and Zach, but a half dozen of the work crew, including the foreman who'd been hired to oversee actual construction.

Cody Gabrielle spotted her and offered a tip of his head even as he kept talking to his crew. The motion was enough to get Finn's attention, and he pivoted on the spot, crutches under his arms and a weary expression on his face.

Zach waved her over. "Definitely need your help."

The crew passed her, headed in the opposite direction. One of the new guys razzed her, low enough his voice didn't carry but loud enough she couldn't miss the dirty comment.

Another joy of working with mostly male crews.

Nipping it in the bud was the best way. She pivoted on the spot and offered a sharp whistle. "Hey."

The entire crew paused, glancing over their shoulders.

"You make another comment about my sweet ass, or you try and touch it, and you'll be wearing my boot where the sun don't shine. We clear?" She glared down the one who had spoken.

His leering expression vanished, his gaze darting beyond her to where his foreman stood.

Shit. Both Cody and Zach had witnessed the scene.

And Finn.

Karen turned and walked away without waiting for a response because continuing to diffuse the situation was the next step.

"Hey, guys. Zach, what's the question?" She deliberately kept her tone light.

Cody wiped his mouth with his hand, glancing at the crew that had suddenly grown wings and was moving rapidly to get started on whatever task had been assigned.

Zach squeezed the hand he had resting on Finn's shoulder then offered Karen his full attention. "We've got an idea but wanted to run it by you. Looks as if the brothel—for lack of a better term—is mostly structurally sound. Just the one part had an issue. Cody suggested we take the building down to the bones then refurbish it as a kind of a row-house dwelling. It could go over really big with singles who want to come out to the ranch."

"Their own room in a cowboy bunkhouse," Cody added.

It sounded like a great idea. She paused. "If you can do it with structural integrity, it sounds like a plan. What do you need my opinion for?"

"You don't think there's a problem rebuilding where we had an accident?" Cody said bluntly.

Karen glanced at Finn. He was still glaring at the work crew industriously pounding nails into new cabin platforms. "Finn. You have a problem with it? I don't think there's any residual bad luck hanging around."

He met her eyes. "As long as you're okay with it."

She would give him a break because he'd been injured and all. "If there's any ghostly residual energy hanging around an old brothel, it would be sexual in nature. Maybe we focus on that part," she teased.

Zach's face underwent a series of contortions, and for a moment Karen thought he was having a seizure.

Instead, he grabbed her hand and pumped it enthusiastically. "You are a genius."

"*Ummm*, thank you?" Karen pulled her hand free and slipped closer to Finn. Some of his rigidity slipped away as she leaned in close and mock whispered, "What's up with Zach?"

"It's the question of the ages." Finn's voice was a rasp, threaded with pain.

"The answer to what we should call this place," Zach inserted. "I mean, really. You've been giving me grief over all the fantastic names I've tossed at you, but now I get it. You were waiting for this perfect moment to arrive."

Finn eased back against the support pillar in a position Karen recognized all too well as the one she used to take when her entire body throbbed.

Still he folded his arms and gave his friend his full attention. "We're listening. I don't know why, but we're listening."

"We've got to use something from the past of this place when we name it. Scarlet Station. Red-Light Ranch. Dance Hall Gertie's."

"Dear God, not Gertie," Cody said quickly. "I had an Aunt Gertie. She had one eyebrow."

Karen paused. "One...eyebrow?"

Cody held one finger above both eyes. He shook his head before looking thoughtful. "And maybe not something quite so blatant as red-light, but I like the idea of scarlet or red in the name."

"Red Boot ranch?" Finn asked.

"That's it. *That's* what we need," Zach said with hyper enthusiasm. He glanced at Karen. "What do you think? It's genius for branding, but it's not really dirty unless people want to dig into the history."

She caught his excitement, wrapping her fingers around Finn's. "I think it's a great name. Let's run a search first to make sure we're not setting up within a hundred miles of some other Red Boot ranch. But if we're not, I think it's cute."

A sigh of exasperation escaped Finn, but he winked at her. "Okay. If it works, we have a name. Welcome to the Red Boot ranch."

It was barely two o'clock, and he was done.

As Finn made his way slowly across the yard and up to the cottage, parts of his body screamed in pain that he hadn't expected.

He made it as far as the living room before a little ball of white fluff attacked the sock covering his uninjured foot. The next moment, the demonic creature had all four claws dug into the thick knit fabric, limbs splayed wide to keep his balance as Finn's leg swung freely.

It was like an elephant getting attacked by a mouse, and in spite of his pain and exhaustion, Finn discovered laughter bubbling up.

"Beast."

He pulled out a kitchen chair and leveraged himself into it. Once his foot was resting on the ground, the kitten made his way upward, climbing Finn like a scratching post.

"Oh, hell no. None of that." Finn grabbed the thing by the scruff of the neck before he could dig his claws into Finn's crotch. He held the kitten in the air in front of his face.

The beast swung teeny paws and offered adorable growling meows.

Finn snickered. "Should've called you Marshmallow Fluff. You're sweet enough to make a man go into shock."

He scratched the little thing under his furry chin then tucked the kitten against his chest. He kept one hand over Dandy's body, cradling him close, and the next thing Finn knew, the kitten was purring, nuzzling his shirt.

"Now there's a sight." Karen stood in the doorway, a soft smile on her lips. "I wondered where you'd gotten to, but now it all makes sense. You knew Dandy needed cuddles."

"Can't have him getting lonely," Finn said gruffly.

Her head tilted as she examined him, obviously reading the signs of pain in his body. But she didn't say anything as she moved into the kitchen.

"Want a drink?"

God, did he want a drink. "Since I assume alcohol is out of the question, you got any kind of juice?"

"No problem." She put two glasses on the counter then dug in the refrigerator as she changed the topic completely. "You know as a woman I put up with rude comments pretty much all the time, yes?"

Finn knew, but didn't like it one bit. "You shouldn't have to."

"I agree one hundred percent, but this is my reality, and I don't see it changing overnight. What does help, though, is me shutting it down real fast. That's all I was doing, and nine times out of ten, that's all it takes. At least in this kind of a setting where we work together on a regular basis."

"What about the one in ten who doesn't know when enough is enough?" Finn took the glass she handed him. "I won't have assholes working around here who don't know how to read no as no."

"And if we get any of that type around here, I swear I will tell Cody, and he'll do his job and take care of it. But I'm not about to have you fire someone for a rude comment that didn't even register on his asshole meter because it was mild compared to what he could get away with on another ranch." Karen was in the chair across from him now, her expression softening. "Do I like having to deal with it? No. But changes are coming. Slowly, *damn* slowly in the agricultural world, but it is happening."

Finn stared into the glass of orange juice she'd handed him. "I don't like bullies or harassers. Never have."

She slipped a hand onto his good knee. "I knew that about you from the first minute when you warned my cousin off for being nothing more than a minor annoyance. You're one of the good ones, Finn Marlette."

If he didn't have both hands full, he would've covered her hand with his own. Instead, he watched a twinkle of amusement rise in her eyes.

She scooped the kitten off Finn's chest and moved Dandy to a box in the corner of the room. "If I'm breaking all the rules and temporarily having an animal in the house, you will learn to behave," she informed the little beast.

Three times Dandy tried to get out, and three times she patiently put him back in the same position. Each time she offered a little pet, and once he relaxed, she gave him a treat.

He opened his mouth in a tiny yawn then laid his head down on his tail and fell asleep.

Karen settled opposite Finn. The room grew quiet for a moment before curiosity rose in her eyes. "Tell me something about the time you were gone."

The whole situation with his family flashed to mind, but no way in hell was he was up to that conversation right now.

But Bruce?

He leaned back in his chair and stared out the window as he considered. "One of the biggest things that happened was meeting the man who mentored Zach and I. Bruce Travers. Damn good man, creative and innovative. A bit of a risk-taker, but very down-to-earth and kind."

She leaned on her elbows. "Mentored you how?"

"He taught us about business. How to invest, what chances were worth taking, when it was better to fold and try something new." Finn sipped his drink as he considered. "Imagine someone who knows pretty much everything about horses offering you a chance to come work with them for a few years. You don't even know what you don't know, but as time passes, you start to understand that it's more than a list of dos and don'ts. It's like a poem or a song, with a rhythm and a rhyme, when you're making a business better or convincing others that what you have in mind is brilliant."

"Sounds as if he was more than a business teacher."

Finn nodded. "He was a friend. Helped me deal with a lot. Taught me a lot. Zach too."

He could talk about Bruce for hours and never finish singing the man's praises, but that would have to happen another time. As sweet as it was to just sit and share with her, he had reached his limit.

"Karen? Do me a favour?"

"Hmmm?"

Stupid how hard this was. "Can you grab me a painkiller?"

"No problem." She slipped past him and headed to the back of the house, trailing her fingers over his shoulder as she went.

She was back a minute later, the pill in the palm of her hand and a bottle of baby oil in the other.

"I don't think that's a good combination," Finn drawled.

Laughter trickled from her as he took the pill and washed it down with the rest of his juice. "You need a rubdown, and I don't have any massage oil. Not unless you want wintergreen foot cream on your chest and arms."

His brain was too numb to think straight. Did this mean what he thought it meant? Dear God, to have her hands on his body—

He went for casual. "Skip the wintergreen. I'll take the baby oil."

She grabbed the towel off her shoulder, motioning him forward in his chair. "Take off your shirt. I'll put this behind you so when you want to lean back, you've got something soft between you and the wood."

Just the thought of her touching him was creating other kinds of wood.

Slowly adjusting position so he didn't cut off blood flow to his groin meant he wasn't undoing the buttons fast enough for her. Either that or she was eager to get him partly naked, because she pushed his hands away. A moment later, competent fingers moved down the placket of his shirt.

He moved obediently as she pushed the flannel off his shoulders, peeling it off his arms. He reached over his head to grab the shirt he had on underneath, pulling it forward and off in one motion.

"Dammit, Finn." She pulled her chair closer, fingers drifting over the bruises on his torso. Over the long line where a jagged board had scratched through everything and left an angry welt, red edges flaring into mottled green and blue.

It was heaven and hell, her touching him with slow, cautious strokes. She put oil on the palms of her hands, rubbed them together, then placed them on his biceps.

Softly at first then with more pressure as she found the knots, Karen massaged his arms, his shoulders, his neck. Long whisper-light drags of skin-to-skin contact followed by pleasure-pain sensations as she dug her thumbs into his abused muscles.

All of it felt spectacular, even the bits that hurt. And how fucked up was that? He didn't care that he was groaning nonstop, he just wanted her to keep touching him.

"You're killing me," he whispered.

"You've had a hard week," Karen informed him. "It's okay to let someone take care of you."

He didn't want to screw this up, but he wanted to be honest. "I want to take care of you. In every way. Makes me feel as if I'm falling down on the job to need so much help."

"We went over this before. If you're still lazing around on your ass three weeks from now, we'll have a talk. Right now, the bruises are still there, and you're doped up to the gills. Give yourself a break," she said sternly.

"Not enough," he repeated. He needed to stop arguing because obviously Karen and Zach had gone to the same school of stubbornness. "Three weeks from now, if I'm still a broken-down mess, kick my ass out of here."

She moved behind him, sliding her hands down his spine and setting goose bumps dancing. "Deal."

He braced one arm on his thigh and the other on the table and let her hands drift over his torso in that haunting, sensual manner. It was gentle and kind, like a friend. Caring for his aches. But it was a flashback to moments in that long-ago summer when they'd stripped each other naked, frantic to come together.

Or the rare times when sex had gone slowly. Those had been few and far between, stolen moments when they'd been sure no one else would be around. Long intimate situations where they'd touched and kissed and connected until they were panting and thoroughly stated.

"Three weeks from now when your hands are on me, it

damn well better be mutual." The words rasped past a throat tight with need. He tilted his head down enough to meet her gaze. "I want to slide my fingers up your naked spine so I can pull you tight against me. Glide them over your hips right before I slide my hand between your legs. Or I'll cup your breasts so I can put my mouth on your nipples and tongue you until you're squirming. I want to…"

Awareness broke through the heat flooding his veins. Hell, he was doing it again.

Finn sat up a little straighter. "Dammit. Those painkillers seem to loosen my tongue more than they should. Sorry."

He forced his gaze to meet hers.

Her cheeks were red, and her neck and the upper part of her chest flushed.

She licked her lips and seemed to fight to find words. "Yeah. You and painkillers are a dangerous mix. I have to get back to work for a while. Need anything before I head out?"

He shook his head, watching as she damn near stumbled over her own feet racing for the doorway.

But before he could finish kicking his own ass, she stopped, squared her shoulders as if readying for battle, then faced him. "Just to be clear, I'm not offended by what you said. It's just a little early in your recovery for me to jump your bones."

Then she vanished, boots clattering at the front entrance briefly before the front screen door slammed shut.

Finn blinked, working through her comment with his slightly muddled brain.

Well, okay then.

It took a while to manoeuvre down the hallway and get himself onto the bed for a nap, but the entire time, amusement and hope mingled to ease the edges of his pain.

His dreams were perfectly dirty.

12

———

*T*he next couple of days passed in an uneven rhythm.
Karen never knew when she got up in the morning
whether Finn would be awake or not. It was easier to leave food
in the fridge than plan on meals at the same time—Finn
crashing when he needed to was a surprising development.

She got into her work, the ongoing evolution of her job
stretching to anything Zach decided he needed help with.

Or Finn, as he took over a lot of the office jobs with barely
any complaining.

Ha on that one.

The man never actually complained, but the way he sat
and glared at the stack of papers attached to the clipboard in
front of him made it clear he wished he was on the back of a
horse instead.

"It's not going to jump up and bite you," Karen teased as
she joined him at the table.

"Don't need anything else biting me. I've already got one
varmint who thinks I'm his glorified chew toy." Finn winked
before gesturing her closer.

In his lap, the snow-white kitten gnawed on Finn's thumb, tail snaking back and forth happily.

"He's terrible. Don't let him boss you around," Karen warned.

Finn shrugged. "I figure he's had a bit of a hard go. I don't mind giving him extra loving right now." He pushed the clipboard toward her. "Save me."

Karen twisted the mess of papers toward her. "What the heck does Zach have you doing?"

"He wants me to make design decisions, which is not my line of expertise."

On top was a sketch of the footprint for the new cottages being erected around the ranch. Mostly one room, with a couple of two- to three-bedroom setups for families. Included was a stack of cutout squares and rectangles, each carefully labelled with *dresser* or *queen-size bed*.

"You should get my nieces to help you with this one. They'd love to play paper dolls and arrange the furniture." Karen took a peek at the inch-deep mass of paper underneath. "What's all this? Did Zach print the entire stock list for Bed, Bath & Beyond?"

"Maybe." Finn offered his most pleading expression. "I said I would deal with the paperwork, but dear God, this is not something I should be in charge of. He wants me to pick colour schemes."

The noise he made brought a laugh to Karen's lips.

"I'm not a good one to help, either. My sisters would probably enjoy it, but...isn't it early to be making these kinds of decisions?"

"We'll be hiring someone as a ranch house mom, as well as a head cook, but probably not until late September. They'll have a say in how much we buy and the supplies we'll need, but it would be good to have at least the styles decided."

Karen nodded. "It'll take me all of three seconds to give you my totally biased opinion. Whatever you decide will fit in each cabin, my cousin Daniel runs a side business for the Colemans building custom furniture."

Some of Finn's desperation faded, replaced by an incredulous smile. "Shit. I am off my game because I totally forgot that. And when it comes to quilts and pillows, you've got a couple cousins who can help with those as well, don't you?"

"If you're willing to splurge for handmade designs. Those you need order from Hope and Becky sooner rather than later, or you won't have them on time. Although they sometimes have a stockpile." A spot of happiness flared inside at solving Finn's problem while helping her extended family.

"I've seen their work. It would be no hardship to feature their handicrafts around the place." Finn pointed to the wad of paper under her hands. "Toss that out. I'll give your family a shout and see what they suggest."

"How about if I give them a call and introduce you? Or reintroduce you—I'm pretty sure both Daniel and Hope will remember your name."

He lost a little of his smile. "Is that a good thing?"

Karen examined his face and the shadows under his eyes as she thought back to five years ago. "I think only one of my many cousins wasn't sure about you. Ashley is now a busy mom of two, so once I give you the all clear, you shouldn't have any problems."

"It's not your guy cousins I'm worried about," Finn said bluntly. "Frankly, the fact your sisters haven't ganged up and offered a death-and-dismemberment warning surprises the hell out of me."

"I'm sure they were planning on it but put it on hold after your accident." She tapped his fingers lightly. "It's no fun threatening somebody who can't run."

To her utter shock and amusement, he stuck out his tongue.

She was still giggling as she called her cousin Hope, owner of the Stitching Post quilt shop in Rocky Mountain House.

Little things like that made her daily work unique and a whole lot more fun than what it had been recently at the Whiskey Creek ranch.

Every moment was different. Like being called to help decide exactly what angle to set the base of a new cottage. Or having to moderate a *discussion* between Cody and Zach over what colour stain to use on the outside of the individual cabins.

They'd painted one wall with the two different choices and still couldn't decide which they wanted. Not even after hauling her into their conversation to proclaim the merits of one choice over the other.

They seemed intent on being a dog with a bone on this one.

Finn swung past on his crutches, eyeing the men as he stopped beside her. "They been arguing like sputtering hens for long?"

"Define long." Karen smirked at Zach, who planted his fists on his hips at her comment. "I told them I already knew the answer, but they won't stop cackling for long enough to listen."

That got a sharp nod out of Finn. "I think I know where you're headed. The barn trick?"

"Of course. Want to help?"

"Glad to."

He waited as she bent and scooped up a couple of dirt clods from the yard, dropping one into his outstretched hand. His eyes flashed with amusement, then without warning, he whipped the dirt directly at Zach.

"The hell?" Zach ducked.

The dirt slammed into the side wall of the cabin, breaking apart and drifting into dust particles that clung to the rough boards.

At the same moment, Karen tossed the second chunk at Cody, deliberately missing so it smashed against the wall about three feet from Finn's.

"You've got a strange way of helping," Cody complained before Zach bumped him on the chest with a fist, pointing at the wall behind them.

The dirt on the left was a vivid round blotch, while the one on the right was barely visible since the lighter brown tone was a near match for the local soil. "And we have a winner. Told you my choice was the right one," Zach gloated.

"Yeah, but you made a lucky pick. You weren't all scientific like Karen." Cody offered her and Finn a thumbs-up. "Good trick."

"Next time, listen," Finn suggested before giving Karen a wink.

The only things wrong in her world were continuing to see Finn in pain and saying goodbye to Dandelion. With her leaving in the fall for school, it was smarter to get the kitten set up with the barn cats, but dropping him off at Silver Stone ranch left her strangely empty inside.

Saturday morning, she rose early to get in a horseback ride before the Canada Day celebrations began. Faint snores drifted through the closed master bedroom door as she passed it.

Yet another batch of wildflowers waited in a glass on the kitchen counter. Just like every morning since Finn had returned from the hospital.

She had no idea when, or how, he was sneaking out of the house to find them, but as she picked up the sturdy stalked bundle with pale purple petals at the top, she had to admit to being charmed.

She slipped the flowers into a bouquet already on the table, discarding a couple of drooping stems. She filled a thermos with coffee, and after leaving a note that she'd meet

Finn at the fairgrounds, headed into the fresh July first morning air.

Morning chores had started. An easy sway of voices and animal noises floated over the ranch as hired help headed to the makeshift mess tent to get their own coffee and breakfast. Horses shifted slowly in the arena. Only a dozen still, mostly ones that belonged to the men bunking in trailers all around the wide work area.

Men waved in her direction as she saddled up Starlight, but no one interrupted her as she tucked the thermos into a saddlebag then mounted and headed to the west.

She hadn't believed her sister Tamara when she'd repeatedly said how different Heart Falls terrain was compared to the land around Rocky Mountain House. Only three hours to the south shouldn't make so huge of a difference.

But it did. The longer she was in the area, the more Karen understood what Tamara had been trying to say.

Here they were already in the foothills, with the Rockies racing skyward and seeming close enough to touch. And while the foothills had some of the characteristic dips into valleys and rolls to heights that were so common around Rocky Mountain House, here the alpine forest had begun to encroach. Pine and spruce trees stood tall, scattered over the nearby hills.

The gullies were no gentle coulees with mudbank slopes. They were granite and sharp, erosion taking the canyon sides down to the bare rock and creating a wilder landscape.

Raw, fresh, dangerous.

Karen rode in the noisy silence of the outdoors. Saddlebags creaked, and her jean-clad thighs rubbed against Starlight's flanks with a soft, shimmering *whoosh*. Birds, wind, and trees all contributed to the music around her.

She let her horse take the lead, wandering where he wanted. He'd found an old game trail, looping out of the ravine and to the north. One impossible puzzle twist later, Karen found herself at the top of a ridge, staring back at what would soon be Red Boot ranch. The town of Heart Falls lay in the distance beyond it with Silver Stone ranch along the extreme southwest corner.

It was a beautiful place, and she took a deep breath and let peace roll over her. What a privilege to be here.

Then why are you so eager to get away?

The thought came unbidden, and she pulled Starlight away from the view, moving up the trail as if that would distance her from the question.

She twisted the reins around her fingers, pausing for long enough to double-check her directions, because getting lost would hardly enhance her reputation when it came to her job.

A soft scuffling came from the right, and Karen froze. Starlight's ears shot up, rotating as he tried to identify the danger.

When her horse relaxed, Karen did as well. Something was in the bush, but it wasn't about to leap out and attack. She slipped from the saddle and tethered Starlight.

Then she moved cautiously through the thicket toward where a brighter patch of light indicated there should be a clearing of some sort.

A small opening between massive pine trees created a little oasis. The mare she'd seen the other day was there. On her side, panting heavily, her belly full of foal.

"Shit."

Karen went back and grabbed Starlight's reins, leading him a little farther until she found a wide enough trail that let them into the clearing.

The only helpful thing in her saddlebags was an emergency kit, and it was soon clear she needed it. The mare was far enough gone that when Karen dropped by her head, she barely moved.

"It's okay, beautiful. I'll help you," Karen reassured her, but at this point, there wasn't much to do.

She took a check, cursing as she discovered the foal was breech. A difficult delivery at the best of times. The mare was small, and the foal—probably from the wild stallion—was full-term and on the large side.

Before she got into anything too drastic, Karen made one attempt at making a call, but as expected, got zero reception. She did the next best thing, which was to write a quick text so it would go through as soon as she did hit cell phone range.

All the while she stroked the mare's flank, calming her. Reassuring her. Praying like hell.

Karen leaned down and pressed her forehead to the mare's. "You and me, we'll see what we can do, okay? Let's give it everything we've got."

She took a deep breath and got started.

HANGING out at the community hall was the last thing Finn wanted.

He'd been pretty much hog-tied and hauled to the Canada Day celebration with the reminder this was a community event, and they needed to play nice. Living in Heart Falls and setting up a business and all that.

At least that was the warning Zach gave him.

"I thought having a broken leg meant I was allowed to be a grumpy ass and recluse for a while," Finn offered dryly.

"Did I say that? I'm sure I never said that." Zach pulled into an open parking space right outside the community hall. "If I said anything, it would've been that you're a grumpy ass, period."

Finn laid a hand on the wheel before Zach shut off the ignition. "You did not just park in the handicap stall."

"I'm dropping you off."

"Move the damn truck."

His friend sighed hugely then moved to a different spot.

They'd barely even entered the hall before being surrounded by a bevy of women.

"We saved you a seat," a particularly fine brunette said to Zach as she batted lashes in his direction. She glanced over at Finn. "You poor baby. You come too."

Finn kept his expression blank as Zach attempted to wave off the encouragement to move in three different directions.

"Ahem."

Finn glanced to the right to discover Julia Blushing standing a little ways off.

He looked for mercy. "Dear God, tell me you have somewhere for us to sit."

She winked. "My sisters saved spots for you, Zach, and Karen." She glanced over his shoulder. "She didn't come with you?"

Well, shit. He shook his head. "Said she'd meet us here."

Julia hesitated then shrugged. "Come on. We'll leave Zach to fend for himself while we track Karen down."

Long rows of tables stretched from one side of the community hall room to the other. Typical metal chairs were lined up at regular intervals, and the whole room was full of laughing, chatting people.

The Stone family had control of a corner. Caleb and Tamara were there with their two girls and baby Tyler. Luke and Kelli chatted with Walker, while the youngest brother,

Dustin, nervously adjusted his collar, glancing over at a group of young ladies who eyed him speculatively.

"Still can't believe they do a bachelor auction at a family event," Finn said to Julia as she led him toward three empty chairs beside Lisa and Josiah.

"If it raises money, anything goes," Julia quipped. "It's okay. You're off the hook for this year."

An entertaining thought struck. "I get to see Zach go up on stage, yes?"

She snickered. "This is a best friend thing, isn't it? Gloating over each other's suffering?"

"It couldn't happen to a nicer guy." Finn adjusted his crutches and eased himself into the chair at the very edge of the table.

Josiah immediately shifted position to join him. "I won't ask how you're doing, but it's good to see you."

"A little like death warmed over, and it's good to see you as well. I expected you out at the ranch this past week," Finn admitted.

"Ended up with a bunch of emergencies, including a middle-of-the-night call that went for nearly twenty-four hours." Josiah fought a yawn before giving in to it. He covered his mouth, eyes screwed tight before blinking hard. He gestured to the coffee cup in front of him. "I might last maybe two more hours before all I'll be seeing are the inside of my eyelids."

They chatted as Finn waited for Karen's arrival. Julia was on the phone, but when he caught her eye, she offered a thumbs-up, so he tried to relax and enjoy the outing.

The potluck started. That's when Finn realized again how much being injured sucked. He couldn't handle his crutches and a plate.

Tamara took pity on him. She dropped baby Tyler into his

arms as an excuse. "Here. You take the babe, and I'll grab you food."

"Thanks."

At three months old, Tyler already had more personality than he'd had a few weeks ago. Finn looked the kid in the eye and straight up told him the truth. "You got yourself a good woman there. Make sure you appreciate it."

A feminine giggle rose behind him, followed by another. Part of Zach's bevy strolled by with plates in their hands, checking him out carefully.

"Too bad you're off the docket." Zach settled into the chair across from Finn. "With the way the women are eyeing you right now, you'd bring in a lot of money. Babies are like magnets."

"I'm surprised you came up for air," Finn said, settling Tyler more comfortably and giving the kid his finger to gnaw on.

"It's all for fun," Zach said, but he grinned.

Julia paused on her way past. She grabbed Zach's cheek, scrubbing red lipstick marks off before offering an epic eye roll and continuing back to her spot.

People returned with full plates, musical chairs ensued, and other than no sign of Karen, it was a perfectly straightforward meal.

Finn kept glancing at his watch.

The microphone clicked on, and Malachi Fields stepped to the podium. "If you'll stack up your dishes and pass them to the end of the table, we'll gather them and get ready for the next portion of our celebration. Nearly time, gentlemen. I need all of our brave bachelors to make their way to the side stairs and onto the stage in the next fifteen minutes."

Good-natured ribbing sounded around the room along with the clinking of plates and utensils.

Somewhere nearby a phone went off, and while it should've been just another part of the background noise, Finn's attention swiveled.

Kelli Stone blinked hard as she scrolled through something on her phone screen. She leaned toward her husband and whispered in his ear before rising and heading straight for Josiah.

She spoke softly into the veterinarian's ear, but Finn caught mention of Karen's name. Damn if he would stay quiet while his curiosity and worry simmered.

He laid a hand on Josiah's arm before he rose from the table. "Karen?"

Josiah glanced at Kelli then tilted his head toward the exit door. "Go. See if you get her on the line."

Kelli took off, hitting buttons rapidly. Concern was written all over her expression.

Only a second passed before Josiah leaned in, but long enough Finn had pictured all sorts of terrible scenarios. "Karen found one of the wild mares in labour. It was a quick message sent before she started trying to help. The fact it arrived now probably means she's on the move. You want to come along and see what's happening?"

No way in hell he was doing anything less.

Josiah led them to the emergency exit rather than trying to manoeuvre through the crowds of people.

Zach caught his eye right before they pushed through the door and held a hand to his ear like a phone. Finn dipped his chin. Soon as they found out what was going on, he'd let his friend know.

Kelli was hanging up the phone and scrambling in her pockets for keys. "Karen's on her way to the ranch. She's got the foal but says it's not breathing very well. You mind coming out?"

"Of course I don't mind." Josiah glanced at Finn before giving Kelli a brisk nod. "Go back in and spend time with your family. Finn and I have this."

"But—" Kelli slammed her lips together. "Yeah. You're right. She messaged me because she didn't want to haul you out if neither of the horses made it. But there's not much I can do more than what Karen's already done."

Josiah squeezed her arm. "It's good to know people trust you that much. And it's well deserved—but for now, go enjoy the event. And make sure you get all the details so we can tease Zach later."

"Deal." Kelli marched off as if she were a twelve-foot-tall Amazon and not a five-foot-nothing, denim-clad whirlwind.

Finn worked his crutches wildly to keep up as they raced across the playground soccer field to Josiah's truck.

"You want to try to call her?" Josiah suggested once Finn had hauled his ass up into the high truck seat.

"Great idea."

Karen answered on the second ring. "Finn?"

"Josiah and I are on our way," he told her. "Where are you?"

"Almost at the west boundary. It'll take me another twenty minutes because I can't move too fast."

Tears coated her voice, which was enough to make all his protective instincts flare. "You okay?"

"I'm not hurt. It's just been a hell of a day."

"Hang in there, *chérie*. Take trail route one, and Josiah and I will meet you as soon as we can."

But by the time they'd covered the distance to the ranch, Karen was nearly at the barn. Josiah swung down and grabbed his kit, moving rapidly to where Karen was getting ready to dismount.

It took Finn too much time to get out of the truck and over

to the barn, and by then Josiah had the foal on the ground and was working it over. He snapped orders at Karen, hands moving rapidly as he did something with the creature's neck.

Nothing to do but watch and wait.

When the little foal finally did that instinctive jolt, legs moving as if compelled to try and rise, Finn took a deep breath.

"Okay. Now it's okay." Karen staggered to her feet, wiping her hands on her jeans, her face ashen.

Finn opened his arms. "Come here."

She shook her head. "I'm a mess—"

"*Karen.*" He waited until she looked at him. "Come. Here."

Her stepping into his arms was a type of surrender. He didn't care that she was coated with mud and smelled as if she'd helped deliver a foal. Her cheek pressed against his chest, and she wrapped her arms around his torso and held on tight, squeezing as if he was the only reason she was able to stay vertical.

He just held her. He didn't stroke her hair or pat her back or any of those things. Partly because he was trying his damnedest to keep his balance, but mostly because this wasn't about reassuring her. It was about being there for her.

Whatever she'd faced, she'd done it with her usual strength. And whatever it was she needed from him right now, he would give it.

Just outside the small circle of two, Josiah shifted back as the foal struggled upright and took its first shaky steps. A miracle, like so many miracles that came before and would come again.

But the real miracle was having Karen in his arms.

13

─────────

Karen: *I miss you*

~

Finn: *I would give anything to be with you.*

~Unsent messages, fall, after Whiskey Creek ranch~

~

Karen was a mess, not just on the outside. She was tired, and dirty, and had a headache from hell. But the most frustrating part was not being able to dissect the tangled emotions inside enough to be able to push them off.

Finn was there, and that part was wonderful.

Once Karen had recovered enough to be able to stand on her own, Josiah gave her an approving nod. "Looks as if this little tyke should be okay. A bit of work in terms of feeding him, but if you want, I can take him over to Sonora's animal shelter.

They're bottle-feeding some calves right now, so adding him shouldn't be a big deal."

The supportive arm wrapped around her shoulders squeezed momentarily. "Might be a good idea," Finn said.

It was a great idea. "I don't have time to take care of him right now," Karen said. "If you don't think Sonora would mind."

The veterinarian packed up his tools, even as he shook his head. "She'll probably thank you for the distraction. She's got a lot of regular volunteers coming in now, and this will give them something to do."

"Thank you." Karen paused. "Wish I'd been able to say that the mare was okay, but she was still down when I decided I'd better leave and bring him in."

Josiah looked a little grim at her announcement and sympathy filled his eyes as he responded, "You know we can't save them all, not even under perfect conditions. You brought the little one in, and that's a wonderful thing."

"Still wish I could've done more." Inside, she ached.

Josiah took off one way, and she and Finn headed the other to the cottage.

He pointed her down the hallway. "Grab a shower. I'll make you lunch."

She drained the entire hot water heater and still couldn't get rid of the chill in her bones. The sensation had nothing to do with the heat of her skin and everything to do with the coyote cries that had echoed around the cottage over the past weeks.

Karen leaned her forehead against the wall of the shower. Predators taking down an injured animal—it was part of life. Chances were the coyotes would put the mare out of her misery if anything.

Still, the idea that she probably left the mare to die didn't sit well.

When she made it to the kitchen, there was a plate of food on the table. Finn was stretched out in a nearby chair with his arms folded over his chest. His eyes were closed, and his head nodded slightly. Fast asleep, sitting upright, waiting for her.

The poor man. He was still in pain and would be for weeks. The last thing he needed was her to weep all over him, and yet that was exactly what she'd done.

She sat down quietly and went to work on the food. Tasteless—no fault of Finn's, she just had no appetite—yet necessary.

All the while she watched him. The slow rise and fall of his chest. The way his lashes laid dark against his cheekbones. Head slowly shifting until his eyelids eased open and his dark gaze met hers.

Instantly alert, he examined her face. "How're you feeling?"

"Annoyed that I dragged you away from time with your friends."

Finn leaned forward, disapproval rising. "Really?"

"Hey, just telling the truth." Karen pushed back her plate, struggling to find an even keel. "It wasn't the best morning I've ever had, so maybe we should let it go for now. Thanks for being there. I appreciate it," she told him sincerely.

He examined her face, breathing out hard as if trying to blow away his own frustration, but he left it alone. Which was exactly what she wanted, even though it meant that mess of emotions was still there and out of whack.

To hell with it. No use in trying to pick apart the ache inside when the truth was sometimes life sucked.

She cleaned up the kitchen, then when Finn slipped out the back door, she headed into the living room to distract herself by going through the mail that had piled up over the past couple weeks. The things she'd had forwarded to her sister's then brought over to the cottage and promptly ignored.

She was in the middle of paying bills when her sister called. "Hey, Tamara."

"Hey, sis. Heard about the colt. Sounds like you had a hell of a day." Noise rattled in the background behind Tamara's voice. Children and a deeper rumble as Caleb answered one of them. "I won't keep you but wanted to let you know Dad's coming out tomorrow. Come for supper. Julia will be here for sure. Maybe even Lisa."

Since the discovery of Julia's existence, George Coleman was now making an effort to be more involved in his daughters' lives.

Karen's relationship with her dad had never been what she would call close, but the last couple months had been the nearest thing she'd felt to having a true father.

Heck, she was here in Heart Falls because he'd insisted she take the time. He'd even written her a glowing recommendation that had contributed to her getting accepted into the training program she was headed for in the fall.

Still, there wasn't a lot of dancing going on at the thought of a meal with him, and wasn't that shitty?

He was trying, so she would too. "I'll be there."

Tamara shared a few stories of what had happened at the Canada Day celebrations, including the tidbit that Zach had come close to being purchased by *two* women. At least until Malachi Fields had reminded everyone that, according to the rules, that wasn't allowed. No matter that the women insisted they were willing to share—although not at the same time.

Amusement broke through the shell wrapped around Karen. "That would've been entertaining to see. How on earth did Malachi explain that in a child-friendly manner?"

"Very, very carefully," Tamara said with a snicker. "Don't bother bringing anything tomorrow but come over early if you can. The girls are off school for summer, and they're eager for time with their Auntie Karen."

"I love spending time with them too." Karen's gaze drifted to the thick yellow envelope that was next in her pile.

Department of Education. Equine Therapy.

Tamara said goodbye, and Karen mindlessly hung up, pulling the envelope toward her. It was a hefty package, a good half inch thick— Probably not the thing she should dig into in her current mood. She pushed it aside and finished the rest of her tasks.

Finn returned from whatever he'd been doing out back, motioning her toward him. "Come on."

He'd started a fire in the circular pit at the base of the deck. Finn lowered himself gingerly into an Adirondack chair. He stretched out his legs and leaned back with a sigh of relief.

Karen grabbed them both drinks then joined him. The arrangement provided a great view of both the fire pit and the mountains in the distance.

"It's too early to see the flames properly, but sitting by a fire is always relaxing." His all-too-knowing gaze drifted over her. "We both need a little relaxing."

It was exactly what she needed. To sit, in silence, staring at the dancing flames as small white clouds drifted across the sky. The quiet passage of time didn't answer any questions or solve any problems, but it was soothing and low demand because Finn made it that way.

Zach showed up with supper just when the rumbling in her stomach had been about to force her to deal with dinner.

"I've got takeout. Neither of you answered your phone, so you're stuck with what I selected from the East Indian menu."

Zach rested his elbows on the railing as he examined them. "If you haven't grown roots over there, come to the table."

Karen got to her feet, stepping over to extend a hand to Finn and help him wrangle his way out of the chair.

His strong grasp wrapped around her wrist, and one sharp tug later he was vertical, smiling down with that unreadable expression. They stared at each other for a moment, the quiet that had surrounded them for the past couple of hours a nearly tangible thing.

She reached up to push away the lock of hair that had fallen across his forehead. "Thanks. Again."

"No problem." He caught her fingers and gently pressed them against his lips.

Her stomach tumbled.

They made their way inside where for the next hour Zach Sorenson provided comic relief by replaying every moment of the bachelor auction with dramatic voices and everything.

Even with the lighthearted entertainment, Karen was ready to call it a night when Zach laid a hand on her arm. "You've had a rough day. I'll help Finn with anything he needs to hit the sack."

"You just want to gloat more about these two women who were fighting over you," Finn grumbled, but he looked Karen in the eye. "I'll be fine. Go get some shut-eye."

Her eyes may have closed, but her sleep was anything but restful. Still, she got out of bed at the regular time to discover someone had woken before her.

There was a new wildflower in a glass on the counter.

The tight knot inside her belly was still there, but a whisper of something sweet drifted in as well. Enough to let her shoulders loosen slightly before she grabbed a cup of coffee and got on with her day.

She put in a solid morning's work before tracking down Finn to let him know she would be out for the evening.

He nodded, frowning distractedly at the receipts he had spread all over her kitchen table. "Zach promised he'd bring food over again, so don't worry about me." He glanced up, focus suddenly intent. "Have a good time with your family. Say hello to your dad from me."

Of all the stupid things... "Shoot. I should've told Tamara you'd come with me. I know Dad would love to see you again."

This time, though, Finn shook his head. "Not yet. Right now you girls are still getting reacquainted with him, and I'm not about to interrupt that. But if you find out when he plans to come down again, we can take him out to dinner."

"I can do that." Karen stood awkwardly in the doorway, uncertain whether she should kiss him goodbye or just leave.

Finn solved the problem by crooking a finger at her. "I know I'm a little distracted, but think of this as a necessary evil."

Which made her laugh. She tangled her fingers around his then leaned in to press their lips together. Brief, chaste.

He caught her around the back of the neck and held her in place, staring into her eyes and then dropping his gaze to her mouth. "I don't think so. Let's try that again."

This time when their lips met, she wasn't in charge. He was. This wasn't the type of kiss that would be approved of in public. It was hot, deep, and dirty, and when he let her go, Karen was breathing hard. Her heart was pounding, and her head was spinning, and—

"You are a dangerous man, Finn Marlette," she said when she finally found enough air to speak.

He winked. "Have a nice dinner."

The time with her nieces was wonderful. Sasha was full of lists of everything she planned to do over the summer. It was amusing as heck to hear "and Kelli says—" repeated a good half dozen times over the course of the recitation.

But what was even funnier was when little sister Emma leaned hard against Karen's side, speaking softly but utterly clear and with confidence. "Mama says sometimes Sasha's Kelli-isms give her conniptions."

Karen stifled her laughter. "Really? And what *are* conniptions?" she asked seriously.

Emma paused for a moment before smiling brightly. "That fuzzy feeling you get when you pet a kitten."

Which was pretty much the best definition Karen had ever heard. "That sounds perfect," she assured Emma even as she met Julia's gaze and the two of them grinned brightly.

George Coleman arrived. Caleb ushered him in, and both Emma and Sasha went wild greeting their grandpa.

Family chaos ensued, the warmth of Tamara and Caleb's home a welcoming hug. The scent of a home-cooked meal and the music of laughter filled the space from top to bottom.

Caleb had served dinner in the Stone tradition when the conversation took a twist. Nothing really terrible, but it brought an uneasy tone.

"You must be excited to head off to school," her father said to Karen. Then he turned to Caleb as he added, "Some of the Coleman boys have stepped in to take her place. They aren't doing badly at all..."

"Have you found out any more about your classes?" Lisa asked while she helped Emma with her dinner.

"I got a package of information," Karen admitted. "I'll dig through it soon, but it's been pretty busy with the ranch work I committed to. Especially now that Finn's in recovery mode."

George Coleman raised a brow. "You're working at a ranch? I thought you left early to spend time with your sisters."

"I am. I mean, we are. But..." A stutter escaped, and she

thought quickly. "I'm sure I mentioned this. Finn Marlette is here setting up a dude ranch. I'm helping them with the horses they need. That sort of thing."

Her father's expression grew tighter as she spoke, and he shook his head as if she had just confessed to some shameful crime.

Then he changed the topic. "What's that boy doing out here? Last I heard he was out in Manitoba."

Karen wasn't about to go into a long explanation when she didn't know all the details herself.

"He's been around for a while." Tamara leapt in with the answer, smiling sympathetically at Karen. "Got his hand in all sorts of ventures these days, not just ranching. He's done well for himself."

It was on the tip of Karen's tongue to mention Finn was doing great, except for breaking his leg, when her father spoke.

"He always was a go-getter. It's good to catch up with people. I should give his father a call. You say hi to Finn for me," her father said pointedly to Karen.

"He said the next time you're in town, he'd love to get together."

Conversation drifted after that, but the uneasy sensation in her stomach remained.

It was still with her when she made it back to the cottage. Neither Finn nor Zach was around. They'd probably headed over to the main house where there was at least a TV to entertain them.

Some strange force of nature pulled her toward that manila envelope. She picked it up again, the heavy weight in her hand triggering zero excitement.

Great, considering you gave up everything for this.

She wanted to growl at the thought.

She pulled out the papers and began reading through them.

A course syllabus, with lists of books they'd be covering, and the hands-on activities of working with experienced trainers.

The tight feeling in the pit of her stomach just got sharper and sharper until she shoved the pile together haphazardly, not even trying to replace the papers in the envelope.

She must've eaten something that didn't agree with her. Or maybe she'd caught a bug, because she was definitely not feeling herself.

She put the whole mess on the bookshelf in the far corner of the room, shoving an old rock that was there for some reason on top of the stack to keep it in place in case—

Hell, she didn't *know* why. Maybe a windstorm would sweep into the living room and the rock would be the only thing that kept everything from tearing apart.

She stomped across the room and headed to bed because there was no way anyone needed to be inflicted with her cranky self.

Something was wrong.

Finn miscalculated a step between the crutches and his good leg, accidentally knocking his cast into the corner of the hallway.

"Goddamn—"

He jammed his mouth closed and stifled his curses.

"Fuck, that one hurt," Zach offered on his behalf. Only he said it in a sotto whisper, which amused Finn enough to mostly forget the pain throbbing up his leg.

Okay, that was a lie. *Nothing* made him forget the pain, but he was capable of more than one thought at a time, and the second one was the business of something being wrong.

"You don't need to babysit my ass," he whispered back at Zach once they'd made their way into the master bedroom.

"But it's such a fine ass, or so I've been told." Zach stepped out of swinging range, holding his hands in the air in surrender. "You know I'm just joking. If we swung that way, we would've done the deed a long time ago."

"I don't know how many times I have to tell you, your chances for a career in comedy are nil."

Finn debated. Drop trou and then crash? Or muster up enough energy to at least brush his teeth before he collapsed into bed?

Zach sat on the mattress, and as patiently as if he were dealing with a two-year-old, he shoved Finn's hands out of the way and helped peel off his pants. "You're about to fall over. Stop fighting and let me help."

"I kind of hate you right now," Finn told his best friend.

"That's okay. I'm big enough to handle mean words." Zach rose from where he'd bent to pull off Finn's socks. "Need any more help?"

"Piss off." Finn paused then sucked in a breath through his teeth. "Thanks."

There was nothing but an amused glint in his friend's eyes. "I'll grab your painkillers."

He was back in the room a moment later, a tall glass of cold water and the requisite drugs in the palm of his hand.

Finn barely had a chance to swallow the pills when, to his shock, he was dragged close and given a brief but thorough back pounding.

Zach stepped back, his grin firmly in position. "Never said it before, but I'm glad you're okay. I mean, you're hurting like hell, drugged up to your eyeballs, and totally confused about what you're doing with your love life. Set on vengeance and trying to meet an impossible challenge, but you're alive, and that's what matters."

Finn pinched the bridge of his nose. "You done?"

He glanced up in time to see Zach glance off into the distance as if considering before he nodded firmly. "Pretty much."

The two of them stared at each other for a moment before they burst into snorts of laughter.

"Get the hell out of here," Finn ordered as he made his way to the bed, amusement still bubbling inside.

The suspicion that something was wrong remained, though. There were still mysteries to be solved, and yes, as Zach had mentioned, there was a challenge to be won.

But there were also things that were right. He had friends —*good* friends. He would heal and be stronger than before.

And he had Karen. A relationship that had so much hope and potential, he was determined neither of them would give up. That was the challenge he was determined to win. That was the most important thing in his world.

Even as the painkillers took him under, his thoughts swirled around finding a way to put a smile back on her face.

To put stars back into her eyes.

To put her back at his side. Forever.

14

Something had come over Finn, and Karen didn't know if she should explain it away as a side effect of the drugs or her current mopey nature making her oversensitive.

He was constantly in her space. Every time she turned around, he was right freaking *there*.

Handing her a cup of coffee. Poking his head around the corner when she came back to the cottage or to the main house for a break. Asking if she needed him to answer any questions.

In the barn.

Waving at her from the deck as she rode past on Starlight.

Hell, she was beginning to think if she crawled into the hayloft of the barn, she would find him there, sprawled out on the bales and ready to ask if there was anything he could do for her.

She stopped outside the horse stalls, trying to regain her equilibrium.

Starlight offered her a hello, nickering to entice her to come and give him a treat.

"You're such a flirt," she told him, but she obediently opened the gate and joined him in the stall. She fed him some lumps of carrot she'd brought along then stepped to the side and laid her head against his warm flank.

She stroked him a few times, feeling muscles twitch under his skin and soaking in his peaceful demeanor in a way that would've surprised a lot of people who weren't comfortable around horses.

He whinnied, lifting his head and adjusting his front hooves softly, as if sensing her mood.

Karen stepped toward his head and wrapped her arms around his neck, breathing in his scent while trying to breathe out some of the frustrations she'd been drowning in for the last couple of days.

Pretty pathetic when even the horses know you're out of sorts.

Knew *and* knew how to offer support.

So be it. Right now, it was either accept the comfort of the big beast or simply find a corner of the barn to sit in and cry. She hadn't been so damn emo since she was a teenager.

There was no such thing as early thirties puberty, though, so this?

Annoying as hell.

"Karen?"

She snorted. It was Finn. She thought he'd been headed to the far side of the construction site where, for some ungodly reason, he checked on the work crew four to five times a day.

"In with Starlight," she called. Because hiding in the stall without saying anything was just childish. Tempting, but childish.

He stepped into view, and she instantly went on alert. "Holy shit, what happened?"

Finn tucked his crutches under his arms to unbutton his

shirt. The flannel dripped, and water ran off the brim of his hat and down his whisker-clad cheeks. "Water main malfunction. I need your help to get cleaned up."

She gave Starlight a quick kiss on his nose and a farewell pat before shutting the gate behind her and joining Finn. "Come. Let's head to the cottage. We'll strip you down on the back deck."

Finn growled his frustration as they made their way outside and across the yard toward the cottage.

"I don't even have to ask where the problem is," Karen said. The entire work crew scrambled frantically in the mud, a tall plume of water spraying skyward like their own homegrown geyser.

"That's a brand-new system," Finn complained. "No way in hell it should've blown like that."

"Super frustrating," Karen agreed before pointing out the positive. "It's still better to find a flaw now instead of a month after you have paying customers around the place."

"Stop being optimistic. I'm cranky," Finn told her.

Gee, that made two of them. A wry grin arrived without warning. "I thought the operative word was grumpy."

"That too."

Undressing the man was pleasantly distracting. Some of the annoyance that had been lingering for the last couple of days began to ease as she helped get Finn naked. He pulled off his upper layers, and she helped him take off his boot, which required him to sit on the tall stool they'd put on the deck just for that purpose.

She peeled his filthy sweatpants over his cast, and by the time he stood there in nothing but underwear—those were wet as well—Karen had gotten a good long reminder of what an amazing physical specimen he was.

There were streaks of mud across his face, the back of his

neck, and his arms. Flecks had fallen on the rest of his torso as they'd undressed him, layering on the beautiful pallet of his skin. Not just muscle and sinew, not just the mesmerizing rise and fall of his chest. Her gaze drifted over the curls of hair on his torso and down that dangerous line leading from his belly button toward the elastic at his waist.

"You keep looking at me like that and I won't be in the shower by myself," Finn warned.

Karen snapped her gaze up from where she'd been admiring the long line of his cock under his underwear. The thick ridge had been growing thicker, probably because she'd been staring in the first place.

And he'd caught her in the act.

She met his gaze. "I should be ashamed, but that's not what I'm feeling right now."

A low rumble rose from his chest as he grabbed the crutches. "Get inside the damn house," he ordered.

She pulled the door open and stepped inside, Finn right behind her. "You know you can't take a shower yet," she warned. "Your cast is waterproof on the outside, though, so it should be okay if we wipe it down."

Then they were in the bathroom. He turned on the taps, grabbed a facecloth and ran it over his hands and upper body before the water had time to warm.

The layer of hair on his arms and forearms rose slightly as the cool water hit his skin. Nipples taut, abdomen muscles forming firm ridges. Karen watched mesmerized for the first moment before realizing that as amazing as the show was, she wasn't helping.

She grabbed another washcloth, dipped it in the sink, and proceeded to wash his back, his shoulders. The dip where his waist went in before flaring to his taut buttocks. She stood behind him in the bathroom and caught hold of his waistband, peeling the underwear down over his rigid fiberglass cast.

His butt was a thing of beauty.

She skimmed her fingers over the indent in one cheek and lower to where it met the firm foundation of his standing leg. Wiry hair brushed her palms as she washed lower, swooped higher.

The upper ridge of his lower back, the taut muscles along his Adonis line.

Finn groaned, and she glanced up to discover he had the edge of the bathroom counter in a death grip. Head hanging down, staring in the mirror at *her* as she touched him.

She hadn't actually been washing him for a good ten minutes. The continued motion of the cloth over his skin was an excuse, and as their gazes met, something in his darkened. Grew heavy and demanding.

He reached back and caught her wrist in his strong fingers. Guided her hand forward, over his abdomen and to where his cock stood upright and thick, moisture spilling from the slit at the top.

Moisture that painted her fingertips when he wrapped her hand around his length and slowly pumped.

Down, then up, rolling her palm over the head where heat and moisture grew.

Again, his fingers wrapped tighter over hers until she knew she never would've gripped him that firmly, but this was good. A sweet and oh-so-dirty connection as he used her hand to bring pleasure to the foreground.

Karen regretted every inch of clothing covering her body because when she stepped closer, heat passing between them, it wasn't enough.

It would have to be, though, because she wasn't stopping what she was doing. Not when the reflection in the mirror showed Finn's eyes closed, pleasure rolling over his expression as he gave in to her touch.

His hand slid backward from over hers until he caught hold of her hips. Fingers dug into her ass cheek as he pulled her against him. Layers of fabric separated them, yet sexual tension joined them together in an utterly different way.

And that *view*—

The mirror image in front of her was every dirty memory and every sweaty dream she'd had since first meeting Finn Marlette. It wasn't as much the perfection of his body as how he let go.

His face. Eyes squeezed tight then relaxing. Lips slightly open as he panted, release edging closer. Muscles of his torso tight, abdomen curling in as she kept the rhythm going.

Karen licked the skin of his shoulder, his arm. Nipping lightly, her gaze fixed on the mirror to enjoy his response.

His eyes—open now and speaking the words that weren't coming from his lips. Need, urgent need. He gasped, hips rocking against her hand in a final desperate surge.

Coming then in long hard spurts that flew across the countertop and her fist as he stared into the mirror and her eyes and let her see everything.

He was still reeling when the truth hit hard. As good as his release had been, and as necessary as it had been, it wasn't the end of what was absolutely vital right now.

Finn twisted on the spot, awkward because of his cast and unsteady on his lone supportive foot because all his damn blood was still centered in his cock.

Still he found the energy to tangle his fingers in Karen's hair to access her lips.

He kissed her as if he were possessed.

He took her deep and he took her hard, and if he weren't hindered by the cast, he would've had her up against the back of the door only a few seconds later.

Maybe the cast was a good thing, because he shouldn't move too fast.

The heat between them flared like a bright flame under a pitch-dark summer sky. Finn fed the passion, licking and biting, holding her against him as her soft curves met the rigid planes of his body.

They fit. They fit so damn well. They were both panting when he let their lips separate.

He grabbed a towel off the rack and dragged it around his neck, tilting his head toward the bedroom. "In there. Now."

Karen backed up slowly, mischief rising in her eyes. "You're supposed to be all relaxed and happy right now."

"I'm very relaxed, and extremely happy, and if you're not naked in about ten seconds, I hope you're not too fond of those jeans."

He crowded after her, fighting to keep from growling when she demurely glanced up from under her lashes.

Then she laughed, reaching for the bottom of her shirt and peeling it up and over her head an instant later.

She went to work on the button of her jeans, but Finn was more interested in ditching the crutches and doing more than admire from a distance.

Only that strip show? Already she was blowing his mind. "Dammit, Karen."

Karen paused in the middle of shoving the denim off her hips, examining him closely.

He hopped forward the half step it took to close the gap, balancing on one crutch as he brushed his knuckles along the edge of her shimmering red camisole. "You walk by in the arena, your hips swaying like the sweetest temptation. I get so freaking hard because you're wearing these sexy things underneath, and I'm the *only* one who knows. Satin and silk, soft to touch, but nowhere near as soft as the skin you're covering up. And I want to strip you bare and touch you everywhere until you're ready to scream my fucking name."

He slipped a finger under the thin silk strap of her camisole and the thicker supporting one of her bra. He slowly brushed his fingertip over her shoulder and down her arm so that the camisole dipped to reveal the smooth creamy swell of her breast, rising and falling more rapidly as the pace of her breathing picked up.

"And this bra should be illegal." The camisole fell away enough the edge of her nipple was visible, peeking out from the supportive bra cup.

Finn dipped his head and slowly licked along the line between her breasts. Up along the curve until he stopped directly over her nipple. Closing his lips, he pulled it into his mouth and pulsed.

Fingers dragged through his hair as Karen moaned, arching toward him.

He didn't have the ability to hold himself on one leg for as long as he needed to enjoy this the way he wanted. Time to get creative. He worked his way up the side of her neck and to her lips, crowding her backward to the edge of the bed.

Easing off just enough to look her in the eye, he spoke hungrily. "Need to take some weight off, but as soon as I do, you're going to give me what I want. I'm not done checking out that pretty bra, and I'm definitely not done making you feel good. Won't be done until you're sitting on my face and my tongue is deep inside, fucking you until you come so hard you forget everyone but me."

Karen moved out of his way, her cheeks red and a flush

covering her chest. "Those painkillers make you very dirty mouthed."

He got on the bed, all the while grinning. "I didn't take any today yet, so let's just say you inspire me. Take off your panties then get up here."

Finn lay flat on his back, legs stretched out. his gaze fixed on Karen. She reached behind her—

"Leave the bra," he ordered. "That's my job. You ditch the panties and come straddle me."

He didn't think it was possible for her to blush any harder, but she did, which set something inside him boiling. Or maybe it was the way she hooked her thumbs into the thin line of fabric covering each hip and wiggled with a natural grace. The silky scrap slid out of sight to the floor, the dark curls covering her sex a bit of nirvana in the bedroom.

Placing one knee then the other on the mattress, Karen carefully centered herself over his abdomen. "Don't you do anything to hurt yourself," she warned.

"When the shoe was on the other foot, I trusted you to let me know if something didn't feel good," he reminded her. "Not going to try anything yet that's too hard and too fast, although the day I get to sink my cock into your sweet pussy can't come soon enough."

She licked her lips, breathing heavily.

He gestured her forward. "Closer. I'm not done playing."

The confusion on her face vanished as soon as she adjusted position. He ran his palms slowly up her torso until his hands cupped her beautiful breasts. A slow circular sweep over the fabric followed by teasing touches of the exposed skin playing peekaboo with his senses.

"Damn if I can figure out how this can be comfortable, but it's one of the sexiest things I've ever seen," Finn confessed.

"The bra gives me a lot of support." Her words slid into a

soft moan as he rolled her nipples between his thumbs and forefingers.

"Bet it feels good," Finn prompted. "When you're out riding and that silky camisole is rubbing your bare nipples, you ever think about me? About my mouth on you? Sucking and biting until you squirm?"

Karen leaned forward, her breasts all but spilling out of the cups. Inches away from his mouth as if offering them like a sacrifice. "Sometimes. Sometimes I come back home and get myself off in the shower. Just let the water slick over me and dream that it's you."

The image was the last straw. Finn undid her bra and stripped it away even as he surrounded one taut peak with his mouth and sucked.

He used his tongue, circling the tender skin until she pushed harder against him. Then it was time to use his teeth, alternating gentle nips with increasing suction. The taste of her was perfect, and he used both hands to press her breasts close enough to alternate from one sensitive tip to the other. She held herself over him, eyes closed, pleasure streaking over her face.

And then it was enough, because it wasn't nearly enough. Finn reached down and caught her hips, dragging her upward.

Karen grabbed hold of the headboard to balance herself, but he held her tight enough she wasn't going anywhere.

He pressed a kiss to the apex of her sex. "Damn, I've missed this."

"Me too." The words were whisper-soft, with a bit of a laughing lilt to them.

Finn met her smiling eyes. "My tongue missed you."

She opened her mouth to say something, but he wasn't waiting any longer. He licked through her curls, opening her. Her flavor rushed him, and he lifted her higher to work greedily. Teasing the bundle of nerves that set her hips wiggling.

He dug his fingers into her ass muscles to grind her down on his face. Stabbing his tongue deep, driving her pleasure higher from the sounds escaping her lips.

He slipped his fingers into her sex and concentrated on her clit with his tongue. Moisture bathed his hand as he teased her entrance. Fucking her slowly with his fingers, she rocked against him, drawing closer to the pinnacle.

The only thing he didn't like about this position was he couldn't see her face, but for here and now, he would take it. Take the sounds spilling from her lips, the moisture coating his fingers, and then as she came, her body clamping tight and squeezing even as he continued to fuck her through the aftershocks.

He left his fingers buried deep, licking slowly over her folds to feel her quiver. The headboard shook as she clenched down again, every motion of his tongue setting her off again.

"Oh my God, Finn. Slow. *Slow*." She breathed out another long gasp, lifting her hips high enough to break contact with his mouth.

He glanced up. Pulled his fingers out partway.

Slowly slid them back in.

Her face contorted as another pulse rocked her. "Oh my God. *Oh my God*."

He did it again, and this time she cursed softly. "I'm going to die."

Finn stilled his hand. Twisted his head enough to press a kiss to the inside of her thigh. She quivered and sighed.

"Want some more?" he asked.

"No. Yes." She laughed. "Later?"

Curling his fingers inside her gently set off another scream.

This time he took pity and slid his hand all the way free. "Later," he agreed.

She carefully lifted herself then grabbed the spare blanket off the chair. She spread it over him before crawling onto the mattress by his side.

Flat on his back, there weren't many options for holding her. But Finn opened his arm, and she curled up next to him, head resting on his shoulder, her arm draped over his torso. Both of them naked except for the hugely present cast.

They lay quietly for a moment. Finn pressed a kiss to the top of her head. "You okay with this?"

"The being naked in bed with you or the part where we got each other off in the middle of the afternoon?"

He went for honest. "Both. The orgasms are fun, but the being with you part is pretty damn important to me. Naked or not."

"Yeah, right. Because I've been so much fun to be around lately." Karen rumbled a little before sighing heavily. "Sorry I've been so damn grumpy."

"Isn't that my line?"

She laughed, but it wasn't bright and clear the way he wanted to hear it.

"I don't know. It's just—" She took another deep breath then shook her head, her hair sliding over his chest and biceps. "We have a goal. To get the ranch up and running, and it's a *good* goal. I'm glad to be able to help you with it."

Her words said one thing, her tone another. For some reason it sounded as if working with him was an item she was determined to succeed at even though it wasn't really what she wanted.

Not being able to look into her eyes sucked. Not knowing a way to reassure her he'd give up the entire damn ranch if there was something else she wanted.

But something told him to wait. He tightened the arm around her briefly. "I'm glad you're here. Not because of the ranch, but because you're *here*."

She softened a little at that, twisting her head to press a kiss to his chest. "Are naps legal on this particular ranch?"

"Definitely. Especially after a good workout."

That got a soft snicker and then quiet. Finn held on as her breathing slowed and they both relaxed.

How the hell would he survive waiting another four weeks until the cast came off to take their relationship to the next level?

But as distracting as thoughts of sex were, he wondered what else he was missing and how to fix it. The miracle of having her trust him again had hit hard.

He still needed to up his game.

15

———

It wasn't as if they'd hit a turning point and it was now all naked fun and full-on *dive into a relationship* time.

Finn wouldn't have minded, but he figured reality wouldn't work that way. And even as he took the time to enjoy the brief nap cuddled up together, he thought she'd likely wake up and find a way to put distance between them again.

Frustrating as that was, Finn didn't fight it. Not as if he could chase her down and demand she stop running from what was between them.

Still, he took the fact that she kissed him sweetly before getting out of bed and pulling her clothes on as a win.

Karen gave him a wink. "One of us has to get to work. My boss's boss is a real hard-ass."

Finn folded his arms behind his head and grinned. "You go on and tell Zach I'm his boss. I want to hear what he says."

She took off with a wave.

He took his sweet time finishing getting ready to restart his day. Thank God for the strange extended clamp tool Zach had

189

bought him that allowed him to get dressed in less than an hour.

Karen had grabbed his wet clothes and popped them in the washer, so he puttered around the kitchen for a bit, getting things ready for the evening. By the time he made it over to the house to catch up with Zach, it was nearly four o'clock.

His friend was looking over lists of something with an atypical frown creasing his brows.

"What's up?" Finn asked as he made his way across the floor, crutches solid on the new wood sheeting being used as a base for the future hardwood floors.

Zach blinked before focusing, answering with a wave of the papers in his hand. "I was checking to see what was on our recent order list, because we're missing a hell of a lot of things. Cody informed me they had to stop the plumbing installations on the cabins because they're short nearly all the elbows they need."

That didn't make any sense. "The contractors wrote up quotes for everything we required. Did a box get stored somewhere it shouldn't?"

"That was my first thought as well. Got some of the guys out looking," Zach told him. "In the meantime, I was double-checking I hadn't screwed up."

"Or me, considering I've been the one doing the paperwork," Finn said bluntly. "Don't spare my feelings. Who knows what I did while higher than a kite?"

"I don't think it's either of us. That's the problem." Zach glared at the paperwork again as if his disgust would scare the truth out.

Finn eased back on the tall stool waiting for him. "Put that down for now. Catch me up on how things are really going. I've been easing off the painkillers. I want to make sure I didn't miss anything important the past couple weeks."

It didn't take long. Partly because Zach knew how to get to the point, and partly because they had a pretty straightforward way of working together. If it was good, that's all Zach said.

If there was a problem—like the missing parts—the issue got put into priority according to the effect it would have on their deadline. Which so far didn't seem to be a problem.

"I think we should narrow down our focus a little, though," Zach admitted. "Alan already told us he's bringing his extended family. That means we need six cabins completed to beat the challenge. Karen said she'll have enough animals and staff to deal with the trail rides. At least the exterior of the row housing will be done—that's more for looks and the fun of it than anything. Once we have everything we need to install, at least."

Finn considered. "Are you suggesting we don't finish this main house?"

Zach shrugged. "We need a place for a cook and to serve up meals. Karen and I were talking about that. As sweet as it sounds to have that in the house, it involves a whole lot more changes than I think we can do in our timeframe. All things considered."

"Probably should've figured that out sooner," Finn said with a grumble.

"Probably would've, but life happened," Zach said brightly. His face lit up as he smiled toward the doorway. "Karen. Awesome. Come tell Finn about your cookhouse idea."

She slipped across the floor, completely professional. It was his own damn fault that he kept picturing that silky red fabric moving under her flannel shirt.

"You want to talk about that?" Karen asked. "It was just an idea."

"It was a good idea," Zach insisted. "Spill."

She shrugged as if not wanting the attention. "Just got to thinking about some of the comments we had at Willmore

Wilderness Park. We had a mess hall set up. Nice big building at the opposite end of the parking lot from the horses—cuts down on the scent of the country."

Finn's lips twitched. "Always a good thing at a dude ranch."

She nodded slowly. "What ended up happening was people started asking to hire out the hall for weddings and anniversary parties. And while the Willmore setup is a little different because we run full weeklong camps which don't leave a lot of downtime, if you made a cookhouse with two rooms for dining, you could rent out one for private parties and still provide for your guests."

"You don't think it would be a problem catering to two groups?"

"Depends on how you set it up, but the people who come out here for a wedding or an anniversary will be horse people, or love the country, or have some reason to pick Red Boot ranch. Heck, they might be interested in a one or two-hour trail ride without staying the night. With how close we are to Calgary, it's a definite possibility. And I hear the rental price on wedding venues has gone through the roof."

Zach pulled out the map of the ranch and pointed to a level spot to the west of the space currently earmarked for the parking lot. "Wouldn't ruin any of the sight lines for the cottages. If we build a nice size deck off a basic building, that would only enhance the experience. I think it would be great."

He was catching the vision of it. Finn considered it from another couple of angles, including how much money it would take to get it done PDQ.

He nodded at Karen. "Great idea. We'll double-check a couple things, but I think you're right. New sources of revenue are always good to include. Zach, see what we have to line up to get it started. Permits, design stamps, etc. We've got that architect who owes us a favour if we need blueprints stat."

Karen hadn't moved. "Really?"

He wasn't sure how to answer that. "Really...what?"

"You're just taking my idea and running with it?" Karen shook her head. "I hope I didn't give you a shitty idea. Don't go wasting money—"

Zach held up a hand. "We just told you it was a really good idea."

"And we will check the money part before we start, but that won't take long," Finn told her.

She shrugged again as if they were both slightly confused. "Oh, by the way. Cody wanted me to tell you guys he found one box of plumbing elbows, but the whole case looks as if it was driven over a few times by a tractor. We'll have to reorder those."

Finn stifled his curse.

"Hey, Zach." Karen changed the topic. Happiness shoved into her tone. "Someone was teasing you earlier about the bachelor auction. I never did hear the details about your winning date. Who bought you? Where are you taking her?"

"Rose Fields," he said with a smile. He raised a hand at the soft whistle that arrived with his announcement. "Don't go getting all excited. She already told me this is not a *date* date. Brad and Hanna's wedding is next week, and Rose wants a date who promises to dance with her as much as she wants. She put that into the auction contract."

"Like that's a hardship," Finn drawled.

Zach laid a hand on his chest and attempted to look long-suffering. "Don't know how I'll survive. A pretty woman wants to spend the evening in my arms? Sheer torture."

They chatted for a few more minutes, then Karen headed one way and Zach another. Finn made his way slowly back to the cottage because he'd had enough.

But Karen's strange reaction kept coming back to mind over

and over again. Why would she be all excited to share an idea yet be shocked when they moved on it?

If Finn had been tracking her down before, he would've had to work doubly hard now. Karen caught herself actively hiding from him.

From going into her bedroom early to getting up while it was still dark—which meant hellishly early at this time of year when by five a.m. the sun had already cracked over the horizon.

Of course, if she knew *why* she was hiding from him, it would make things easier.

The little touch of sex had only whet her appetite, so it wasn't that. She couldn't wait until he lost the cast, or at least wasn't popping painkillers on a regular basis, because she knew from experience there were ways to get creative even while he still wore the awkward contraption.

She just felt *shitty*.

He certainly didn't need somebody with a rotten attitude stomping into his world and making life more difficult.

She took herself off to Silver Stone to chat with her sister and visit with Kelli.

The cool sweet scent of the Silver Stone barn made the tension inside ease slightly. Karen found her step slowing as she wandered through the barn in search of her friend.

One of the barn cats paced slowly on the ridge of a stall. It paused to stare at her with glittering green eyes, slowly twitching its tail.

Some of the peacefulness inside Karen slipped away.

"Hey. Didn't expect to see you today." The voice drifted from above. Kelli stood at the edge of the hayloft, her arms folded on the railing. "Come to visit Dandelion Fluff?"

It was as good an excuse as any. "Partly. Partly to see you."

Kelli gestured toward the ladder attached to the nearby wall. "Come on up. You can kill two birds with one stone, so to speak."

The top of the ladder opened into a loft like any other, with neat rows of sweet-scented hay arranged with military precision. Kelli sat on a low section, and as Karen approached, a mess of kittens came into sight, all crawling around the natural playpen formed by one slightly lower bale.

"You've been the Pied Piper," Karen teased.

"I had early chores. This is one of the treats I give myself when I finish," Kelli said. "Sasha and Emma always want to know where the babies are. That's my excuse for why I track them down."

Kelli caught one of the tabbies, lifted it to her face, and rubbed noses.

"It wouldn't at all be because you're a soft touch for a cuddly creature, because, of course not." Karen scooped up Dandelion. "Hello, sweetie. Did you miss me?"

She got the most satisfying *meow* as he opened his little pink mouth. She pressed him against her chest, and he nuzzled her throat, little paws digging in.

The tightness inside returned with a vengeance, and now it was at the back of her throat, making it difficult to swallow.

"Hey. You okay?" Worry painted Kelli's expression.

Karen shook it off and forced a smile. "Wanted to know if you've heard anything more about the wild horses. How's the gelding you pulled from the pack?"

"Marmalade. He's doing okay. Still a little willful, but he's behaving better since we started giving him jobs to do." Kelli leaned back, absently piling more kittens onto her lap as she spoke. "I was hoping to get out and check on Thor and his harem sometime next week. You want to come? Love to have you along."

"If it works," Karen said slowly. "It'll be busy during the next couple of months. I swear Finn and Zach hired all the seasonal workers in the community, and they all want my opinion on things."

"No problem. I'll let you know when I end up with a free day to go exploring, and if it works for you to join me, great." Kelli cursed softly, peeling a kitten off her arm that had started using her as a climber.

Dandelion was sound asleep in Karen's arm.

She stared down at him, the little bundle of warmth. So trusting. So fragile.

At some point she had to stop avoiding the day. She carefully placed him back with his adoptive siblings, the mama cat meowing as she adjusted position to let another kitten latch on for a meal.

Peaceful. Sweet and content.

A million miles away from the sensations swirling inside Karen.

"Well, I guess I should get going. I haven't finished *my* chores," she said brightly as she got to her feet.

"Anytime. If you get a break in the afternoon, I'll probably be working with Marmalade. You're always welcome."

Karen was just about to vanish below the level of the loft when Kelli called after her again.

"Oh. And I'll see you at Tansy's."

Her pause was just long enough to feel uncomfortable, at least on Karen's end. "That's right. Girls' night out is tonight, isn't it? I can't make it. Something came up."

"That's too bad. We'll miss you," Kelli assured her. "I'll see you around soon. Tell Finn to heal up fast."

"Will do."

Karen kept moving, slipping into her day and forcing herself to work extra hard because when she was working, she wasn't thinking.

And when she wasn't thinking, that tight knot of frustration inside didn't hurt as much.

Incredibly, she avoided Finn the entire day. It helped that at some point he and Zach took off to the bank to deal with paperwork regarding an error in charges that had to be dealt with in person.

Around five she got a text from Finn, but even that was easy to push off.

Finn: *headed to Longhorn's for dinner. Will swing by and grab you.*

Karen stared at her phone for a minute before responding: *not really hungry. You guys have fun.*

She wandered around the house aimlessly for a good fifteen minutes before getting angry. That damn envelope was haunting her from the shelf. She felt like crying for no good reason, and she'd deliberately made it so that she was all alone instead of spending time with her friends or with the man who said he wanted nothing better than to be with her.

Foolish, irresponsible, and certainly deserving of having a shitty evening.

Something drove her outside to the fire pit. Finn had set it up with kindling, so it was a one match job to make things light. She sat in her chair, staring into the flames while the sun inched its way toward the mountains.

The stillness in the air felt unnatural. No birds chirped, and even the long grass beside the road seemed to be silent, the wind so light the strands were barely moving. Overhead, a hawk cried out. A lonely, eerie sound that brought goose bumps to her arms.

The predator on his own, looking for dinner.

Karen stared at the sky, one step away from crying.

Nearly an hour later, the familiar sound of crutches and a solo footstep carried across the deck then to the grass that led to the fire pit. The chair beside her creaked, and she opened her eyes but still avoided looking at him, staring instead over the distant mountains dusted with orange and pink.

Finn stayed silent for a bit, and then he held out a hand over the edge of his armrest. The chairs were far enough apart she had to be willing to reach the other direction and meet him in the middle.

She lifted her fingers to his.

A second later, she was tangled up tight in his firm grip, and the warning signs about imminent tears grew sharper. Dammit, this had to be hormonal, because she *wasn't* this weepy and out of control.

When he didn't say anything for a bit, Karen slowly relaxed.

A different kind of tension rose. The kind where she realized he'd been honest about what he wanted, and while she wasn't sure what the hell was going on, if she was going to give more than lip service to this relationship, she had to be honest as well.

"I feel as if there's this big black cloud hanging over me." The words came out through an aching throat.

She glanced to her left to find Finn still staring into the fire. Nodding slowly.

"That's not typical. Or it wasn't, not five years ago. You got any idea why?" he asked.

She shook her head before realizing he couldn't see her.

"No. I don't." Frustration struck as well. "Okay, I know one thing that's upset me, but I just need to get over it."

He lifted his head and met her gaze. "Want to talk about it? You know I can keep a secret."

His comment hadn't been meant to make her laugh, but it did. "You definitely can keep a secret." She grew serious. "I know my dad's trying, but every time I'm around him, I keep expecting the same old responses I've had for the past umpteen years. I don't enjoy spending time with him, and that's absolutely shitty."

His grip on her fingers tightened. "It's not shitty. It's real."

"I feel so guilty. I mean, Julia wants to get to know her dad, and to her, this earnest guy is the only one she's ever had to deal with. Tamara focuses on him being grandpa, and that seems to help. Lisa is like a duck and water just runs right off her back. But I don't *like* him." The admission nearly caught in her throat. "I worked with him for too many years. I know he's done some really nice things lately, but..."

The understanding on his face didn't wash away any of the guilt but at least didn't add to it.

"A little while back he explained to Lisa he was trying, in some twisted way, to protect us. He figured being chased off the ranch would keep us from being hurt or killed, like the accident that took Mom. Which is fucked up and not right. It hurts to think of the time and energy I spent trying to make the ranch better, and all the while, he never wanted me there."

Silence echoed for a moment. The fire crackled while her heart pounded after the harsh confession.

Then Finn tossed a grenade of his own. "I'm angry—so very angry—at the thought of how you were treated. And while your father did some things right, I don't respect how he treated you. It makes it tough to think about doing anything with him, and

I'm only feeling this secondhanded. I didn't have to put up with the bullshit you did for so many years."

Karen pulled her hand free to dig in her pocket for some tissue. This was no longer a no-crying zone, although—for now at least—her eyes were only leaking instead of her having full-out sobs.

Finn's expression went stone-cold. "Don't answer if you don't want to. Did he ever do anything sexually wrong to any of you girls?"

Shock slammed her system. She shook her head vigorously. "*Never*. We've talked about it, too. My sisters and our cousin Anna. A no-holds-barred type of conversation when the whole Me Too topic started, so I know that's not a secret hiding in the Coleman family past."

The hard ridges of his expression softened slightly. "I'm glad. But don't go thinking just because you didn't have to deal with that issue that it means what you did put up with is minor. Because it's not."

His warning came at the exact moment she'd already been heading down that path.

He was right.

Didn't make it any easier to ignore the rush of guilt. She'd had a roof overhead, food on the table, and a job to do. There'd been plenty of good things in her world—

She still hurt inside.

Karen spoke slowly, trying to put into words her biggest issue. "I spent a lot of years being told I wasn't good enough, and that sinks in, no matter how much I didn't want it to. And it doesn't matter *why* he did it, it was wrong."

"It was totally wrong. You didn't deserve it then, and you don't deserve this now." Finn leaned forward, looking to catch her gaze again. "This isn't something that will change overnight."

"I know."

He dipped his chin. "Your dad's not the only person I'm angry at," he admitted. "I have to be careful to not let the anger inside come out at the wrong moments. It's something I've been working on over the last couple of years."

Karen waited, but he didn't say anything more about the source of his anger. She figured he would when he was ready. The more important point now was the other part. "How do you work on it? Punching bags? Ballroom dancing?"

He snorted. "I do a mean tango."

"Especially now." She glanced at his cast.

Finn leaned back, staring toward the sun as it dipped behind the rise, disappearing from sight. "I went to a therapist for a bit. We came up with some questions I run through when I hit the issues that set me off."

"Go on."

"Might sound basic, but it helps. I ask *what's my endgame?* Usually that offers some different paths to head down instead of just blowing up."

Karen thought about it. "When I get asked to go over for dinner with my dad, my end goal is to be a good daughter, so I should suck it up and go."

He shook his head. "Fuck that. You *are* a good daughter. The endgame is for you to be happy and healthy, which means sometimes you'll say no to dinner because you don't have the energy to deal with him right then. Sometimes that means you might tell your sister you'll come over but you're leaving right when the meal is done. Or that you want to sit with your nieces."

"But I should—"

"Be miserable?" Finn shook his head. "*Ma chérie,* it's not your job to teach him how to be a good father."

The words hit with the weight of an anvil.

Finn carried on softly. "You say he's trying to do things differently, but he's had so many years of being another way—he'll fuck up at times and instinctively fall back into bad habits. You don't need to volunteer to be in range while he practices not being an asshole."

The tears that had been hovering were no longer willing to wait, and the floodgates opened. Because it was true. Every word scalded her soul and wrung her hard.

Curses drifted from him, then the sound of his stern voice broke through her misery as she wept, face in her hands.

"I can't do this," Finn growled with a rasp. "I can't fucking watch you cry without holding you. And I can't get up and scoop you into my arms, so *chérie*, you gotta come here. Come sit with me and let me hold you. We'll get through this. We'll find a way."

A million and one excuses why it was a terrible idea shot to the surface, all of them knocked away with a firm memory of how gentle he'd been with her when she'd been the injured one. Karen rose from her chair, crossed the short distance between them, and eyed him with concern.

He caught hold of her, dragging her into his lap. Her hips settled on his good leg, and her body twisted toward him until she was cradled in his arms.

In his arms, her world adjusted. The darkness was still around her, but there was a protective layer as well.

Finn Marlette, lighting a candle in her heart that sent out thin tendrils of hope into the aching night.

16

___

What Finn wanted most was to be her hero. An impossible task considering his injured leg and the utter inability to change the past.

Regret struck at having fucked up five years ago and not coming back sooner to change her world.

Yet he knew those choices were not only in the past, they were impossible as well. He was the man he was today because of the past five years. And dear God, he hoped what he'd learned was enough to make their tomorrows what she deserved.

She was still crying, but softer now, hands clutching his shoulders, face buried against his neck. The sound of a broken heart.

He nuzzled his lips against her temple. "Cry all you want, *ma chérie*. Get it out so when you're ready, we can look to the future."

Finn stroked her hair over her shoulders and down her back. Soft, sweet petting until she relaxed. Tension slowly drained away and left her pliable in his arms.

She tilted her head until their gazes met. "I'm not like this. I'm strong, and I get shit done and move forward."

Her voice was a whisper, sorrow and dust.

"Crying is strong," he insisted. "It's your body saying enough pretending you aren't hurt. Admitting you're not Teflon takes a lot of strength."

Sadness lived deep in her eyes. "I don't want to feel like this."

"No one wants to feel as if they'll never measure up. And I get that you had that told to you an awful lot. Either in words or deeds." He stroked his fingers under her chin. "It wasn't true. It's time you stop telling *yourself* that you're not enough. That's a good place to begin."

Karen looked shocked. "I'm very competent at what I do."

"Damn right you are," Finn agreed. "I think you tell yourself that sometimes. But after observing for the past month, I've noticed you don't always let other people say the same thing. And it's not modesty but denial."

Her mouth opened then closed as she considered. She stroked his arm, absently caressing him as if the touch helped center her. "So, my endgame is to admit I'm awesome?"

"That's a good goal. But let's talk for a minute. I use that question about endgame when I face a situation where my temper's taking off. It works even better if I think ahead of time about what I'm working toward. You said you're stuck in a cloud of darkness. I know you want to get rid of it. Aiming at a target makes it easier to step away from negative emotional distractions. It's one of the first lessons our mentor taught me and Zach."

Karen paused and glanced into the sky for a moment before speaking firmly. "I'm going away to school in the fall. Right now, I'm here in Heart Falls, spending time with my sisters and helping you guys get the dude ranch going." She took a shaky breath. "I'm spending time with friends and going for horseback rides, which means I have zero reason to complain about anything because all of those things are fantastic."

How the hell to make this clear? "Those aren't goals, that's a laundry list of what you're doing. What do you *want*? When you look deep inside yourself, what do you see yourself doing five years from now? Or if that's too far off, think about a month from now or tomorrow. What are you doing to put a smile on your face? I don't mean a shits-and-giggles smile like life is a constant party. Work isn't always fun, but even when Zach and I are dealing with the knottiest problem, there's a satisfaction to getting it done if it's a step toward the real goal I want to achieve."

"I can't declare my long-term goals that easily," Karen complained, pushing away from him slightly. "I mean, I have to analyze what I've done in the past, then—"

"Screw being systematic, go with your gut," Finn ordered. "Close your eyes."

She gave him a dirty look but followed his instructions.

Her slightly damp lashes rested against her cheeks. A crease lay between her brows, and tension gripped her body.

Finn wanted to fix it all.

He gently caressed her cheek. "Take a deep breath then picture yourself waking up tomorrow morning. What's the first thing you think of that would make you happy, deep down in your gut? What are you looking forward to?"

"Dandelion Fluff jumping on me."

The words shot out of her as if jet-propelled. Her eyes popped open. The expression of shock that followed made Finn's lips twitch into a smile.

"Why don't you have him anymore?" Finn asked gently.

"Because animals don't belong in the house," she said automatically.

"Some don't," he agreed. "Some do. Why can't Dandy be your *in the house to cuddle with* pet?"

Her lower lip trembled. "I'm going away to school in the fall," she repeated. "I can't take a kitten to college."

"Maybe not, but that's a problem for down the road. If you want, we can go out and grab the furry beast tonight. I'm sure he'd love to jump on you first thing in the morning."

Damn. The expression in her eyes was tearing him apart. As if she couldn't believe she was allowed the simple pleasure of a cat in her house.

He pushed his luck. "What else do you want when you wake up tomorrow? Don't think about if it's on your current to-do list, because you didn't make that list when you were thinking about yourself."

Her gaze dropped to his lips. "I want to be in your arms."

Hell yeah.

She straightened slightly, hand rising to cup his face. "I want to wake up in the morning in bed with you, but even as I say that, I know it's a crazy idea considering you're still hip deep in a cast, and there's—"

"Yes." His fingers tightened on her chin. "The thing you want. I'm saying yes to that. Screw the excuses that instantly popped to mind saying you can't have it, or you shouldn't have it, or you need to do something before you get to have it. That's the stuff you need to say *fuck it* to."

"But—" She slammed her lips together. Breathed in slow and deep then tried again. "What I want is you, Finn. Period. It's what I've wanted since forever. I've done a shitty job showing that. I don't know what I'm doing going forward, but if this is *teach Karen new tricks* night, I will absolutely say that when I picture tomorrow morning and the morning after that, what would make me smile is to have you beside me. And Dandy."

Finn had zero problem ranking up there with a handful of fur, especially considering exactly how big a change it was for her to admit that particular desire.

"Then you've got me. I'll worry about how to deal with my damn broken leg. Now wiggle up here a little more and give me your lips because someone just set an outstandingly clear goal. She needs a reward."

Karen pushed up on the arms of his chair, still trying her best to keep her weight off him. But when she tilted her head and leaned in close, it was all warm breath and sweet offering, no holding back. Their lips pressed together slowly. Softly. Tentatively, not because they weren't certain they should be doing this but because it was a moment to savour.

Finn threaded his fingers into the hair at the back of her head and cradled her close. Tasting and teasing, slowly bringing up the heat until she squirmed so hard he caught hold of her hips.

He broke them apart only to look into her eyes. "Time to take this inside."

"Your leg—" Karen paused. Her expression firmed. "I'm not going to be a pushover, even though I'm now second-guessing every one of my comments. I want to be with you, which means I want you to hold me. And I want to hold you, but I do *not* want you to hurt yourself."

"You plan on hogging the entire bed or pushing me onto the floor in the middle of the night?" He lifted her in the right direction for her feet to hit the ground.

"Only if you deserve it," she said with barely a hint of amusement in her tone. He accepted her outstretched hand, making it to his feet in one moderately smooth motion.

He gestured her toward the house. "Inside. We have unfinished business."

SHE'D BEEN LIVING in the cottage for over a month, sharing it with Finn for over two weeks, and this was the first time she'd felt awkward. At least until he crowded behind her, pressed his lips to the side of her neck, and nuzzled softly.

"Need to turn off that busy brain of yours," he whispered. "Anything dire you need to take care of tonight?"

There were messages from her sisters on her phone, considering she hadn't told any of them she wasn't coming to girls' night out. She considered the possibility of continuing to ignore them but decided that wasn't a smart idea. "Give me a minute to head my sisters off at the pass before they all show up here."

"You want to pick up Dandy?"

She had her phone out, opening a group message instead of responding to everyone individually. "I still can't believe you're encouraging me to get a pet."

He leaned around and got in her face. "I figure he picked you. We can go grab him, no problem."

Her thumbs moved over the keypad even as she shook her head. "I doubt Silver Stone security would enjoy finding us the barn in the middle of the night trying to track down an errant kitten."

She double checked her message then hit send. Hopefully it was enough to keep her sisters at bay.

Had a rough day, but I'm okay. Hitting the sack—I'll see you all tomorrow. XOX

She stabbed the send button then laid the phone aside, twisting on the spot to cup Finn's face in her hands. "Tomorrow we will go and get Dandy, because as awkward as it feels to admit it, I really want him around."

"Then you get to have him." Finn kissed her softly. The corner of her mouth. Her cheek. A long slow tease along her jaw until he reached her ear. "Tonight, I get you."

A shiver struck.

"Is that a yes?" His hands moved to her hips, busily untucking her shirt.

"I think so," Karen answered. "You don't plan to just cuddle, do you?"

His lips tugged on her ear briefly before his mouth latched onto the tender spot on her neck that always drove her wild. He sucked lightly, his tongue doing dangerous things to her blood pressure.

His fingers slipped beneath her shirt, calloused fingertips skimming gently over her skin before one heated palm pressed against her lower back. He tugged her toward him, and their torsos met. His firm muscles rubbed her shirt, which in turn teased skin that was far too sensitive.

"We might have to get creative," Finn warned her. "But I don't mind starting with a repeat of where I finished last time."

"Where was that?"

"Between your thighs with my tongue on your pussy."

"Oh. There." It wasn't that she didn't remember, but that words were beginning to lose all meaning. "Okay."

Finn chuckled, scooping his hand between her shoulder blades. He hummed happily. "No bra."

"Woman home alone, having a pity party? Trust me. No bra."

His amusement rippled over her skin along with the goose bumps formed because his hand slid forward and he cupped her. Her breast rested in the palm of his hand, and his thumb teased circles over her nipple.

"Are we doing this here?" she asked.

"Doing what?" Finn murmured.

He was going to make her say it. "Having sex."

"Right now I'm playing with your tits. Which is part of having sex, I suppose." His grin grew wicked.

She was tempted to grab his ears and shake him. "You're enjoying this."

"Yep. I hope you are too." He stared down at the fabric moving over his thumb. "I suppose we should either go to the bedroom or close a few curtains."

"Great idea." She made sure he was balanced before she stepped away. "I vote we stay here. One second."

It only took a moment to shut the curtain over the sink, and when she'd locked the two doors, front and back, she returned to the kitchen to find Finn leaning on the counter, grinning at her.

"I like it when you take charge," he told her.

She whipped her shirt off over her head and tossed it on the chair.

A low growl escaped him. "Come here."

Instead of joining him, she slipped off her sweatpants, stripping down to her underwear.

Then she hopped up on the sturdy kitchen table, opening her legs wide as she reached up to cup her own breasts. "I thought you liked it when I took charge. This might work best for our purposes."

Finn lost his shirt even as he crossed the short distance between them. With one hand braced on either side of her hips, he leaned their bodies together as he took her lips.

The next minutes vanished in a haze of rising sexual heat. His big palms were all over her, teasing and caressing. He kissed her as if it had been years and she was saving his life.

Karen gave in to temptation and let her fingers explore as

well. Ridges and dips called to her, teased her senses, and made her heart pound.

He kissed her mouth. Kissed her breasts. Dragged over a chair and sat, hauling her hips forward. "You didn't think this through," he growled.

An instant later, her underwear was on the floor, the elastic snapped at the hips. Then his mouth was on her, licking and sucking and biting, and watching only made the sensations that much more intense.

Pleasure streaked upward, whirling around her. She dug her fingers into his hair and dragged him even closer.

He lifted her, and Karen fell back onto her elbows. The bristles of his beard dragged against her inner thighs as his tongue on her clit went wild.

"*Finn.*"

The orgasm started in the usual place, but it seemed to develop tendrils, wrapping around her body in increasingly thick waves. Her entire body tingled, pulsed.

Finn lowered her hips then stood to shove down his pants and underwear. His thick cock rose toward her, and Karen curled up enough to wrap a hand around him and stroke.

He swore, grabbing for his pants to pull out a condom. It was one of the speediest suit ups she'd ever seen, but she didn't care. She was so ready.

Her feet on the tabletop, thighs spread wide. He notched his cock against her sex, rubbing up and over her clit. And again, aftershocks made her gasp.

"Dammit, Finn. Do it already."

His expression grew darker. Serious. "You want this?"

She wanted to scream in exasperation, and yet she knew what he was asking. "Yes. I want you. *All* of you."

His hips eased forward slowly, the thick length of his cock pressing in an inch at a time. Mesmerizing, sensitive. Perfect.

When he was fully buried, Finn caught hold of her hips and tugged her even tighter. Pleasure flared again. His gaze slid up her body from where he'd been watching his cock disappear into her, paused on her breasts, and slid higher until he met her eyes.

The rocking motion continued. This was so much more than just a connection of his body and hers. Karen grabbed hold of his wrists and held on as ecstasy spiraled.

For a man balancing on one leg, Finn was doing a damn good job of blowing her mind. It was everything in combination. His expression, the caress of his fingers now sliding to rub against her clit.

His words.

"Come on my cock. I want to feel you grab me tight."

She didn't need to come for this to be perfect, but she did. The explosion was unstoppable and inevitable because of the way he looked at her, the way he teased her exactly right. Because he knew her, he wanted her.

He cared for her.

Maybe even loved her.

Karen gave in to the demand, arching her back and calling out his name.

Finn grimaced, pushing her thighs apart farther, speeding up again. He pumped into her, thrusting madly. Every drive set off another aftershock, and she cried out over and over.

He stilled with his cock buried deep, his cry echoing off the walls. The ironclad grip he had on her thighs eased slightly. A little more. Finn gasped, drawing back slowly, pressing forward so she felt every inch.

He collapsed over her, elbows resting on the table, forehead against her body as he breathed heavily.

Quiet. Peaceful. Connected.

He pulled out, dealt with the condom, and was right back over her a second later before she'd had a chance to get cold.

"I missed you." Finn spoke against her belly, kissing her softly, and for a moment, she was headed toward being a weepy mess again.

Then he blew a raspberry, and all bets were off.

She reached down to tug on his ears, and he wiggled out of her grasp. Karen curled her way upward, wrapped her arms around him, and squeezed tight.

She kissed him. Long and lingering before moving far enough away so they could stare at each other. No words, because they didn't need any.

What followed was laughter and kisses and a sweet time together until they ended up in the master bed. No more serious words, just two people getting to know each other all over again. Comfortable, quiet.

Intimate silence.

Karen woke in the middle of the night, the stillness broken only by Finn's gentle snore. She leaned up on one elbow, the moonlight sneaking in the window just bright enough to let her examine him closely.

That night had not been what she'd expected. And yet, Finn had been the catalyst for change—that part she could have guessed.

Five years ago, they'd been together because they'd gotten along and they'd both had an itch to scratch. But the reason she'd fallen so hard in the end was because of more than chemistry and charm.

Finn Marlette was a good man.

A good man for *her*, she corrected mentally, because even as he'd been gentle tonight, he'd been blunt.

As she replayed conversations in her head, it became far too clear that he was right. Not much use in arguing about the fact horses liked her. She was good with them—damn good. If anything, she was overconfident in that area.

But even with that talent, she still didn't expect people to take her suggestions seriously. That first day working with Zach —each time she'd offered up an idea, he'd nodded and moved to the next point.

She'd been floored to discover he'd actually taken her ideas and run with them.

Counterpoint to that, she didn't always follow through when she *did* have a good idea—didn't fight for what she really wanted.

She didn't want to wake Finn while she pondered, but not touching him was impossible. She brushed the back of her fingers whisper-soft along his shoulder, sliding up to push back the hair on his forehead.

He smiled, still sound asleep.

Tonight's discussion might have been a turning point, but she felt a little as if she'd gotten off the main thoroughfare and suddenly her GPS had gone silent.

What *were* her goals?

She'd done goal setting on a regular basis, but perhaps the truth was she needed to emphasize that question slightly differently. Because everything up to now had been based on expectations of others and working toward the common good of the Whiskey Creek ranch and the Coleman clan.

What were *her* goals?

She snuggled against Finn's side, stretching her legs away from his to be sure she didn't bump him when she moved.

His arm curled around her, drawing her to his body. Even asleep, it was clear he wanted her as close as possible.

What do I want?

What makes me happy?

When I wake up in the morning, what do I want to aim at that will bring me joy?

A snort escaped. She stilled instantly.

Finn didn't move, which was good.

The amusing thought remained.

All she could think of was that show her cousins-in-law were obsessed with. The one about downsizing possessions where this incredibly smart woman kept asking the people she worked with, 'does this spark joy'?

Karen had never quite understood the purpose of the question before—but then she'd never had a problem with possessions. What it seemed she did have a problem with was picking *activities*, daily and ongoing, that were truly important to her.

She was already half-asleep as the questions tumbled in her brain and images mixed with them.

The last thing she remembered on the edge of falling asleep was a dream where the tight knot in her belly was gone. She wandered through her day, picking items up one at a time and watching as some lit up hard enough to make the entire room shine.

So be it. It wasn't quite as original as Finn's question about endgames, but it just might work.

Tomorrow, she would start looking for sparks of joy.

17

---

*I*t was like watching springtime come to the prairies. That slow change of seasons when the snow would keep trying to hang on a little longer but determined green growth insisted it was time to move on.

That's what Finn saw as Karen slipped into the day.

She seemed slightly distracted, and she hadn't wanted to talk about anything too serious that morning. He knew how that was. Once he'd made up his mind to try something new, he needed some time to do it before analyzing all over again.

Waking up next to her hadn't sucked. It made it impossible for him to sneak out and grab her flowers, but she didn't seem to mind that they weren't there.

When they chatted over coffee, the one thing she did want to talk about was the kitten.

"We're definitely picking up Dandelion today, but I promised to give Zach a hand this morning. Do you want to come to Silver Stone with me later? We're not getting a lot of horses from them since you don't need racing stock, but there're a couple of retirees that might work well."

Finn placed his coffee mug aside as he leaned back against the counter. "You know I trust your decisions. But if you want some company, I'd love to join you." He tapped the cast on his thigh. "I'll be assessing them from a distance, though."

She slid into his arms, smiling. "No riding. Not this time. But having you with me would make me happy."

"Good girl," he whispered as he kissed the tip of her nose.

She swatted him lightly on the butt, winking at him as he turned to walk away.

It was a bit of a scramble, but he found time to pick her a flower so it was there when she showed up for lunch.

He was working at the table, giving his leg a rest, when she came in. She glanced at the kitchen counter and the small white offering he'd scrounged up.

Wildflowers near the cottage were in short supply.

"Thank you for my bit of wilderness," she said. "It's really sweet you've picked that up again. Bringing me flowers."

She settled into his lap, hands on his collar.

"I still remember you telling me how not being able to ride meant not getting to see some of your favourite parts of the ranch as they went into bloom." He pulled her closer and nuzzled against her neck.

"The first morning, when I found that crocus on my second-storey windowsill, I thought the pixies had come to visit." She breathed in slowly, eyes closed as she brushed their lips together. "I'm not prone to flights of fancy."

"Damn near needed to fly to get up there," Finn told her. "That apple tree still outside the window at Whiskey Creek?"

"Don't think you'd be paying me any visits the way you are right now, Hopalong."

He stared at her lips, hunger for more than lunch rising. "You'd be surprised what a motivated man can accomplish."

She laughed before giving him the sweetest kiss for his

labours. Sweet that turned into a full-out, enthusiastic Karen kiss which involved full body contact between her breasts and his chest, distracting him hard.

Dear God. That wasn't the only thing that was hard.

"I'm game to retest this kitchen table for stability," he offered.

She skipped out of reach, digging into the refrigerator and placing items on the counter for lunch. "Hold that thought. I'm starving."

"Me too," he growled with as much innuendo as possible.

That triggered a laugh. They fell into the rest of the meal with an easy companionship. Karen seemed a lot more lighthearted than she had been lately, and he was glad.

They headed to Silver Stone, and she caught him up on what he'd missed that morning in the yard and gave an update on one discovery. "You know the supplies we were short on when the last shipment arrived? The stuff the construction crew has been complaining about?"

"Did they show up?"

She shook her head. "Not the missing stuff. The replacement order came in. Zach and I got to chatting with the delivery guy. He was trying to figure out what on earth we were doing that required so many support joists and toilet seals. He swears he dropped them all off. Said someone would've signed for them."

Finn nodded. "We already checked that. That's one problem with having so much going on at the same time. Somebody did sign, but we can't read the signature. What the heck would they have done with all that stuff, anyway?"

A gentle shrug lifted her shoulders. "I don't know. Sell it on the black market?"

"I never knew there was such a call for toilet seals," Finn said dryly. "I suppose it's possible we got somebody with sticky fingers with the rapid hiring we did. We'll get Cody to keep a closer eye on things."

She turned down the driveway at Silver Stone, parking expertly in a space right outside the barn. "In the meantime, Zach estimates we're closing in on a third of the way done. Most of the outbuildings are to lock up, which means the entire place looks like some bad Western B movie, without the false fronts on the plain-board buildings."

"Somebody else gets to decide how to make them pretty," he reminded her as he pushed open his door and gingerly lowered himself to the ground.

"Zach said he got some good ideas when he talked to Julia a while ago." She motioned him toward the arena. "I'll go grab Ashton and tell them we're ready. Oh, and I'll find Dandelion."

She took off with a skip in her step.

He tried not to dwell on the fact he was tottering along at a snail's pace. By now the whole crutch thing should be getting easier, and it was, in terms of balance and his muscles not aching like crazy.

Having to use them in the first place was getting old, and he still had three weeks left before the doctor said he *might* be set free.

Finn looked around the yard for a while, activity in all the nooks and corners like any well-run operation. Voices echoed along with the sounds of animals, and over it all lay a thick sense of peace. The familiar noises soothed something inside him.

He missed having a working ranch.

"You look ready for a drink." Josiah Ryder stepped from the barn, a small white bundle of fluff cradled in his arms. He leaned on the railing beside Finn as he looked him over. "Maybe a double."

"Feeling better than I have in a while." Finn motioned for Josiah to pass over the kitten. "What are you doing here?"

Josiah gestured toward the three horses being led from the barn. "A bunch of tasks for Ashton. Then Lisa and I are staying for dinner. Her dad's in town tonight."

A detail Finn had not heard earlier. He glanced at Karen, who was leading one of the horses into the arena.

He wondered if she knew.

He ignored the question and instead enjoyed the time chatting with Josiah. He and Zach had only recently moved out. While the three of them had been roommates for only a few months, it had been enough for Finn to realize how much he enjoyed Josiah's company.

And since Josiah and Lisa were most definitely an item, and Finn planned on being with Karen long-term, the relationship between him and the veterinarian would be around for a long time. He wanted it to be a positive one.

The women laughed as they worked, putting the horses through their paces as he and Josiah, and eventually Ashton, watched.

The older man was head foreman at the Silver Stone ranch, and probably as much a fixture as the worn boards on the side of the building.

He offered Finn a firm nod before all his attention turned to the animals. "I hear you might want some of our old-timers."

"If Karen says so."

That got a grin out of Josiah. "She trained you fast."

It was tempting to grin back, but Finn knew nothing was officially settled, so nothing was guaranteed yet. "She built a good foundation. Easy to get the ones who are well-trained back into behaving when you start them off right."

A bright laugh sounded from inside the arena. Lisa wore a smirk that stretched from ear to ear as she led a grey mare up to the railing. "Always good to hear you know the true way the world operates."

"You say *jump*, and I say *your bones*?" Josiah offered.

The older man beside them snorted, attempting to turn it into a cough. Ashton straightened, eyes twinkling as he shook his head. "I think this conversation is a little over my head."

Finn gave Josiah a wink, turning to Ashton as Lisa moved out of earshot. "I'm sure Karen will have a list of exactly what kind of animals we'll need from you. Been wondering something—you heard how Sonora is doing with the animal rescue? She got a decent turnover rate happening yet, or she struggling?"

"That woman's a damn miracle worker. I swear she puts a spell on anyone who comes in her door, because ninety percent of them leave with an animal." Ashton lifted a hand and got into lecture mode. "She needs to not be so stubborn, though. Plenty of people around here would give her a hand with the hardest parts of the business, yet she's all determined to do it on her own. Makes no damn sense."

"She's independent, all right." Josiah was grinning now, elbows leaning on the railing.

"Best kind of woman there is," Finn agreed. He and Josiah exchanged another glance, because over the past while, it had become all too clear that Ashton had a major crush on sweet Sonora Fallen.

It was equally clear the man would swear up one side of the barn and down the other that no such thing was true.

Teasing on the sly to make the sixty-year-old admit the sheer amount of time he spent with her—or thinking about her —had become an amusing pastime.

Ashton headed off to give Kelli a hand. She offered Finn a wave from across the yard before leading the animals back into the barn.

Karen came to join him. Contentment on her face, she stepped in close and wrapped an arm around Finn's waist. With a happy sigh, she cradled the top of Dandelion's head and pressed a kiss to his furry little nose.

"Public display of affection. I like this," Finn told her, tipping her hat back to turn it into a true PDA.

"Icky." This from Lisa, laughter in her voice as she climbed over the railing and all but threw herself at Josiah. "Cover my virgin eyes, they're kissing."

Josiah swung her in a circle, a laugh booming out over the landscape. "I don't think that word means what you think it means."

"*Hey*. You're supposed to be on my side." Lisa wrapped her legs around him and kissed him thoroughly. "There. Now I have boy cooties as well."

Karen laughed softly as she stood beside Finn, arm still around his waist, head leaning against his shoulder, and Dandelion cradled against her chest. "We should get going."

"Talk to you tomorrow. We'll pass on a hello to dad from you," Lisa said cheerfully before she grabbed Josiah's hand and tugged him toward the house. Josiah waved over her shoulder.

Which left a very confused and yet content Finn standing at the railing with Karen.

She reached for his crutches, extending them to him. "I've been plotting about what would make me happy tonight, and it involves you taking me out to dinner. Think that's possible?"

He followed her to the truck. "I think that's very possible. Anything in particular you're hungry for?"

She didn't answer until they were on the road heading north. Dandelion was curled up in Finn's lap, a small warm puddle of fur. "Steak would be good. We can drive to Calgary if you want some good Italian or something other than East

Indian." She glanced at him, a wry smile twisting her lips. "I'm sure you caught that bit. About Dad being in town."

"Josiah told me."

She stared at the road for a minute and then blew long and hard. "I actually practiced that one this morning while I was working because I figured it would happen sooner than later. I thought of what it would feel like the next time I got an invite to dinner. That knot in my stomach got tight again, and instead of feeling happy about getting to spend time with my family, I was dreading it. So, for right now, my answer was no. But *then* I figured out what I wanted to do instead."

She reached across the space between them and caught his fingers in hers. Smiling shyly. "Imagining a nice dinner with you made the knot go away."

He squeezed her hand. "Good for you."

"Imagining coming home with you afterwards made fireflies dance in my belly, so there's that as well."

The image made him laugh. "Is that a good thing? Fireflies in your belly?"

She hummed. "A very good thing. You interested?"

He lifted her fingers and pressed them to his lips. "Let me wine and dine you, and we'll see about finding some fireflies later."

KAREN STARED at the clothes hanging in her closet and hesitated. It wasn't as if the wedding was a highfalutin affair. For their mid-July vows, Hanna Lane and Brad Ford had decided to get married up at his family ranch, outdoors, with a potluck dinner. The number of people invited was probably under fifty, and they were either Hanna's friends or the people

Brad worked with, which meant the guest list was made up of farmers, ranchers, firefighters, and other blue-collar workers.

People would dress up nice, but it wouldn't be fancy.

She still didn't see anything in her closet that made her happy. Definitely nothing that sparked joy, not for this event.

If she was brutally honest, part of the reason why she wanted a special outfit was to keep in line with that *looking for things she loved* attitude.

It hadn't been easy, but over the last week, Karen had practiced pausing before making a choice and before responding to a comment or question. She was pretty sure sometimes it looked as if she'd been frozen.

But it was getting easier to make a quick decision about *yes* or *no* on the path to what she truly wanted.

That morning, she had finally taken the step to deal with the biggest source of stress in her world. She still alternated between being absolutely sick to her stomach that she'd done it and being ecstatic she'd been brave enough to take charge in a decisive way.

Surely after all that she could find an outfit for tonight.

"Is there something hiding in your closet?" Finn stepped through the doorway and swung his way to her side.

"Looking for an outfit that's dressy without dressing up." She patted him on the arm. "Even those of us who are content to spend our lives in jeans have these moments."

"Sounds as if you have the same problem as me," Finn told her.

"Closet full of clothes and nothing to wear?"

He tapped his leg. Lips twisting at the corners. "Pretty much. Don't think I should show up in sweatpants."

She snickered. "You could set a new fashion trend. I'm pretty sure as long as they're made out of flannel, it'll go over big time."

He glanced at his watch. "What about we go into town and see what we can come up with?"

"*Really?*"

His nod was slow and teasing. "I know it's a small town, but they do have a few things. Let's check out that new consignment shop."

"You're taking me on a shopping date? Cool."

Finn made a face. "Let's just say I'm taking you on a date, and we'll see what happens."

Which is how they ended up on Main Street not even half an hour later, strolling, such as Finn's crutches would allow, side by side down the old-fashioned boardwalk. They peeked in windows, discussed the merits of the fishing and tackle shop's location, and made a pit stop at the candy store.

That meant they had to stop and sit for a moment at one of the tiny tables against the building wall.

"Crutches and ice cream are a dangerous mix." He licked his ice cream cone and made a noise that ought to be illegal. "This stop alone was worth the trip."

"Yeah. For me too."

Was it terrible that she couldn't take her eyes off his tongue? Probably not, considering she knew exactly how talented it was.

Envious of an ice cream cone. Awesome.

He must have caught her drooling, because his gaze grew heated and that dangerous smolder was back. Totally distracted, the next thing she knew, her ice cream was running down the side of the cone and over her fingers.

"Let me help." Finn grabbed her wrist and tugged her hand close to run his tongue over her skin.

News alert. Spontaneous combustion outside ice cream shop in small-town Alberta. Yep. That would be the feature headline in tomorrow's news stories.

Eventually, she and Finn ended up at the consignment store where, to Karen's absolute delight, something special was waiting at the far end of the store.

She stopped dead in her tracks, lifted a hand, and pointed. "Finn?"

"Coming. Narrow aisles are a little bit hell on—oh, *hello*. Do they fit?"

She took the pair of red cowboy boots off the shelf, snooping around until she found a place to sit. And when her foot slipped in, there weren't only joyful lights going off around her but an entire stage with spotlights.

She stood and gave a little twirl, her feet cradled in sheer comfort.

Finn cleared his throat then tilted his head behind her to the far wall. "Is that your size?"

The dress displayed on the wall had enough frills to make it swing as she moved, and it fit her perfectly.

The man in front of her was quieter. But his eyes... Oh, his eyes said a whole hell of a lot.

Two days later, outside the main house at Lone Pine ranch, Finn sat beside her, their fingers linked as they waited for the wedding to start. He'd found a pair of black pants that fit over his cast, a dark shirt, and a red vest.

How he'd found a vest that exactly matched her boots in so short a time, she didn't know.

But they looked like a couple, and they felt like a couple. The sensation in her belly was a lot more like fireflies than anything else.

The usual chitchat and discussion drifted around them as they waited for the event to begin. Eventually Brad made it to the front of the area where the chairs were arranged as an outdoor sanctuary. He stood under the apple tree with Malachi

Fields at his side. The older man looked slightly amused about something.

Hanna's little girl, Crissy, came down the aisle, a silver bucket in her hands full of all sorts of flowers from the masses blooming around the house.

"Hanna has the same good taste in flowers as you," Finn whispered in Karen's ear.

She squeezed his fingers as Hanna walked past. Little white flowers dotted the braid on top of her head. She wore a simple white dress and an expression of utter adoration on her face as she stared at Brad.

Then Brad and Hanna were promising to love each other into the future. The vows included a whole bunch of other sweet words, but Karen was too busy trying to deal with the image of her and Finn doing the same thing to focus on the actual details.

Something inside burst like a dam that had received its final blow.

Screw it. Finn had said he wanted more. If she wanted to hunt fireflies, then she should look for the biggest, brightest, most incredible fireflies in the entire world.

Which meant telling him what she truly wanted and then making it happen.

The wedding moved from orderly to chaotic. There were more than enough people willing to direct the crowd from the ceremony to the party. Karen caught up with her friends, chatting with the girls she'd so naively cut herself off from the last time they'd gathered.

There were no hard feelings, though. It was clear that when she stepped into a conversation, she was welcome.

Once the meal was over, they all headed outside to where music had begun playing.

Rose all but bounced in place with excitement. "Excuse me. Now is when my bachelor pays his dues."

Her sister, Tansy, rolled her eyes. Karen laughed.

"You know what she did?" Tansy asked.

Karen nodded. "Come on. I'm pretty sure there're guys willing to dance even if you didn't purchase them."

The crowd gathered around the far side of the yard. Karen went to where Finn stood talking with a beaming Brad. The newlywed had his arm banded tight around Hanna as if he had no intention of letting her go any time soon.

"Brad and Hanna." Brad's father, Patrick, weaved across the distance where he stood next to a set of speakers. "It's time for you to break in the new dance floor."

The newlyweds stepped onto the low wooden platform constructed outdoors. Brad led Hanna to the middle. He caught her fingers and kissed them before pulling her into his arms as the beginning strains of music drifted over the air.

Finn tucked an arm around Karen, bringing her close as his heat slid against her.

Brad and Hanna danced slowly, eyes fixed on each other as if there weren't another person for miles around. Sheer love in their expressions.

Little Crissy came running from the side. She threw herself at the two of them and clung on tight like a kitten.

With a huge laugh, Brad lifted the child into the air. He gave her a kiss before adjusting position to hold Crissy as well as Hanna.

The three of them danced, officially starting their life together.

The music changed, and Finn twisted Karen against him, swaying slightly while more people made their way onto the dance floor to join Brad and Hanna.

"*Finn.*"

"I'd love this dance." He held her perfectly, that connection rising like always. Far from the crowd and in their own private world.

Why on earth would she complain when this was exactly what she needed? The tension in her belly wasn't the type she got from wanting to run away. It was a knot like a person got when they wanted to say words that were big and important. Words that were true down to the core of her soul.

Like love. Like forever. She held those back, mostly.

"This dance and all the rest you want." It wasn't a confession of how she felt, but it was close.

His grip tightened, then his lips were on her temple, kissing her sweet and light. "I'm holding you to that."

She was ready to let go and trust. Maybe it wouldn't work in the end, but like he'd said, if they didn't aim at what they wanted, they'd never find out.

18

Finn and Karen abandoned the party just after midnight.

Zach was still on the dance floor with Rose, along with a half dozen other diehards who looked ready to dance the night away.

Karen was quiet on the drive home, which in a way was good because Finn's brain was whirling in a million different directions.

His leg had healed enough that dealing with the cast was the worst part. He was no longer popping painkillers like jellybeans, which meant what was rattling in his brain couldn't be explained away by confusion or chemicals.

He'd started the summer with the intention of being with Karen no matter what it took, wherever the journey led. The way she'd leaned against him this evening, giving every indication she was ready to get fully on board—

He actually hadn't expected that miracle to take place until sometime in the fall. They were both stubborn, and they had baggage. Their time years ago had been sweet, but more like a solid base than a settling of roots.

Fuck it, did he even know how to grow roots? All he knew was he wanted to be with her. It was time to tell her that again.

Karen turned off well before the road to what eventually would be Red Boot ranch. She glanced toward him. "I have something to show you. If you haven't been there already, that is."

He mentally calculated where they were and figured it out pretty quick. "The lookout over Heart Falls pool?"

She nodded. "This time of year, it's pretty. It's only a short walk to the bench."

"Not a problem."

They walked the well-worn trail in silence, the moonlight overhead shining a clear path. The sound of the falls grew louder, from a faint trickle to a rumbling laugh as water burst over the top of the cliff and descended to the heart-shaped pool at its base.

When they reached the bench, Finn glanced into the valley, surprised to see more than moonlight shining on the water. "Somebody put up spotlights?"

Karen sat on the bench, and he settled beside her, grabbing her fingers and holding on tight.

She leaned her head on his shoulder and laughed softly, gazing out over the glittering reflections on the water's surface. "Tamara said her youngest brother-in-law, Dustin, was mucking around out here a while ago. He said he was doing something to enhance the natural ambience. She thinks he was setting it up for skinny dipping."

Finn laughed. "That's usually done in the dark, but I can see why putting a little light on the subject would be entertaining. We'll have to come back here once I get my cast off and give it a try."

"Two weeks left?"

He squeezed her fingers. "Counting the days."

"Me too." She twisted slightly, careful of his leg but adjusting to make full eye contact. "I've got something to tell you."

His breath caught, but he did his best to act as nonchalant as possible. "Shoot."

"I've been thinking lots about what things I want, and you were right. I set a lot of goals over the years, and I've been successful in getting stuff done, but many times, I don't know that what I accomplished was the right thing. I mean, you said that as well. Work's not always fun, but it should be valuable. Doing something because it's another person's priority can't be how you run your life, can it?"

He stared into her big brown eyes. "Whose goals have you been aiming at that you think need changing?"

"Karen's." She snorted. "I know, that makes no sense. But it's like there's this part of me with a set of rules and ideas that are so built-in that they dictate everything. Every choice I make and every target I set."

"Those aren't the choices you want to make?"

She made a face. "That Karen wouldn't have Dandelion in the house. New Karen thinks he's the sweetest thing, and I'm so glad he's around."

The whole conversation began to make sense. It wasn't the confession he'd hoped for, but he was still pleased. This would make a huge difference in her world.

"Good for you." He rubbed his thumb over the back of her hand. "What other changes is New Karen planning?"

"You." Her voice was husky and low.

It seemed those fireflies she'd mentioned before were an epidemic, because his damn belly flip-flopped as if he were full of them. "Go on."

She took a deep breath then handed him her heart.

"I want to be with you. I want to give us a real chance and not sit here with Old Karen. She's worried about how hard it will hurt if we have to walk away from each other again. I want to work full-out to make sure we stick."

Hell. He wrapped an arm around her and pulled her into a tight embrace. "I want that too. And I'm so damn sorry you were hurt when I left."

She clung to him, but her head shook gently. "It wasn't your fault. It was *no one's* fault. Not really. It was a matter of place and time and there was not much we could do about it."

A deep flash of anger rose inside him because that was true, but it was also easy to point a finger at *one* of the reasons he hadn't returned to get her after he'd realized walking away was wrong.

But that confession was for another time. Here and now he was hearing the words he'd hoped for since he'd made his way to Heart Falls, and damn if he wasn't eager to accept every bit of it.

Time to flip her world upside down as well. He met her eyes before he spoke. "I'm all in. Everything you said about striving to make us work... *hell* yes. If you need space as you figure out what you really want, I can give you that, but I will not leave you. I swear I will *not* walk away again."

Her fist bumped against his chest with about as much impact as Dandelion with his little furry paw.

"I did *not* want to cry tonight," Karen complained.

He placed his fingers under her chin and lifted her face. Kissed her eyelids. Tasted the salt in the tears streaking down her cheeks. "You have to cry for us both."

She wiped her cheeks, pushing the corners of her lips into a smile.

He leaned their foreheads together. "I love you. I have for a very long time."

Lightning danced in her eyes. She took a shaky breath. "I love you too."

The hug was spontaneous. Karen twisted on the bench so she was once again as close as possible even with his leg sticking out awkwardly like some mannequin they'd had to haul along.

But the cast faded to nothing because what she'd just said outweighed all the frustrations and all the anger.

She loved him. He would move mountains to make sure that stayed true.

But for now, he kissed her. One hand cradled the back of her head as he took her lips. He nibbled until she gasped, then he slid his tongue deeper. Tasting her and sending his own senses reeling.

Her hands were busy at the front of his shirt, opening buttons until her palms pressed against his chest. Fingernails teased, sending his skin dancing.

He teased her earlobe into his mouth. "I want you. Right now."

She leaned back slightly, her eyes wide. Her first glance went up the trail toward where the truck was parked, but it was brief, and the next thing he knew, she'd pulled herself to vertical. She slid her hands under the skirt of her dress and wiggled her way out of her underwear.

All of that done with a slightly shy, innocent attitude.

The effect was completely undone when she took her underwear and swung it saucily before offering them to him.

"*Ma chérie*, you're killing me." He didn't fucking care where they were. "Come here."

He adjusted his position and spread his legs wider. More than enough room for Karen to step between them, staring down with a definitely naughty expression.

He ran his hands up her hips, her waist, over the sweep of her breasts. "First we get you ready."

"I'm ready," Karen insisted.

"Prove it." Finn undid the row of buttons down the front of her dress. He pushed aside the fabric to reveal skin and a pretty bra sheer enough that her nipples showed even in the moonlight.

He undid the front snap—best damn invention ever—and cupped her breasts. Eagerly, he leaned in, sucking and lapping and biting from one side to the other while she ran her fingers through his hair and moaned.

"I'm ready."

He was past ready but nowhere near done. "Put your fingers in your pussy and show me how wet you are."

A gasp escaped, but she slid a hand down her thigh, crumpling her skirt as she raised it.

"*Finn.*"

Her complaint came as he once again placed his mouth on her, enjoying the lush beauty of her breasts. His hum of amusement danced against her skin. "Didn't say I was done. You touching yourself yet?"

That got him something between a growl and a groan. Finn slid a hand down her hip and hit bare skin.

It was nearly his undoing, because a bare hip meant a bare ass and a bare sex, and he was inches away from being able to pull her forward and sink into her wet heat.

Karen straightened, a vision of sensual debauchery. Her hair lay tousled around her shoulders, naked breasts framed by her open dress. Her bare thighs were pale as she clutched one side of her skirt. The other hand she held out, fingers glistening in the moonlight.

He couldn't get any harder. "Good girl. Let me double-check."

Her head fell back as he pulled her fingers to his mouth, licking them clean. Then he moved them down again, pressing against her sex. Rubbing firmly over her sensitive clit.

His fingers were wet now as well, and together they built her pleasure. Just a little more was needed.

"You keep doing that," he ordered. "Rub your clit. I'm going to fuck you with my fingers. And once you come, hard, you climb on board and I'll sink into you so deep there'll be no you or me, just us."

Her eyes went huge. Her fingers faltered for a moment then picked up speed. He slid a hand lower, careful not to interfere with her motion as he teased her entrance. Small circles until she squirmed on the spot, and only then did he slide his fingers deep.

MOONLIGHT MAGIC WAS the only thing keeping her vertical. No way was she still standing under her own strength, not with Finn staring at her with that look in his eyes.

They'd moved beyond *smolder*. It was pure sex.

His hands drove her to the pinnacle so quickly. Should she complain that it would be over too soon or be excited because the next thing was sure to be just as wonderful?

Even more intimate. Although, having his hand on her— and his fingers in her, and his gaze burning through her—was as intimate as they could get.

His voice thrummed in her ears. "That's it, *ma chérie*. Squeeze me. So fucking good, but it'll be even better when it's my cock inside you. I'll make you see stars."

She tilted her head to the clear night sky, grinning as galaxies twinkled down on them. "So good."

It was right to be there. To finally have admitted part of what she needed to tell him. The most important part. The rest were minor details, and they'd figure it out as they went along, but now with his hands driving her onward, Karen dug a little deeper, increasing the speed of her fingers over her clit as sparks flew.

"*Finn.*"

The hand on her hip tightened, and the fingers inside her slowed. Which was good, because her body attempted to trap him in place, and the slight motion was just enough to drive her orgasm even higher.

His fingers slid out. The next bit got a little messy between dragging a condom out of his pocket and opening his jeans enough to free his cock and get it covered.

Then she was up on the bench, straddling him, gazing into his passion-filled eyes.

He pressed a kiss between her breasts.

Her skirt hung over his thighs, and if it weren't for the pornographic view of the open bodice of her dress, no one would've known what they were doing. Maybe they could guess as she rose and fell over his thick length, rubbing the wetness of her sex over the rock-solid temptation rising skyward.

Finn caught her hips and stilled her, adjusting until his tip pressed between her folds.

Then he kissed her, wild and hungry, fire flaring. She was sure he would drive himself deep, but he waited, teasing with just enough pressure that she knew he was there. Impossible to ignore, perfect anticipation rising.

She was breathless when he finally let her pull her lips away, panting as she met his gaze, and it was then that he pressed her down. A slow, inevitable joining that finished with her soft sigh of satisfaction.

The last bit of Old Karen vanished in a baptism of new hope.

Finn brushed a hand over her cheek, wiping away a lingering tear. "I love you," he said again. "I know I'm broken still, but I plan to do everything I have to so you'll know it's true. Inside and out."

Her heart sparkled. "You're doing pretty good for a broken guy. Just saying."

That rare grin of his appeared. "I'd better live up to your expectations."

She didn't know how he did it, considering he wasn't the most mobile at that moment, but it only took a few minutes for him to begin to blow her mind.

His grip on her hips provided the pulse of motion that set her strumming again.

"Put your fingers back on your pussy, *ma chérie*. I want to feel you with me again."

She didn't care if she came again or not, but with him looking at her as if she'd actually hung the stars, the whirl of sensation inside was inevitable.

She'd talked about fireflies, but this was sensual pleasure mixed with the light in her heart, and all of it together meant, as she teetered toward the edge, the physical and the emotional mixed solidly.

As her body gave in, it was only an echo of what was in her heart. Pleasure—connection. To this man.

Finn made a noise as she clamped down on his cock. A happy, grunting, *laughing* sound.

Amusement rushed in. She snickered in response, and suddenly there they were, an orgasm still rippling through her body but laughter surrounding them as well.

His hands on her hips eased, sliding around to her back, caressing now. Lips coming together as they kissed with smiles on their faces. Slowing, still connected physically, and definitely connected on an even more intimate level.

When she pressed her cheek to his and squeezed her arms tight, it felt right. Coming back to earth after having visited the stars.

Cleaning up and heading back to the truck brought a little more laughter because she made him bring the condom rather than bury it somewhere in the bushes.

She put the truck in gear, heading back to the cottage. "My sister brings my nieces up here, and none of us want to explain why there's funny deflated balloons tucked in the trees."

Finn snickered. "If you think we're the ones who broke in that bench, you're delusional."

She gave him a tap on the arm. "Let me keep my innocence."

"*Ma chérie*, you just debauched me on a park bench. Your brand of innocence rocks my socks off."

They held hands and listened to the radio on the short trip home.

They weren't done talking yet—she still needed to tell him the rest of her news. She grabbed them drinks while Finn went outside and got the fire pit burning. This time instead of side by side in Adirondack chairs, she settled on the bench across from him so she could see his face.

The sun was well and truly gone behind the mountains, and the stars glittered overhead. To the north, the lights of Black Diamond made the distant horizon glow faintly.

In the barn and arena beyond main house, the horses and animals they'd started to assemble moved quietly. Nighttime noises that fit so perfectly with this location.

Karen fell a little bit more in love with Heart Falls.

Or maybe it was the man across from her. Flames from the

fire between them flickered, highlighting his satisfied expression.

"You look content," she teased.

He leaned back, breathing slowly as his eyes flashed. "Building a good memory is a fine thing."

She raised her glass lightly. "Here's to building many more."

He offered her a toast in return. "I can't get this cast off soon enough. I don't want you sitting way the hell over there. I want you in my arms where you belong."

"We have plenty of time for that," she reassured him.

Concern drifted into his face. "No more working so hard," he said. "We're taking the time we need for us. Especially since you're only around until the end of September. At that point, you'll get busy with school, and all, but I will be there with you. The first few weeks it'll be a little touch and go as I get things tidied up around here—"

Oh my God. Karen held out a hand as if stopping traffic. "Wait. *What?*"

Determination flashed. "I told you I wasn't ever walking away again. Since you've got to go somewhere for your training, I'm going with you. I'll give you your space, but—"

"Finn. *Stop.*" She shook her head hard. "This is what I had to tell you. I'm not going to school."

He didn't say anything, just sat there staring at her, shocked.

"This is what started this whole thing. I think the program is a fantastic one, and, yeah, I was excited at first. It's a good job, and *maybe* it's something I want to do down the road. But I think Old Karen latched on to going away to school because it was something people would approve of as a good enough reason to abandon the Coleman clan."

He wasn't laid-back anymore but leaning forward, listening intently.

And now she had to run off at the mouth, but whatever. It wouldn't be the last time she had to explain.

She stared at the fire. "I liked working for the family to some degree. But because it was tough to deal with my dad, even the family who appreciated my skills had to walk on eggshells to make sure they weren't stepping over boundaries with him or with the other old-timers in the community. Whiskey Creek ranch was filled with so many bad memories that I wanted out. Applying for equine therapy hit all the right buttons to get everybody's approval. It was horses, and giving, and a fantastic service to others. Part of me feels horrible for not following through, but every time I imagine going, I nearly get sick. And not nervous sick, like a thing that I haven't experienced before, but physically sick in that I know it's not right for me."

"Not right for you now, and maybe not right for you ever. That's not something you need to apologize for." Finn said it softly but firmly.

She met his gaze. "New Karen knows that. Old Karen is kind of shaking in her boots and wants to apologize left, right, and center." She straightened. "But more to the point, I'm not going away. I'm staying *here*. So you don't have to drop everything or give up your work for my sake. Because I don't want you to do that either."

"Oh, *ma chérie*. You amaze me. And you humble me, and I'm so glad I don't have to live without you." A whisper, but so, so sweet. He held open his arms. "You know the routine."

She crossed the distance between them quickly, carefully resuming her position in his lap.

Finn curled his arms around her, tilting her head to kiss her. Gently this time. Sweet, like a sugary icing on the top of the cake. Then he pressed her head against his chest and sighed softly. Just holding her.

Another thought struck. "By the way. I plan to get the wild foal back from Sonora as soon as possible."

A small sound of amusement escaped him. "You plan on keeping him in the house along with Dandelion?"

"Maybe." She tilted her head back to smile up at him. "*Nahh*. I've already got one awkwardly limbed creature in my house. I don't need two."

A sharp pinch nipped her butt.

She laughed softly then snuggled in tight again.

In front of her, the fire danced, yellows and golds reaching skyward toward the twinkling stars overhead. There were still decisions to be made, and her not-so-secret school news to share with others, but right now, she'd told the most important person and made it clear what her priorities were going forward.

The most important *people*—Old Karen had been given her walking papers that night.

It was time to take a leap of faith and push all the secrets aside.

19

---

*I*t seemed a queen-size bed wasn't big enough for him, Karen, his cast, *and* a two-pound bundle of fur.

Finn knew exactly which of the four he wanted gone. He was counting down the days until he could roll over in bed and pull Karen into his arms the way he wanted to, no awkwardness or fiberglass involved.

Still, waking up to see happiness shining on her face was amazing. Karen giggled as she shifted her fingers slowly under the quilt while Dandelion Fluff stalked the moving bump. Outright laughing when the kitten pounced.

It was a bit of perfection, and Finn soaked it in.

Her gaze slid upward. Her happiness grew brighter. "Morning."

"Morning, *ma chérie.*" He crooked his finger. "I'm afraid you'll have to come to the mountain."

The evil woman grinned. The next thing he knew, a hand was sliding across his hip, and fingers rested oh-so-teasingly on his morning wood. "Definitely a mountain."

One thing led to another in the best way possible, after the kitten had been put firmly on the floor.

They were sitting across each other at the breakfast table an hour later, Karen's expression still something sweet enough to make everything in him vibrate with happiness.

"I asked Zach to come over this morning," Finn told her.

Shock flew across her features. "*Okaaaaay.*"

A chuckle escaped. "Don't worry, I'm not sharing bedroom secrets, but there are a few other secrets I do want to spill."

"And Zach's part of them?" Karen looked thoughtful at his nod. "Just so you know, he truly is a good friend. He's never once talked out of school about you. He thinks you're amazing."

"Of course he does." Finn poured himself a top-up on his coffee and leaned back in his chair without saying anything else.

Across the table from him, she snickered. "I love you."

He knew he was grinning, which wasn't usual for him, but the fact she got his sense of humour and would still admit she loved him made her even more perfect. "I know."

The comment earned an epic eye roll as she rose. "Excuse me while I go buy you some new cheesy lines."

"There's no cheese like old cheese."

She stripped off the shirt she wore, tossing the balled-up fabric at his face before turning and heading to the bedroom.

"If you're starting a floor show, you're walking the wrong way…"

"Zach's coming over," she called over her shoulder. "I'm not greeting him in my pyjamas, aka, your shirt."

He leaned forward to enjoy the view of her hips swaying the entire way down the hall.

Damn, he was a lucky bastard.

She showed up, fully dressed, right as Zach arrived.

The doorbell buzzed. Karen opened the door, her amusement clear. "What? Are you not feeling well?"

Zach paused on the welcome mat, carefully removing his boots. "Not sure what you're talking about."

She made her way back to the chair Finn had dragged to his side, settling next to him like a dream even as she teased his friend. "That's the first time I've actually heard you use the doorbell. Oh, wait. You knocked once but opened the door and walked in before anybody answered."

"You told me to make myself at home," he reminded her. He spun the nearest chair around and sat on it backwards. He folded his arms along the top rail and tossed them a broad grin. "You two have fun at the wedding last night?"

"Shut up," Finn rumbled softly. "What about you, twinkle toes? What time did you roll in last night?"

"And you better have treated Rose right," Karen said, smiling with bared teeth. "Otherwise her girl posse will get you."

Zach's hands shot in the air. "I did my as-per-purchase duty and danced the girl's night away. Then I took her home and dropped her off." He leaned forward as if about to tell a terrible secret. "The instant I parked Delilah, Rose turned and said she'd had the best time, and I was a great dancer, and if I ever wanted to let her drive my car, she was fully on board."

Finn offered Karen the head tilt. "Girl's got good taste in cars."

A deep *ha!* burst from Zach. "And *then* she said there was no need for me to get out of the car, because her sister was right there, and this wasn't the kind of date that ended with a kiss."

"*Awwww.* That's sad," Karen said.

Zach looked startled. "You *wanted* me to kiss her?"

"Well, I can't see you ever allowing her to drive Delilah, so she should've gotten some bonus out of the evening." Karen wiggled away from Finn's fingers. "Stop tickling. Just calling them as I see them."

Considering how important Zach was in Finn's life, it was good to see his people bonding.

Now for a test of how quick Zach was on his feet. Finn deliberately linked his fingers with Karen's.

His friend's gaze flickered down then back to Finn's face. A slow smile curled Zach's lips, but he didn't say anything. Just waited.

"Been a few changes around here, but this one affects you," Finn said. "Karen's all in on the dude ranch. She's sticking around permanently, which means adjusting plans for hiring once she figures out exactly which job she wants full time."

His friend's pleased grin said it all. He knew this announcement wasn't just to do with Karen staying at the ranch but staying in Finn's life.

Zach's gaze shifted to hers, and he dipped his head. "Never been happier to hear any news in my life. Welcome aboard."

Karen looked a little wild-eyed. "Thanks." She glanced at Finn. "That wasn't what I expected."

"That's just the start, because now we get to the meat and potatoes. Remember I told you about Bruce Travers?"

She nodded instantly, looking at them both. "Your mentor."

Zach's face brightened with understanding. "Is this about that thing we weren't talking about?" he asked

A snort escaped. "I damn well hope so, because if it wasn't, that was a dumbass thing to say."

Karen's fingers tightened in his. "Secrets?"

There were still a few to spill, and Finn was determined to get them out. "Remember that fancy-schmancy car that was here at the start of summer? The lawyer from Bruce's estate gets in touch with us every now and then. He's a good guy, Alan, but this time something in the will triggered, and it turns out we have a deadline to get Red Boot ranch up and running."

Confusion was trickling in, but she still held his arm in a possessive grip. "I thought Bruce passed away a couple years ago. How can he do that?"

"Lawyers are brilliant at finding ways to make their billing charges last longer," Zach drawled. "The whole deadline is not that huge a deal. Not if we keep things rolling."

"When do we have to be operational?" Karen asked.

That was nice, the way she so easily accepted she was part of this.

"Thanksgiving."

She uttered a particularly foul curse, and both he and Zach blinked.

"Seriously, guys? You've heard me swear before."

Zach leaned forward and spoke softly. "I was just admiring the complete conviction with which you said it."

She folded her arms over her chest and glared. "Back to the point, why on earth would you agree to that kind of a deadline? I mean, it's not impossible, but rushing doesn't seem the way you guys like to do things."

The little tidbit about losing everything to Brandon got another burst of sailor-worthy salty language.

Zach's grin grew bigger by the minute. "I really like you," he told Karen.

"Stop flirting with my woman and get your own," Finn grumbled, but he agreed one hundred percent.

"No way in hell is Brandon getting our ranch," Karen said.

"That's what I said." Finn squeezed her fingers. "So. Load the cannons and full speed ahead. Nobody else knows about the deadline, but by Thanksgiving, we need to be ready to impress the socks off Alan and his family."

"Nothing we can't handle." Karen's phone went off, and

she wrinkled her nose. "Sorry. That's my dad. After skipping dinner the other night, I should take it."

She slid from the table and went out on the deck, leaving Finn and Zach alone.

His best friend let out a heavy sigh. "It's always so emotional when the fledglings leave the nest."

"Shut up," Finn muttered.

Zach leaned forward, honest pleasure spilling across his face. "I'm happy for you. I mean, I'm happy for what I think you're telling me, which hopefully is that you finally fessed up and told the woman you couldn't live without her."

"Something like that," Finn said.

Zach paused, looking thoughtful. "I thought Red Boot ranch was just another step along the way. Another project before you moved on again. I mean, I'm glad it's not, but it seems like a big change. Sounds as if you're planning to make this home."

Well, hell. Finn's brain had been so full of everything else that this little detail hadn't quite registered. Yet, damn if Zach wasn't right.

But when Finn thought about it, *really* thought about it, that sense of belonging in this community had been growing over the past months.

It wasn't just about finding a place for Karen but a place where he felt at home as well. A place for the two of them to grow together. That was kind of—unexpected.

Perfect, really.

"It's been building for a while," Finn admitted.

"It's been clear you missed the ranch," Zach shared. "Finding a new home makes sense. Where you grew up isn't a place you can ever go back to."

"It's not the idyllic, safe place I thought it was," Finn added in agreement. He glanced out over the land, all the way to where the Rockies rose to the heavens. The summer day was full of beauty and happiness. "I need to build some new memories, and this place has got the potential."

That got a laugh out of his friend. "And Bruce would tell you that potential is the most important thing to see." Zach spoke softer, gesturing toward Karen standing out on the deck, one hand driven into her hair. "That's a memory that needed to become more. I'm glad you've got her back."

Finn watched Karen carefully, the feeling in his heart big enough to push against his ribs. "She's the very top of my list," he told Zach. "Everything else got moved down."

"Including me," Zach returned firmly. "I've got zero problem with that. It's exactly how it should be."

Damn if Finn didn't have everything he needed in his world. A beautiful woman who said she loved him, and a best friend who understood him to his core.

Finn wordlessly reached a hand across the table toward Zach.

Zach ignored it. Instead, he rounded the table then pulled Finn to vertical to give him a bro hug and a back pounding. "Me too, buddy. Me too."

As far as conversations went, chatting with her dad went smoother than expected. He caught her up on a few of the goings-on at Whiskey Creek, including a shocking second of praise regarding her past work with some of their herd. That part was nice, and the part where she heard some of the family gossip.

But then he began bellyaching about his oldest brother, Uncle Mike, giving more and more responsibility and decision-making over to the next generation...

That's the point where Karen reached her *enough*.

"Hey, Dad. It's been great, but I was just finishing lunch, and I've got an appointment in fifteen minutes. Let me know the next time you plan to be in Heart Falls. Finn and I will take you out for dinner."

Her dad grumbled for a moment then latched on to the topic change. "That reminds me. I tried to get hold of Richard Marlette the other day. The phone number I've got for him is out of service. Ask Finn for some new contact info, will you?"

"Sure. I'll send it to you. Gotta run. Love you."

The last bit of the conversation made her brain stumble for a moment. It only took a second to shove her phone back in her pocket and return to the kitchen, scooping up Dandelion to use him as her own personal touchstone. Stroking the little creature's soft fur eased the tension while she leaned back against the door, eyes closed, searching for peace.

The truth was she did love her dad. She just didn't *like* him very much, not right now.

And that was okay.

Unexpected sounds caught her attention. The loudest noise was Dandelion purring against her chest. Karen opened her eyes, suddenly aware the kitchen was unoccupied. Finn and Zach were nowhere to be seen.

Shouts echoed from the front of the house, and she carefully put the kitten down before hurrying to the front door.

Smoke billowed from the roof of one of the newly constructed cabins. She jammed her feet into her boots and headed out at a full-out run.

The work crew poured into the yard from various places around the ranch. Karen caught up with Finn as he swung forward on his crutches at an alarming rate.

"I hope you don't think you're going in there," she informed him briskly.

He gave her a quick glance before pulling to a stop. A sheepish expression slid over his face. "Of course not."

She wrapped her arm around his biceps to make sure. "Someone call the fire department?"

"Might not need them." Two or three men had hoses out and were soaking both the corner of the burning building and the nearest cabins. Smoke billowed up thicker, a greyish tinge forming like thunderstorm clouds.

Meanwhile, Zach stepped from the cabin. He raised a fire extinguisher in the air as he shouted reassurances. "It's okay. It's out."

He made his way over to where Finn and Karen waited. Karen had never seen Zach look so serious as when he stepped in close, speaking softly. "Are the security cameras up and running yet?"

Finn stilled. "Some. Why?"

Zach glanced over his shoulder before reaching into his pocket and pulling out a partially burned chunk of cardboard. About two inches high, the unburned section had a familiar image on it.

"That's a fire starter box. Was someone already lighting the woodstove?" Karen asked.

"Doubtful, considering the stove wasn't hooked up. That's the only reason we spotted this before everything inside the cabin went up in flames—the smoke escaped through the partially open chimney." Zach's expression grew darker. "The fire started under a worktable. I found the piece of box and the remains of way too big a pile of sawdust."

"You're saying it's arson." Finn stared hard at his friend.

"It's possible it was an accident. If someone swept up a lit cigarette butt with the sawdust, it would've smoldered for a while before catching fire." Zach glanced at Karen then back at Finn. "Want to call the cops?"

"Check the security footage first," Finn said.

Karen shook inside at the idea somebody had deliberately lit a fire in a brand-new construction. "Catching somebody red-handed on the security tape would be great, but why wouldn't we call the police right away?"

Zach wrinkled his nose. "We want to keep moving forward," he reminded her. "Arson investigations can take a while, which means shutting down construction for an unknown period of time."

She hadn't thought of that. "You really think somebody deliberately set the fire?"

"I don't know. I honestly don't know," Zach said.

Beside her, Finn's unreadable expression was firmly back in place. "Let's check the cameras first and see what we find. I don't want to jump the gun and assume." He laid his fingers over Karen's. "We'll make sure you're safe. Just in case something is going on."

"Not just me. Everybody, including you guys." Another concern she hadn't even considered until this moment. "What about getting some guard dogs for the property?"

"Security personnel as well." Finn glanced at Zach. "First priority. Right now."

His friend nodded. "I'll tell Cody about this so he knows to be on his guard, but beyond that, let's keep it quiet. I'll meet you at the house ASAP to check the video feed."

But the cameras were a bust.

Finn sat back in his chair, disgruntled after having pulled all the stored data from the cloud. "Had to be a dozen guys in and out of the cabins along that row, and with no clear shot at the front door of that particular unit, I'm not ready to start an interrogation."

"Then start where you can," Karen said. "I agree. I don't think we should call everyone in and start asking questions. Get some security in place, and that should discourage any more of this kind of thing."

"Hopefully it's enough." He met her gaze. "You feel worried about anything, any time, you let me know."

"I will."

The rush of adrenaline slowly faded as Karen and Zach worked together on the cleanup for the rest of that morning. The task turned out to be reassuring. Nothing seemed super suspicious inside the cabin. Plus, other than it smelling like the inside of a smokehouse, there hadn't been enough time for structural damage to occur.

When they were finished, they carried their supplies and the couple of bags of wood scraps and sawdust onto the porch then propped the door open to let it air out.

"It all seems pretty clear-cut." Zach shook his head. "I'm just a suspicious bastard. I shouldn't have said anything in the first place."

Karen shrugged. "Bringing in security isn't a bad idea. We need it up and running before Thanksgiving, anyway. We think living in a small town means nothing exciting ever happens, but people get desperate here as well."

"And desperation leads to mistakes and bad decisions." Zach nodded, offering her a sly smile. "By the way, how did you manage to convince Finn to leave the cleanup to us?"

"Me, convince him? He volunteered to cook lunch after he dealt with contacting your usual security guys." When Zach's jaw dropped dramatically, she raised a hand as if swearing an oath. "I know. I will take cleanup duty any day if means I get to go back to a home-cooked meal."

"As long as he's not making mac and cheese," Zach teased.

She punched him in the arm good-naturedly then headed home to her man.

The house smelled wonderful. The bit inside her that said

this was a strange thing fought against the part that said it was a perfect thing and she should appreciate every moment.

"Hi, honey, I'm home," she called as she kicked off her boots and marched toward the kitchen.

"Perfect timing."

After stepping through the doorway, Karen paused to take a good look in light of that *full appreciation* thing.

He'd set the table with placemats, pretty plates, and an actual vase with fresh flowers. Tall glasses waited by each setting, but thankfully a very solid hint this wasn't anything too far out of her wheelhouse was there as well—an industrial-size bottle of ketchup sat on the table.

"You get to work for your lunch," Finn informed her as he turned away from the counter. "It's ready, but I didn't want to juggle bowls and my crutches.

"I have zero problem being your waitstaff." She gestured him toward the table then hurried to grab the food.

A moment later they were both seated at the table with steaming bowls of tomato soup and grilled cheese sandwiches with crisp, perfectly browned surfaces in front of them.

The smell alone made her stomach growl in anticipation. "It looks awesome," she said.

"It's a comfort meal." Finn grabbed the ketchup and put a healthy portion on his plate. "Usually I keep soup to wintertime, but it felt like a good thing to serve today."

Karen laid a hand on his arm. "It's been a good day when it comes down to it. There wasn't much we had to do to fix the damage. Zach now thinks it was just an accident after all."

"That's good. I still have a call coming in from the security company, though. Should have them in place in the next couple of days." He twisted until he could squeeze her fingers. "Eat."

The food was delicious, which got Karen to wondering.

"We never did get a chance to do things like cook together. I mean, back at Whiskey Creek."

"I was too busy trying to figure out how to crawl in your bedroom window without being caught," Finn reminded her.

She laughed. "We got up to mischief in so many places other than my bedroom, Finn Marlette."

"If by mischief you mean fooling around and sex, you're right. And that doesn't count all the places I *thought* about taking you." He caught her fingers and brought them to his lips. Kissing them before turning the tease into a nibble. "I've got a list of all the things we're doing once I get this cast off."

"I can't wait," she told him honestly. "But I'm serious about the cooking part too. It's nice that we both like to cook. We're not going starve."

"Is this when I'm supposed to say something cheesy like 'we can live on love'?"

"I would snicker, but I'm too busy enjoying my grilled cheese—what did you put on here? It's delicious. Some kind of jam?"

He pressed a finger to his lips. "I'm not giving you my secret grilled cheese recipe."

Karen leaned forward on her elbows. "Which means that you get to make them any time I get a craving."

Finn stuck out his hand. "Deal."

With a snicker, she linked their fingers and gave his hand a firm pump. The instant he let go, she snatched the final sandwich triangle off his plate, scooting from the table to where he couldn't reach her.

"Hey, give that back." Amusement danced in his eyes.

"No way." A little sad that she didn't have any ketchup to dip it in, she gobbled the section down, moaning as her taste buds lit up.

Finn folded his arms over his chest and gave her a pretty good mock glare. "I ought to paddle your butt for that."

"Promises, promises." She swung back to his side and wrapped her arms around him. The next step was to press a noisy kiss to his cheek. "That was yummy. Thank you."

He dipped his chin. "Thanks for the work you did this morning."

"Not a problem. It interrupted my—" Which brought back to mind another interruption from earlier in the day. "Shoot. Hey, when my dad called this morning, he said he's been trying to get hold of your dad. You got a phone number I can pass on? Seems the one he's got is no longer current."

Amusement drained from Finn's expression, leaving his face grey under his tan.

Karen pulled back with concern. "Finn?"

He shook his head. "Last night you said something pretty powerful. About you and me and making this stick, and I'm with you all the way on that. Which means there're no secrets between us. No real secrets, anyway."

Worry raced through her belly. "What's wrong?"

"There's something I need to tell you."

20

Karen pulled her chair closer and grabbed his fingers. "You're kind of scaring me, Finn. Are you in trouble?"

"What? No. This isn't actually about me." He made a face. "Okay, it is, but the trouble is the secret isn't mine, so I had to get permission to tell you."

No way would she untangle that one, so she just sat and waited. She knew well enough that sometimes tough stories didn't progress forward in a linear manner.

Finn looked pensive. "The instant I left Whiskey Creek, I knew it wasn't right. But you couldn't leave either, so I had to go figure things out at home before I returned."

This wasn't where she'd expected the conversation to go. "I don't hold anything against you from back then, Finn. You made a promise to your parents. Kind of like I made a promise to the Coleman clan. Neither of us could up and leave."

Uncomfortable in a way she'd rarely seen, he took a deep breath and met her gaze straight on. "We went home. Me, Levi, and Duncan. Levi, as you heard, discovered he was soon to be a

257

daddy, which has been nothing but a blessing in his and Chelsea's life. But Duncan—the closer we got to being back at the ranch, the quieter he got, which is saying something."

Karen nodded. While she and Finn had been tangled up tight with each other that summer, and Levi and Lisa had run wild like colts, Duncan had been a quiet ghost who seemed content to be alone.

Finn tore his gaze away and stared at his cast. "Levi and Chelsea got together. It was decided they would move into the ranch house with my parents until the baby arrived. There was plenty of room for them to stay. Then Duncan came to me and said he couldn't keep quiet anymore." Finn paused. "He said dad had sexually abused him. He didn't trust the man to leave Chelsea alone or, down the road, to be around Levi's kids."

An aching rock pit opened inside Karen. "Oh my God. Poor Duncan."

Finn met her eyes again. "I talked to him this morning, by the way. He gave me permission to tell you. Told me you needed to know as well, and he hoped you would try to understand."

She lost the thread at that one. "I don't— Understand what?"

The expression in Finn's eyes reflected both red-hot anger and icy frustration. "Duncan refuses to press charges. He doesn't want the attention or the media circus that sharing the information would involve. He said he couldn't take it, but with Levi and Chelsea in the picture, he wouldn't risk *not* saying something and potentially allowing it to happen again."

The entire situation was a tangled web. Being thrust into it the way Finn had must have been hell. And brave Duncan, struggling between hurting as a victim yet trying to save others.

Karen squeezed Finn's fingers hard. "I am so sorry Duncan had to deal with that. It's just not right."

"It was a fucking mess," Finn admitted. "Duncan was close to the edge. We almost lost him. I was so scared he would do something drastic, no way would I push him to be hurt any further. Levi had no idea, and as far as Duncan knew, neither did Mama."

Karen cupped Finn's cheek, willing strength into him. "Your parents aren't on the ranch anymore."

A single shake of his head as his expression hardened. "I only saw one solution that didn't involve hurting Duncan more or leaving anyone vulnerable. I got my father alone and told him that I knew. He didn't even bother to deny it. I told him he had one choice. He needed to leave the ranch immediately but make it seem as if it was his idea. I didn't care how thick he had to spread the lies, he would convince Mama that they needed to move far enough to have a good excuse for never visiting."

The answer to Karen's question was clear, but she asked it anyway. "And if he hadn't agreed?"

Finn didn't hesitate. "Then he'd be dead, and I'd be in jail for murder."

The confession should've horrified her, but a rush of unexpected fire struck. "I'm glad you're not in jail, but it's no loss that he's still alive. Which may sound heartless, but I keep picturing sweet Duncan. He didn't deserve that. *No* one deserves that."

Once again, Finn hauled her into his lap, but this time instead of offering her comfort, it was her arms that curled around him. It was her murmuring soothing words and pressing kisses against his tear-dampened face.

They sat together for a couple of quiet minutes before he gave a shaky breath. Easing back slightly.

He pressed a kiss against the side of her mouth then dipped his head firmly. "It was the right thing to do, but following through was hell for all the reasons you can imagine. On top of it, I had intended on cutting ties as quickly as possible to get back to you, but the situation made it impossible."

"I'm so glad you were there," Karen insisted. "I mean, what if you had stayed at Whiskey Creek? Oh my God—"

"We can't ask 'what if,' but I needed to tell you. I wanted to be back at your side not even an hour after I left."

She was a mess inside, and yet the pulse of love just beat stronger and stronger. Karen ran her fingers through his hair and stared at his face, memorizing the lines that hadn't been there years ago. Understanding better where they'd come from, that they were the marks he'd earned doing a task no one could honour him for.

"I love you. And we're together now. Everything you did just makes you more *you*," she insisted.

He curled a hand around her nape. "Only a few people know Duncan's story. You, me, Zach. One other person—Alan, actually. Bruce knew as well, because I got started with him while I was dealing with the legal details of removing my father from the ranch. I spent a lot of time keeping an eye on my father in those days until my parents officially moved, and Bruce needed to know why. Hell, in the end he helped me set up things via Alan to be airtight from a legal standpoint."

She wasn't really curious other than wanting to know for certain that Levi's babies were safe. Yet... What about other kids? "Where did your parents move to?"

"Québec City. They're in an adult-only condo where Mama is completely happy. She enjoys city life and getting to socialize anytime she wants. Three or four times a year, she flies to Winnipeg where my brother picks her up to stay at the ranch for a week or so. My father is always too busy to join those visits. Mama believes it's too difficult for him to go back to the ranch because of the memories. And my father is not allowed to work with children or be in a private setting with anyone but

Mama. I have someone watching him—that's part of what Bruce helped me arrange."

His words faded as if he had run out of energy to continue. His palms pressed against her back and pulled them closer together, not with physical hunger but a desperate, urgent need for connection.

Karen held on as tightly as possible, giving with her touch, offering what she could with her words.

"No more secrets. Just one step at a time toward our future." She leaned back slightly, pressing both palms to his cheeks. "We'll build a safe, happy place right here, together. Red Boot ranch will be our home. Levi and Chelsea and the kids will come and visit. You'll tell Duncan he's welcome to drive his eighteen-wheeler into the yard and stay anytime he wants. We'll be all the family they need."

He dipped his chin firmly. The breath he took was still slightly shaky, but the love in his eyes was solid. "*You're* all I need. All I've ever wanted."

Exhaustion rolled in as if she'd been working chores for hours instead of sitting in the kitchen having a conversation. She gave Finn a brief kiss then tilted her head toward the door. "Come on. I need some fresh air, and I want you with me."

They walked in silence for a while, following the path that headed toward the river at the bottom of the pasture. It was wide and smooth, which meant Finn's crutches worked fine.

He grumbled his disgust, though. "I want to hold your hand and not deal with this nonsense of being close by but not touching."

"Newsflash, cowboy. Even when you do get your cast off, we're not going to spend twenty-four seven attached at the hip."

It was good to hear a soft chuckle, and Karen glanced to the side to find he was smoldering at her again. "I plan to do my best. Oh, wait. It's not quite *hips* I'm thinking of."

"Bad boy." She raised a brow. "I thought you liked cowgirl position."

"Love it," he agreed. "Anytime you want, I give you the go-ahead. But more variety will be fun."

The conversation drifted then, deliberately becoming lighter as they avoided talk of the serious matters that had blown up their day. There were plenty of other things to discuss, between ongoing plans for the ranch and Karen tentatively exploring possibilities for the future.

Those ideas needed to be talked through with more than just Finn, which is how a couple days later she finally built up the courage to share her news with her sisters.

They'd gathered at the cottage, supposedly to introduce one of their favourite family traditions to Julia. Karen figured the interactive, hands-on meal would be a good distraction after she'd dropped her bomb.

It also meant cooking and cleanup would be a snap, and with the long days they were putting in at the ranch to keep things moving at an accelerated rate, right now Karen was all about easy.

Julia stepped through the door. "Sorry I'm late. Where do you want these?"

She held out a block of Swiss cheese and a carton of eggs.

Lisa grabbed them then headed to the kitchen. "That's the last we need. I'll get the omelet mix together. Karen, slice the cheese."

It was like old times. Karen exchanged a glance with Tamara. "I'm not in charge of my own home."

"Get used to it. I have." Tamara admired Tyler, who was conveniently eating before they started their meal. "Auntie Lisa is a bossy pants, isn't she? Yes, she totally is a bossy pants and we love her for it."

Karen snickered as she joined the other girls in the kitchen and obediently cut up the cheese as per Lisa's instructions. Ollie wander under Lisa's feet, sweetly begging for treats until ordered to the pillow Karen had placed in the corner.

As soon as the dog settled, Dandy crawled from under the couch like a wild tiger, intent on stalking Ollie's tail.

By the time they gathered around the table, Tamara had finished feeding the baby, burped him, and put him down to sleep. She rubbed her hands together. "I'm starving. After nine months of not eating, I'm still playing catch-up."

"I can't believe you were actually nauseous your entire pregnancy." Julia hesitated. "Okay, technically and scientifically, I believe it. I just mean that was a pretty shitty hand to be dealt."

"I hope it doesn't run in the family," Tamara said dryly.

"I nominate Karen to be the next guinea pig to get pregnant," Lisa said instantly.

Karen gasped. "What? *No.* I just got into a serious relationship. It's obvious you're the next to fall."

Tamara gently tapped her fingers against the side of her glass, just enough to get their attention and not loud enough to wake the baby. "Instructions for Julia so she knows what we're doing. This is a raclette."

"Raw food meets hot surface, cook till it's done." Karen pulled one of the little pans from underneath the top broiler plate. "You can cook little omelets in here or melt cheese to pour over top of your food. Eat until you're ready to burst."

Lisa lifted a pair of chopsticks. "The only other family rule you need to know is even if you put a piece of food on the top surface, it might not be there when you go back for it. It's kind of a free-for-all when we get rolling."

The newcomer watched for a while as the three of them started eagerly. They passed around sauces and dips, and easy conversation drifted while tidbits were consumed and laughter danced in the air. The animals made the occasional forage attempt before being sent back to their *no begging* zone.

It was comfortable, and it was family. Karen's concerns about sharing her change of plans eased when confronted by how sweet the connection between them felt.

Still, the deed had to be done.

She waited until everybody had food in motion then laid her utensils down and sat up a little straighter. "Got a couple things to let you know. All of it good, and I hope you'll be happy for me."

Three sets of eyes turned on her, filled with curiosity.

And eagerness. "Are you and Finn engaged?" Lisa asked.

Karen restrained from rolling her eyes. "Jump the gun a little? It's way too soon. We're—" What the hell did she call this? He was more than her boyfriend. More than a lover.

He was...*hers*.

"You're together." Julia dipped her chin firmly. "You guys fit. And I understand there's history, but you seem pretty solid in the here and now. Good for you."

"What will happen when you head out in the fall?" Tamara looked uncertain. "Long-term relationships do better when you're in the same postal code area."

Karen put both feet forward and jumped.

"There's the other thing I want to let you know. Ever since I got here, I've been considering my options. Thinking about what would make me happy not just down the road, but right now. And that might sound a little backwards, but it's been pointed out that it's okay to do things that make me happy. I've decided school is not on my short-term list. Instead, I'm staying and working the ranch with Finn and Zach." She wondered if she would have to fend off a mass of questions, so she hurried to finish. "It's what I want. I'm excited to stay in Heart Falls."

The entire time Karen had been talking, her sisters' expressions had grown more surprised, eyes widening.

Lisa pressed her fingers over her mouth. Then damn if she didn't burst into tears. Tamara followed, and suddenly Karen's eyes filled as well.

It was far too easy to get a group of grown women to end up watery messes.

Julia was the one who finally voiced her discomfort. "I don't even know why I'm crying. I mean, I'm happy for you. Sounds as if you gave it a lot of thought. Besides"—she jerked a thumb toward Lisa and Tamara—"getting to set up here in Heart Falls with these two is pretty perfect."

"I'm crying because *she's* crying," Tamara insisted as she pointed at Lisa. "Dammit. Pregnancy and nursing hormones are *hell*. I'm really happy for you, Karen. And not only because it will be so much easier to hold family get-togethers."

The little cream-coloured terrier, Ollie, was up on her hind legs, scratching lightly at Lisa's leg, trying to figure out what had gone wrong so she could fix it.

Lisa soothed her, slowly petting the puppy's head. "It's okay, sweetie. This is one of those weird things humans do when they're happy." She held her hand out to Karen and gave her fingers a big squeeze. "That's a hell of a destination change, but I'm hardly one to talk. I'm so glad you're sticking around."

"Now we need to find Julia a full-time job in the area so we'll have all the Whiskey Creek women in one place," Tamara pointed out.

Julia shrugged even as she wiped away tears. "I wouldn't mind, but right now the job only lasts until the end of October. But no matter what, this will make it a whole lot simpler when I come visit. I'll find all three of you in one spot."

They returned to their meal while questions and teasing about every other topic under the sun continued. Laughter rose and love and support surrounded Karen like a warm blanket on a cold day.

It might be a different story when she had to explain to extended family, but really, at the core, did that matter?

The women around her right now—*they* were the ones in her heart. They were the ones whose opinions mattered, and with them by her side, she could do anything.

21

———

Things smoothed out after that in a way that made the momentary upheavals seem like distant memories. Finn was fine with that.

Security teams were hired, and there were no more unexpected losses or fires. Which meant as the end of July rolled around, things continued to progress at double-quick pace.

Karen drove him to the hospital for his appointment to get the cast removed. He was antsy. It was a couple days later than he'd hoped, plus he was so done being chauffeured everywhere.

In the driver's seat beside him, his woman didn't even try to hide her amusement.

"Stop smirking," Finn grumbled. "Admit it. You're just as eager for me to get this cast off as I am."

"Oh, I don't think *that's* possible." She offered him a sweet smile before turning her focus back on the highway. "I'm absolutely amazed you didn't take a hacksaw to it yourself yesterday. You're to be commended for your restraint."

"Damn doctor shouldn't have said August first when she

267

knew she wasn't coming back from holidays until the third," Finn complained. "And putting on my chart that no one else was allowed to take the cast off without her approval was just nasty."

"I know. It was a terribly mean thing to do." Karen patted his hand with mock sympathy. "Shall we go for a celebratory horseback ride when we get home?"

He kept hold of her fingers, tugging them to his lips. "Maybe second thing."

If anything, her smile got wider. "You're right. You really should go on a full inspection tour of everything that's been accomplished over the past couple of months before we try anything fun."

"You just carry on like that. See how well fucked it gets you."

She gasped. "Language."

He shifted as much as possible in his seat, turning toward her and playing with a strand of hair that had fallen loose from her ponytail. "I can't wait to get you home and strip you naked. After I use my mouth and fingers to make you scream a couple of times, we'll move on to something totally wild."

"Really? And that would be?" The question came out a little breathless.

He leaned forward to get in her line of sight. "Missionary position."

As hoped, he got a loud laugh, but the twinkle in her eyes said she was just as eager to mix it up.

Having her in his arms each night had been a bit of a miracle. Yet since rolling over required his full concentration and the equivalent of a damn workout, their sex life had remained limited.

The doctor took pity on him, pushing through the X-ray results quickly, which put him back in the waiting room in double-quick time. Being stared down by that minuscule woman with the attitude of an Amazon would've been highly amusing if there wasn't so much on the line.

"You've healed well," Dr. Jerimiah told him. "Congratulations. You graduate to walking on two legs."

Finn grinned over the doctor's shoulder at Karen. "Ready to go dancing, *ma chérie?*"

"Good idea," the doctor told him. "In moderation. You need to build up your strength again. I'll give you a set of exercises and a prescription for physiotherapy if you need it. I have a feeling your biggest issue will be not overdoing it." She glanced over her shoulder at Karen. "Keep him off his feet when you can."

"She already promised to." Finn caught Karen's gaze, and when he spoke again, his voice had gone lower. Needy, full of anticipation. "Frequently and enthusiastically."

That might've come out a little dirtier than he intended. In front of the doc and all.

The young woman laughed. "That's pretty much what I figured. If you have any troubles, come back and see me. Otherwise, stay out of collapsing buildings, and I hope the rest of your summer goes well."

He pumped her hand with real gratitude. "Thanks."

Finn and Karen took a slow stroll to the parking lot, but when he pulled open the passenger door for her, she shook her head and pointed at the seat. "One last time as passenger. I insist. You have presents to open."

It wasn't worth grumbling about because—*damn.* Without the cast, he felt fifty pounds lighter and yet slightly out of kilter. "Okay. But tomorrow I drive."

She hadn't been kidding about the presents. A pile of them rested on the seat.

He waited until she'd pulled out of the hospital parking lot and had them on the highway headed home to Heart Falls. "What's all this?"

"Everybody wanted to celebrate your getting-out-of-jail moment." She pointed to random packages. "Zach, Cody, Josiah. Those two are from Tamara and Lisa. Tansy sent over a black forest cheesecake, and Julia and the crew at the fire hall picked up some ribeye steaks for us to enjoy sometime this week."

A strange knot developed in his throat. He stared at the boxes, all brightly wrapped, and wondered at the weird sensation in his belly.

Karen glanced over. "Finn? You okay?"

He picked up one of the packages, opening the tag on it to see it was from his brother Levi and family. "I'm a little choked up right now, to tell the truth."

"Because people are happy you're feeling better?"

He shrugged. "Hell. I figured they would be happy knowing I won't be begging favours anymore. I'm just not used to— I don't know."

She threaded their fingers together. "Not used to having visible signs that people appreciate you show up on your doorstep? Or in this case, truck seat?"

He nodded. "Pretty much, yeah."

"Well, they do appreciate you. And they're happy for you, and I need you to start opening presents because I'm dying of curiosity."

Even as he worked the wrapping paper on the one in his hands, he lowered his tone a notch. "Thank you for what you got me. It's exactly what I wanted."

She snickered. "My present isn't even here."

"Oh. I was talking about your promise to sex me to death."

"Oh. That. You're welcome." She gave him a love tap on the shoulder. "You're a terrible present opener. Get going."

The box from Levi and Chelsea contained cards from the kids— typical small people productions made of crayon scrawls and hearts—and a picture frame.

Levi and Chelsea sat on the front porch of the house Finn had grown up in, surrounded by their family. The kids wore matching outfits with cowboy hats and boots. The three little tykes looked happy and well loved. His brother had an arm wrapped around Chelsea's shoulders, the smile on his face sheer perfection.

The house itself had a new paint job, and somehow it looked a lot shinier than the last time Finn remembered being there.

He carefully put the frame aside, soaking it in as a new memory to help wash away some of the bitterness of the past.

Then he worked on the next present, warmth growing in his chest.

"Zach got me a new deck of playing cards. Probably figured the other set we use is marked, considering how bad he's been losing lately."

"You shouldn't be so mean to your best friend."

"Hey, if he wants to help finance our next vacation, I have no problem taking money from him." He opened the bag from Josiah and laughed. "The man gave me a jar of Bag Balm."

"That should help with all the chafing you plan to get," she teased.

They grinned at each other.

He picked up the package from Tamara and gave it a shake. Something slid inside. "You want to wait and open this when we get home?"

They were still a good forty-five minutes from the ranch. "Keep going. This is entertaining," Karen told him.

Inside the paper was an old-fashioned tobacco tin. "She wants me to take up bad habits," he informed Karen. He wiggled off the lid, and laughed out loud. "Scratch that. Your sister just gave me a couple dozen condoms."

"Get out." She glanced over quickly as he tilted the container toward her. "She's terrible."

"She's brilliant," Finn said. "Now I can be prepared for the days ahead."

Only when the present from Lisa also made the same suspicious sliding noise, Finn started laughing even as he tore the paper off. "Oh, look. Another tin. I wonder what's inside?"

"I'm going to kill my sisters." But her laughter joined his, and when he poured the contents into his open palm, the colourful packets like a rainbow, she tossed him a dirty grin.

When she pulled off the road and headed down a gravel path toward who knew where, Finn sent up a thank-you to the heavens.

"Tell me you have some ulterior motive in taking me for a ride."

She pulled the truck to a stop on a narrow path hidden between tall trees. "You think you can handle that missionary stuff in the back of the truck?"

He met her at the tailgate in under three seconds.

She hoped this wasn't going against everything the doctor had warned Finn about, but they were both too eager to wait.

He took the blanket she'd grabbed from the back cab and, with one firm snap, spread it out in the truck bed. Then he caught hold of her and pulled them together, lips meeting eagerly, hands moving freely as they gave in to desire.

He got her jeans undone, pushing them and her panties off her hips seconds before he lifted her to the surface of the open tailgate.

Hands on either side of her legs, Finn leaned in. "Hold on tight. I'm about to take you to church."

Which meant it wouldn't be long before she started singing with the choir. The thought made her giggle, the sound turning into a moan as Finn opened her knees and pressed a kiss to her inner thigh. Another one, higher, hands stroking in advance of his mouth until his thumbs teased against her core.

Soft, slow strokes that ignited her senses and built a spiral of need deep within her.

The warmth in her heart was rock-solid—the connection to this caring, giving man had grown steadily over the past couple of months. It seemed a mere whisper of time but was compounded by their earlier summer and all the moments over the past five years when she'd thought of him. Hoped for him.

Wished for him to be with her—and now it was real.

A nip against her thigh made her gasp.

He leaned over her. "Someone's daydreaming."

Her fingers drifted through his hair. Stroked the crest of his cheekbone. "Dreaming about you. Always about you," she confessed.

He twisted his head to drop a kiss on her fingers. "I love you, *ma chérie.*"

Her heart welled with happiness. "I know."

The usually stoic and quiet man who owned her heart laughed so loud his joy echoed off the trees around them.

Then he put his energy back between her legs. Teasing and touching until the spiral inside her tightened then uncoiled in a rush. Pleasure streaked from her core outward as he climbed over her, his jeans pushed aside, a colourful condom wrapper abandoned beside them.

He crawled between her thighs, and the broad head of his cock nudged against her sex.

He paused, notched against her, powerful arms holding

their torsos apart as he hovered over her. Staring into her eyes and letting her see everything in him. "You're mine."

"Always." *Forever* echoed in her head as he slid deeper. Impossibly slow. Wicked sensations built between them as he touched her perfectly.

The blue sky ranged above them, tall trees waving slightly in the wind. The scent of summertime and the hazy heat coming off the asphalt mixed into a symphony of countryside experiences.

As Finn drew his hips back, cock teasing over sensitive skin, Karen breathed out, *"Home."*

The corners of his lips curled, and he pressed in faster. Harder on the next thrust, catching hold of her hip and changing the angle to drive deeper still.

Each time the word echoed in her mind and from her lips. This was coming home.

He was her home.

The pulses sped up, and she reached around him, fingernails digging into the soft fabric of his flannel shirt. The rough scratch of his jeans played against her inner thighs, and where they connected, it was heat and fire and perfection.

"Finn." She lifted her legs around his hips, digging her heels into his ass as he made a final thrust and threw his head back, calling her name to the sky.

Then he was kissing her. Nuzzling his lips along her neck. Pressing sweet endearments against her mouth. Lowering his torso over hers until she felt him along every inch.

Over her and in her. A part of her forever.

"I like my present so far," Finn told her as he licked her earlobe delicately. "We might need to stop a couple more times along the way to make sure, though."

Happiness welled. "You goof. We'll never get home."

Joy lit his face. "From what you just said, we're already there."

Now that Finn was a hundred percent mobile, Karen never knew when he would show up, eager for her. Eager to be together. Delight danced every time she stole away with him—something far beyond what she'd felt that long ago summer during their fling.

This wasn't a temporary thing, and the mere idea of that sparked a massive amount of joy.

As the week moved forward, work fell into a smooth routine. The guys barreled ahead on the construction parts of the ranch while Karen concentrated on staffing.

They still took time to spend with their friends and family. Finn insisted on it, which Karen appreciated because it would've been too easy to go overboard striving to meet the deadline.

She did her own share of wrangling to make sure *everyone* important in Finn's life was included. Like the day when Finn's phone rang while he and Karen had stopped for lunch.

Duncan ended up on speakerphone.

They chatted with him the entire meal. Duncan caught Karen up on the latest and greatest innovations in trucking. Told them all about the online games he played in the evening with friends from around the world.

"Right now I'm doing a run from Toronto to Detroit, but I asked to get moved to a more western route," he told them. "If it happens, I hope you don't mind me dropping by more often."

The expression on Finn's face was worth the effort it had taken to track down his brother.

"You're always welcome," Finn assured Duncan. The words came out a little rough.

After Duncan hung up, Finn came around the table and

scooped Karen into his arms, squeezing her tight. "Mischief-maker. You did something, didn't you?"

No use in pretending. "I got hold of Levi. I wanted Chelsea's number to update my birthday calendar with the kids' information. He was really excited to talk to me and instantly invited us to come out for Christmas. I told him we weren't sure of our plans this year, but we would definitely find a way to get together at some point."

He nodded slowly. "I think I'd be okay to go visit them. They're making the ranch theirs and filling it with new memories. It might be good to see that in person."

She agreed. "And I called Duncan. Didn't bring up any specific topic but let him know we've got lots of nice, quiet places around here, and we'd love to see him. Anytime. It seemed to be all he needed."

Finn kissed her then, and what with one thing and another, they didn't get back to their work list for over an hour.

Zach wore a constant smirk any time he came around. Which Karen figured they probably deserved.

The only bad part hanging over their heads was the deadline. Construction progressed at its own pace. If they wanted to hire quality people for permanent positions in and around the ranch, that required giving *them* time to organize their lives.

Karen muttered her frustration at Finn as they stood side by side in the little cottage kitchen, washing dishes after dinner. "I know exactly who I want to hire as a house mom, but until we have a place for her to stay, there's no use in getting her to start work. All she needs is two weeks' notice, though, and she's willing to join us."

"This is the hard part that always comes into play with Bruce's challenges," Finn told her. "If it was just us, we can turn on a dime. Tossing other people into the mix makes it tougher. We'll figure it out," he promised. "Tonight, don't worry about it. You enjoy your outing with your girls, you hear me?"

Warmth scooped into her belly again.

What a difference a month had made. Barely thirty days ago, she'd skipped out on her friends and been moping around the house, confused about her future and where to go to find happiness.

Impulsively, she wrapped Finn up in a hug, wet hands from the dishwater pressed against his back. "You remember that day I told you I felt all gloomy inside and didn't know why?"

He held her tight. "That night is etched in my memory."

She bumped her nose against his. "I don't feel like that anymore," she assured him. "Thank you for being a good listener and for giving me some pretty damn good advice."

"You're welcome. Now get your ass in gear. Your sisters will beat us to the barn if we don't get a move on."

He was partially right. Kelli was already there, carefully coaching Tansy, Rose, and Brooke in the fine art of patting a horse's nose. Hanna was the only one of their friends not joining in. Brad had stolen her away for a birthday weekend in the mountains.

Kelli spotted Karen first. "Getting our greenhorns warmed up," she informed them. "Your sisters are about ten minutes out."

"Perfect. Now we need a few more horses, a bit of moonlight, and a touch of magic, and we'll be ready to go." Karen twisted to go finish preparing the horses and spotted Finn already coordinating the task with some of the hands. Zach showed up as well, chatting easily with her friends, his handsome face lit up with his usual smile.

As Lisa, Julia, and Tamara joined them, it was clear the one thing Karen already had in her life was magic.

22

With Starlight nickering happily under her, Karen led her friends into the fading light. Twilight fell as the animals moved at a steady gait along the wide access trail toward their first destination.

Her sisters were competent riders, and she'd made sure to give the less experienced friends bombproof horses. With Kelli bringing up the rear, Karen was confident they'd have no problems on the trail.

Julia nudged her horse forward enough to be able to chat easily at Karen's side.

"I've missed this," Julia confessed. "I mean, I like being a paramedic, but after growing up constantly around horses, not having access twenty-four seven kind of sucks."

Karen knew exactly what she was talking about. "You're welcome to come over any time you need a fix."

Julia nodded. Sitting easily in the saddle, she stared at the mountains looming over them. "I'll take you up on that offer, as long as I get to ride *with* you at least some of the time." Her smile was a little cheeky. "I do want to get to know my sisters, not just take advantage of their awesome access to horseback riding."

It had been a good thing, getting to know Julia better. "You fit in with us," Karen assured her. "I hope you've been enjoying yourself and not feeling too overwhelmed."

"It's been okay," Julia assured her. "Except for the learning how to deal with diapers. I could've done without that part. So gross."

Karen laughed. "Are you sure you're a paramedic? I thought that meant you had an iron stomach."

"Blood and guts? No problem. Toxic baby poop? That stuff requires an entire hazmat training level I haven't aspired to yet."

They rode on the gentle trail for about forty-five minutes before reaching the lookout spot Karen had found. With the fire pit ready to be lit and the stash of supplies for s'mores and thermoses of hot chocolate in her saddlebags, her girl gang gathered around.

Soon they were all happily roasting marshmallows as they waited for moonrise. The conversation went in a dozen different directions at one time, chatter looping and overlapping in a way that only made sense in a close-knit community.

Karen sat in the middle and soaked it all in.

"No, I'm not going on another date with him," Rose repeated in response to Tansy's teasing. "Zach was nice enough, but I'm not looking for a steady boyfriend. I told you I wanted to dance, and he delivered. That doesn't mean I have to see him anymore."

"Wait. That's right. I had a question about this," Brooke spoke up. She reached back and tightened her dark ponytail before turning an inquisitive gaze on Rose. "I was totally shocked when I saw you with Zach at Hanna's wedding. I thought you were dating Alex, the ranch hand from Silver Stone and volunteer firefighter. You know, another tall, dark, sexy dude."

"I did. For a while. We had fun, but we're just friends. We didn't want to get serious."

"Heaven forbid you get serious," Tansy muttered.

Rose glared at her sister. "Don't you go making any comments about my sex life."

A chorus of snickers went around the campfire.

Brooke deliberately placed another marshmallow on her stick, grinning as she held it toward the fire. "Didn't hear anybody mention sex until *you* brought it up."

"It's Tansy's fault." Rose said through her teeth.

A slow chin dip from Brooke, along with another sly smile. "Probably. Usually is."

"Hey," Tansy protested.

Which brought another round of laughter from the collected group. Ties were being built; friendships strengthened.

"Speaking of sexy..." Tamara leaned toward Brooke. "How's that firefighter of *yours* these days?"

"We're good. Slow and steady, but that's fine. I was thinking—"

Julia shot to her feet, hand pointed toward the east. "Sorry, Brooke. What's that?"

The group quieted as they peered in the direction of Julia's pointed finger. The moon had risen, the full circle overhead shining like a spotlight toward the meadow between them and Red Boot ranch.

By ones and twos, wild horses slipped out of the trees toward the broad expanse of river. Silver sparkled on the water's surface as the herd of a dozen and a half made their way through the meadow.

"There's the stallion, far left at the lead," Karen said. "What a beauty."

"He's *huge*," Rose said. "Is he dangerous?"

"If you got directly in his path, possibly. Otherwise, I'd prefer to face him over a cougar," Kelli said quietly.

The herd wasn't going anywhere at any great speed, so the group of women stood in silence, admiring the animals as they grazed across the meadow to the water's edge.

That's when Karen saw her. The mare with the off-kilter gait. The one whose foal she had rescued.

Instinctively, she caught Lisa's fingers and squeezed, her throat tight with emotion.

Lisa made eye contact. "You okay?"

Nodding gave her a moment to pull herself together. "I just spotted Moonbeam's mom."

Lisa wrapped an arm around her, comfort in the touch. "She made it. I'm glad."

Lightness rushed through Karen's body, washing away the final bit of sadness that had been nestled against her core in spite of all the good things that had happened. She leaned her head on her sister's shoulder. "I was so tangled up at having to leave her there."

The arm around her waist tightened. "Oh, sweetie, I get it. Just because you knew it was the right thing to do, that didn't make it any easier."

That magic Karen had thought about earlier—it was out in full force right now. Seeing the wild horses in their element filled her soul with a peacefulness and beauty that couldn't be defined.

The stallion jerked alert, pawing at the ground and shaking his mane before letting out a shrill call.

"What's going on?" Rose asked. "He sounds upset."

"I'd say he was serenading some new ladies, but that

shouldn't be possible." Karen moved to the side to get a better look at the overall area.

Julia swore softly, pointing in a new direction. "Unless someone left the barn door open after we left."

Karen dug in her saddlebag and grabbed a set of binoculars. With only moonlight shining down, it was hard to pick out the individual animals as they crossed the field toward the river, but some of them were familiar beasts she'd brought from Whiskey Creek. She'd recognize them their movements anywhere.

And then—

"Son of a bitch."

Literally. Someone was down there, standing beside a gate that wasn't supposed to be open.

She pressed the binoculars against Lisa's chest then dug in her pocket for her phone. "Give me a second."

"Those horses aren't supposed to be there, are they?" Tansy straightened. "What do you need us to do?"

Karen lifted a finger in the air. "Finn? We've got trouble. Someone just let out a bunch of our mares. They're headed straight toward the wild stallion."

IT HAD BEEN A PERFECTLY LAID-BACK evening. Finn and the guys had pulled out a card table and a deck of cards with a plan to play once they finished shooting the breeze. They'd hauled in Cody as their fourth, and the man turned out to be a great addition. Easy going, entertaining.

An hour and a half after the girls had taken off, they still hadn't dealt the first hand.

It felt good, though, to catch up. Not just a *what the hell do we need to get done next?* type of conversation, but relaxed. No agenda. Guys who truly enjoyed each other's company.

The only thing missing was a good glass of scotch, which Finn planned to enjoy once Karen returned.

"Every time they have a girls' night out, we should get together." Josiah leaned his chair back far enough he was nearly horizontal, boots propped up on a hay bale.

Cody lifted his beer in the air in agreement. "You've got my vote."

"Boys' night in," Zach suggested.

"What is it with you and this irresistible urge to name things?" Finn asked his friend. "Can you not find your way to a place unless you label it? Somewhere down the road, you'll have a house called Green Gables, and I will gag every time I visit."

"You're just jealous because—" Zach paused as Finn's phone went off. "You're just jealous. That's all."

"A superior naming ability is a highly sought-after skill," Josiah offered.

"Everybody shut up for a minute," Finn ordered so he could hear Karen. "Say that again."

"Somebody's got at least eight of our horses out in the far west field. This isn't the animals breaking away from the rest of the herd and wandering off. I see a person as well, waving their arms and shouting to get the horses to head outside our fences."

"Shit."

Three sets of eyes were on him now, all amusement vanished as everyone went on alert, probably freaking out that something had gone wrong with the girls.

Karen continued, "In a stroke of bad luck, the wild stallion is in the area." Even as Finn swore, she moved to reassure him, confidence in her tone. "Yeah, that's what I said. Don't worry, we're close enough to head down and make sure he doesn't grab our girls. But you need to go deal with the jerk who let them out in the first place. Bastard's got some explaining to do."

"Don't take any chances," he ordered.

"We'll be careful. You watch out—that person isn't where they should be. Who knows what they're up to or if they're alone."

That issue hadn't even occurred to him.

The instant she hung up, Finn headed toward where he and Zach stabled their horses. "Someone is trespassing and stealing our horses. Is it still called horse thievery if you're shoving them toward the wilderness instead of the back of a trailer?"

Cody started getting his horse saddled in double-quick time. "If it's one of our crew, I swear I'll skin the bastard."

"You'll have to get in line. Sounds as if Karen is ready to do that with her bare teeth." Finn told them what little she'd shared before looking at his best friend. "If I remember correctly, there are two ways to get to that field."

Zach tightened the cinch on his horse. "You want me and Cody to come in along the north fence line?"

He considered the route, even as he placed the bridle over Mywaye's head. "Josiah goes with Cody. You and I will approach from the south. If by some chance the guy tries to escape straight east, we'll have security waiting."

"I'll give the guards a shout as soon as we're riding," Cody promised.

"Are the girls okay?" Josiah asked. He sounded more concerned than expected. "I mean, this was supposed to be a fun moonlight ride, not a roundup."

Finn thought over the list of women who had headed out that evening. "They've got three newbies but also five highly-skilled horsewomen. They can handle it."

It seemed to take forever, but he knew they were out of the barn faster than usual. He led Zach to the same path he and Karen had walked only days before. They moved cautiously, but the sense of urgency was there. And it wasn't about the horses, and it wasn't even about whatever the hell was going on at the ranch.

It was about making sure Karen was safe.

Hoofbeats rang loudly against the hard-packed dirt.

The instant Karen got off the phone with Finn, she started handing out orders. "Finn's taking care of our mystery man. We need to make sure Thor doesn't take off with our mares. Tamara, are you good to stay here with Tansy and Rose and make sure everything's dealt with?"

Tamara nodded. "We can head back to the ranch the same way we came once the fire's out. You've got the trail well marked. I'm okay if we go slowly."

"Someone will come back to meet you as soon as possible," Karen promised. She turned to her other sisters and Kelli. "We'll deal with the herd."

Three heads nodded, all of them moving toward their horses without any questions.

"What about me?" Brooke asked.

She'd been the most competent of the three inexperienced riders on the trip up, and Karen needed one more set of hands. "You okay coming with us? You'll ride with me to the bottom of the hill and then work as a backup."

"No problem."

The smooth grace with which everyone responded made Karen proud.

Starlight had done the trail enough times that he moved

confidently even in the darkness. It gave time for Karen to talk to Brooke about what her task would be.

Once they hit the bottom of the hill, Karen helped Brooke to the ground then directed Lisa and Kelli to the trail leading north. "Julia and I will go south for ten minutes then head toward the river. I'm hoping with the fuss over by Red Boot ranch, the stallion won't be interested in moving in that direction. He'll wait for the mares to come to him. We should be able to cut them off before they join his herd."

Brooke held up her phone. "And if the wildies head in *this* direction, I set off my alarm so they don't take the trail up past the fire pit and spook the rest of our group."

"Just don't set the alarm off unless you have to, because *none* of the horses are going to like that sound."

The five of them headed in different directions. Karen was amazed at how quickly the group had gone from laughing and joking to dead serious and a competent team.

But then again, she'd worked with some of these women most of her life. She knew what they were capable of.

Maybe that was part of what had called her to Heart Falls. Called her to make this home, because even in the midst of not knowing what the hell was going on, it seemed she was in the right place and with the right people.

As she and Julia moved quietly along the trail, Karen took the time to loosen the straps holding her shotgun in place.

Julia noticed. "You think that's necessary?"

"Hope not, but I don't want to have to scramble if I need it."

"Understood."

They rode across a new section of land, the low brush backlit with moonlight that turned the edges of green leaves into shimmering silver where the dew had begun to gather. It was beautiful and surreal considering they were currently sneaking up on a herd of wild horses.

The murmur of the water grew louder as they moved in.

"How deep is the river here?" Julia asked quietly enough to not carry farther than Karen's ears.

"We can ford it if we have to." Karen strained to make out details as the moon played peekaboo behind clouds. She lifted a hand. "The stallion."

"Your herd." Julia pointed farther to the east. "That's good. They haven't moved very much. They're still close to the fence line."

"Your eyes are better than mine," Karen said, hauling out her binoculars to check.

She'd just got them in view when the quick *crack* of a gunshot went off. Instantly, the mares panicked, turning to run. They left behind the fence and headed toward where Julia and Karen stood on the far side of the water.

"It's that idiot again," Karen said even as she urged Starlight forward. "Come on. Let's stop them before they hit the river."

Water sprayed upward as she and Julia ran their horses across the shallows then up and across the land toward the panicked mares. To the east, the fence line was clear except where a batch of trees blocked her sight line.

There was no sign of the shooter. After checking to be sure they were far enough away to not be a target without a person visibly moving toward them, Karen concentrated on the horses.

Julia pivoted to the left, Karen to the right. The mares instinctively moved together, slowing their motion and circling back toward the familiarity of their new home.

Another circle, and the horses slowed again, heads and ears twitching as they tried to figure out what to do next.

Across the river, Kelli and Lisa eased toward the wild herd

to push them back toward government land and the wilderness where they belonged.

FINN AND ZACH left their horses in the shelter of the trees and made their way to the fence line, sneaking up on the man who just stood there, shouting every now and then at the horses who weren't doing what he wanted.

"Tackle him?" Zach murmured softly.

"Take him down."

Then the bastard pulled out a gun and shot into the sky, and everything went sideways. Zach grabbed Finn, hauled him to the ground, and settled into one of the low-lying dips not even thirty feet from where the man stood.

They both lay motionless, expecting to be discovered at any moment. When nothing happened, Finn cautiously poked his head up to discover the man still had his back toward them, staring at the horses.

Zach took a peek as well, and when he laid back down, his friend pointed toward the mountains. "Horses to the west," he whispered. "And the girls."

Ice-cold terror ran through Finn's veins. "How close?"

"Far enough for now." Zach tilted his head toward the man. "Rush him?"

It was agony to lie there, making a plan instead of getting it done. "Can he shoot the girls?"

Zach shook his head. "Too far. Not even a lucky shot."

Then that was the answer. "We wait. He moves, we move. He shoots, we move."

His friend dipped his chin in agreement.

They sat in silence. One minute. Two.

Time inched like slow-melting water down the side of an icicle.

~

ANOTHER CRACK WENT OFF, only this time the horses didn't bolt. Just shuddered as if they really wished Julia and Karen would make this night go away.

"What the hell is going on?" Julia asked. She glanced back toward the fence line. Pointing again. "Over there."

It was the briefest moment where a single form was silhouetted by moonlight. A second man came running out of nowhere, tackling the first to the ground, while again gunshot echoed.

Karen glanced at the herd, but they were milling around Julia as if she were the holy grail. "Stay here," Karen ordered before turning Starlight and heading at a run toward the batch of trees closest to the fence line.

"What the hell?" Julia's voice faded in the distance.

Maybe this was a stupid move, but every instinct Karen had told her to do it. She put her head down and rode.

~

FINN HIT the ground with a stranger under him, pain streaking along his weak right leg. Fists pounded against his ribs as the man attempted to throw him off.

Zach cursed in the background, a gasping sound, and Finn was distracted for just long enough that the man under him kicked him off. The stranger scrambled for the gun that had been knocked from his hands.

He lifted it, pointing directly at Finn's midsection.

Goddamn it.

Finn slowly raised his hands in the air. "Careful."

More curses sounded, but this time they were from the man in front of him. A familiar voice, completely unexpected.

Anger flared. *"Brandon?"*

His mentor's son pushed back his hoodie and glared. "What the hell are you doing out here?"

"Talking to a piece of shit horse thief." He turned his back on Brandon and hurried to see what was wrong with Zach. He knelt beside his friend. "You okay?"

Zach was on the ground, clutching his shoulder. "I dove the wrong direction," he said, his voice shaky. "Fuck."

Finn moved Zach's torn jacket aside to see enough to infuriate him. The shot hadn't gone through his friend, but it was a bad enough graze it probably hurt like hell.

He put Zach's hand back over the wound and pushed down hard. "Pressure. We'll get someone to fix you up right away."

He pulled out his phone to call Josiah while Brandon kept shouting random bullshit in the background.

Rising to his feet, Finn snapped at Brandon, "Shut up, right now. I don't know what the hell's going on, but we'll figure it out after Zach's been fixed up. Put that damn gun on the ground and get your ass over here."

Brandon just stood there, hand shaking, gun still pointed in Finn's direction. "Did I shoot him? I didn't mean to shoot him."

He was on the edge of tears, definitely not coherent.

"You don't pull out a gun and point it at a person unless you intend to shoot them." Finn roared the words. "Put the damn gun down *now*."

Nothing changed. If anything, the gun wiggled even more.

"I didn't mean it," Brandon cried again. "It was an accident."

Hell. Finn raised a hand, trying to calm the man, but it was no use. Brandon grew more hysterical, the shotgun waving in the air with zero finesse as he shouted *accident* over and over.

"Of course, it was an accident. He's fine," Finn said loudly, trying to break through the panic.

"It's your fault, you know." Brandon raised his gaze to Finn, and the damn gun rose again.

In spite of the man being an absolute chickenshit, at that moment Finn was convinced he was about to be shot anyway. When a loud *crack* rang out, he even flinched, waiting for pain to rip through his body.

Instead, Brandon screamed. He fell to the ground and clutched his lower leg.

All the breath whooshed out of Finn.

He glanced at Zach.

His friend shook his head, pointing toward the river. "I'll be damned."

Out from the nearby cluster of trees, Karen Coleman stepped cautiously toward them, a rifle in her hand and a steely look in her eyes as she made her way forward.

Finn met her at the fence line, stopping en route to remove the gun from Brandon's proximity.

"Good shot," he told her.

She raised a brow and answered without a trace of irony. "He looked like he needed shooting."

A comment which for some reason struck Finn as absolutely hysterical.

Behind him were two men in need of medical help, but in front of him was the woman he loved, who had been willing, and able, to put a bullet in someone for his sake.

He brought her over the fence and into his arms.

23

———

*T*he next hours passed in a blur, and Finn's hand in hers was the only thing that kept Karen centered.

It wasn't even the shock of having shot a man. There had been a gun pointed at Finn, and Brandon's obviously increasing stress had made that move a given.

It was everything *else*. The interrupted trail ride, chasing down the wildies. Finding out Zach had been shot—

Thankfully, it was only a surface wound. It had only taken a couple minutes for Julia to bandage him up. "You'll have a nice scar, but it shouldn't affect your range of motion."

She took care of Brandon's calf wound as well, and the EMT had been perhaps not quite as gentle in her caregiving as Karen had seen her with other patients.

Now Brandon sat on a chair in Cody's office, being watched closely by their foreman as they waited the arrival of yet another visitor.

Another visitor who wasn't the RCMP, which added more confusion on top of the rest of it.

"You sure we don't have to call the police?" Not that Karen

wanted a record or any of the rest of it, but contacting the authorities just seemed the thing to do after shooting a man.

Well, technically *two* men, since Brandon had shot Zach as well.

"Alan said not to, and considering who did what to whom, we'll just wait until we hear what he has to say for right now." Finn pressed a kiss to her temple and poured more tea in her cup. "Relax."

It wasn't as if everybody knew, either. Right now, Julia, Zach, and Finn knew she'd taken the shot. The rest of them assumed Brandon had been injured with his own gun during the wrestling match. Finn had not gone out of his way to correct the assumption.

Karen's friends and family had gone home after everyone had returned from the wilderness and the mares had been led back to the barn.

Now she, Finn, and Zach waited in her living room for their bigshot lawyer to arrive.

"You know this is weird, right?" Karen told the two of them pointedly. "Most people don't have this kind of relationship with a lawyer."

"You mean the type where the man hops on a private plane in the middle of the night to come deal with dicey situations?" Zach lifted his glass in the air, the bandage on his shoulder pushing against the fabric of his T-shirt. "Welcome to the family."

"I should be drinking what you're having and not this tea," Karen muttered.

Finn offered his glass. "All yours if you want."

"I need my head about me in case this lawyer of yours expects me to be coherent." She stole a sip before she handed the glass back, though.

Once the burn of liquor faded, she cuddled up against him.

The room went slightly hazy as her eyes drooped. Finn and Zach continued to talk softly while the fire crackled in the stove.

She must've fallen asleep, dropping after the adrenaline rush, because the next thing she knew, there was light on the horizon and someone rattling around in the kitchen.

She was still on the couch and in Finn's arms, which struck her as pretty much perfect.

Karen glanced up to find him gazing at her contentedly. "Hey."

He bumped their noses together. "Hey. Want to go get freshened up? Alan's about two minutes out. He'll talk to Brandon first, then we'll get this dealt with so we can move on. Okay?"

Which is how half an hour later she ended up at her kitchen table with a stranger in a five-thousand-dollar suit to her right and the man she'd shot directly across from her.

There had to be a better way to phrase that. Because really, she'd only shot him a *little*.

Alan's expression screamed disapproval as he stared at Brandon before focusing his attention on Zach and Finn. "Here's what it comes down to. Brandon's been trying to sabotage your plans to be operational in time to win the challenge."

Zach mock gasped. "Colour me shocked. Brandon? Deceitful and underhanded?"

The lawyer continued. "He paid someone else for the first while, and then when you increased security and his hired help ran, he decided he had to come out and mess with you himself."

"You rat bastard," Zach said softly, his amusement vanishing. "You had someone light the fire and steal supplies, didn't you?"

Brandon stared at the floor.

Alan spoke firmly. "He also personally booby-trapped the building that fell in on Finn."

The entire situation had been unreal, but that comment broke through her incredulousness. Karen's palms hit the table. "*What?* What did you just say?"

"It was only supposed to make you fail the challenge so I could get what I deserved." There was zero trace of repentance in Brandon's voice.

The numbness inside flared to fury. Karen found herself on her feet, staring at the man who'd caused Finn so much pain. "I should have shot you three feet higher. You might have killed Finn."

"It was supposed to collapse when no one was around," Brandon insisted. "It was an accident."

"Just like you *accidentally* shot Zach?" The fury inside her wasn't healthy. "We're pressing charges."

"Wait, you can't do that. You *deliberately* shot me," Brandon whined, his gaze darting around the room as if hoping someone would take his side. "You'll be charged too."

She leaned in, staring into his frightened eyes.

This *asshole* had caused Finn to be hurt, and while the man she loved had recovered, he'd suffered needlessly.

She was beyond pissed.

Every bit of the protective anger roiling through her rang out as she snapped her response. "*Bring it.* No jury on earth would convict me."

Finn caught her fingers in his, tugging her into his lap. "Let's hear what Alan has to say."

His grip was less of a restraint and more a claiming. Holding himself in a circle around her, yet allowing her power to remain visible—and she had to be vibrating at the moment. She was ready to reach over and pull Brandon's head from his shoulders with her bare hands.

Finn's arms were possessive in a way that made it clear he was proud to have her there with him.

That they were together.

Alan straightened, dipping his chin toward her and Finn before returning his attention to the bastard on the far side of the table.

"Obviously, there will be consequences. But when we spoke privately a few minutes ago, Brandon agreed that *he* will not press charges for the incident that caused him to be *accidentally* injured if you will not get the police involved regarding his actions, including horse thievery and sabotage."

Finn stroked his hand over her thigh, soothing her. It took everything in her to not shout at Brandon a little longer.

What she did manage was a fairly reasonable tone as she directed a question at the lawyer. "And those consequences you mentioned?"

Because hiding the body was on her list.

Alan met her gaze. "Brandon will get a very small monthly stipend from his father's estate under the condition that he never contact any of you again. If he breaks that rule, or interferes in your lives in anyway, he will lose all future income and at that time will be charged with every crime we can lay at his feet, which I promise *will* involve jail time."

Zach cleared his throat, his expression not so cool and collected as she'd come to expect from the man. He was as pissed as she was. "So he gets a reward for having tried to ruin us."

"There are reasons," Alan said blandly.

At that comment, Finn straightened slightly. He leaned forward to whisper in her ear. "That means we'll get the real story soon. Stop sharpening your knives—I think Alan has a plan in our favour."

Karen glanced at Zach. The man had leaned back in his

chair and was now eyeing Brandon as if he were an interesting bug on a pin. No more fury. As if the strong prairie wind outside had wiped it clean.

"We need your approval before this is a done deal." Alan met her gaze straight on. "Are you willing to trust me?"

Clearly Finn and Zach did, so as hard as it was to let her urge for more punishment go, she nodded.

"I'd suggest Mr. Travers avoid accidentally crossing paths with us. I'm sure your justice would be thorough." She stared the man in his pasty white face and let her anger shine bright. "Mine would be quick."

"Bloodthirsty woman," Finn whispered again. He tightened the arm around her waist and eased back enough to let the heat of his body wrap around her.

"I'll be back." Alan escorted a limping Brandon to the door. Zach rose to his feet to accompany them.

The instant they left the room, Finn had her turned, hand controlling her nape as he stared into her eyes with amusement. "You are one seriously sexy hellion. I'm tempted to haul you into the bedroom right now and fuck you boneless."

"He *hurt* you," Karen said firmly. "He deserves to suffer."

"*Hmmm*, there we go again. Bloodthirsty looks good on you." Finn covered her mouth with his own before she could laugh, and then fire and heat rushed them.

Bedroom? If she didn't know they'd have returning company in a few minutes, she'd have taken him right there in the kitchen.

The kiss would have to be enough for now. Possessive and wildly intimate, he stroked his tongue along hers and set her nerve endings tingling. She thrust her fingers into his hair and pressed their torsos together.

"Jeez, guys. Give me a break." Zach said as he came back in, amusement in his teasing tone. "I'd tell you to get a room, but Alan is just sending off the Asshole Achievement Winner of the Decade and then he'll be back."

Finn separated them slowly. "We will finish this. Soon."

"Definitely," Karen agreed before sliding off his lap and retaking her own chair. Without a blush, she met Zach's laughing eyes. What burned between her and Finn was undeniable. "So. This whole 'operating outside the law' is part and parcel for you guys?"

Finn shook his head even as he pulled her chair closer to tangle their fingers together more easily. As if willing to give her some distance, but only so much. "Usually we're very legal-minded. Alan, you've got some explaining to do." He turned to the door as Alan returned to the kitchen.

Lawyer man leaned back on the counter and folded his arms over his chest in a surprisingly relaxed pose considering everything that had just happened. He looked the three of them over before nodding firmly. "I suppose I do. And then we need to talk about you, young lady."

His gaze settled on her.

Yeah. That's what Karen had figured. At some point, the shit had to hit the fan.

Only Finn was smiling, and Zach's eyes had widened, and the tension seemed to fade from everyone else, only to pool in her toes.

She lifted her chin and braced.

It had never been boring. The time spent with Bruce and the ensuing years of lessons had meant Finn was kept on his toes, but this night had been one bizarre twist after the other.

Still, when he glanced at Zach, his best friend waited

patiently, a broad smile on his face and absolute chill in his body language. No concern from that quarter.

Of course, the man was hell at the poker table...

Taking charge of the room as if it were his office, Alan got their attention then dove in.

"I'll put you out of your misery quickly and get this list out of the way. First, the challenge is off. You no longer have to have the ranch up and running by Thanksgiving, although I still plan to bring my family out to be your first guests, whenever you feel is a reasonable time-frame to open." Alan held up a hand to stop Zach's sputtering. "Whether you want to go double time or not is up to you. At this point, you've already satisfied the conditions of Bruce's challenge. If I may?"

He pulled a long envelope out of his pocket and handed it to Karen. "Would you read this, please?"

She looked spooked, and rightly so considering Alan's earlier pointed comment about her, but she went ahead. Glancing over the words quickly before reading in a clear, firm voice.

"Once again, I can picture you boys, and the thought makes me smile. Of course, right now you're probably cursing me a little, but you'll see reason in a minute.

I wrote up three letters this time, but I bet you're reading this one. The second was a letter congratulating you on completing the challenge (I know you could do it if you had to). The third was commiserating that you hadn't, and to be honest, I didn't put any effort into that note because it was a one in a hundred chance that you'd fail.

Does it make it easier if I say this challenge wasn't for you?

I know my son. After all the chances I gave him, he's probably been making your life hell since I died, demanding "what he deserves." Which is a swift kick in the pants, but at this point he's made his choices and it's hard to change when he doesn't think there's a need.

Now that he's got steady money on the line, he should leave you alone. If he doesn't, he loses that portion of his easy life. I hope he'll make the smart decision this go-round.

Alan will tell you the rest of the details, but know that I'm proud of you. I'm counting on you to use your inheritance to build up your community, not just enjoy the easy life.

Raise a glass for me, boys. You're my arrows shot into the future. Make them count."

Karen folded the paper back up slowly. "The challenge wasn't for Finn and Zach. It was for...*Brandon?*"

Alan nodded as he took back the envelope. "That's why I brought him here when we started. He knew exactly what was going on and what you were dealing with. If he'd left you alone and you'd succeeded, he would have gotten a settlement as well, but twice as big. Now, he should be out of your hair, and mine, hopefully forever." Alan made a face as he met Finn's gaze. "I'm sorry about the accident, though, and that stupid incident with the gun. Totally out of character for the man."

"It *was* an accident," Finn acknowledged, hoping to keep Karen from flaring into protective mode again. "I agree. Brandon was not his usual wishy-washy self. No way you could have known, and frankly, if we go forward without ever having to see him again, I'm good with it."

Zach leaned forward. "To clarify—the challenge was to see

if Brandon would be an inferring asshole. He was, and we have proof, so the deadline is over."

"Correct."

Zach shook his head. "Wild."

"Next detail," Alan continued. "You will find that your holdings have now doubled as the side funds drop into the corporate accounts."

Holy hell. Finn and Zach gaped at each other. "That part is real?"

Alan nodded. "Now that we're fairly certain Brandon will never be an issue, Bruce felt it appropriate to expand your control."

Karen looked confused, so Finn went for the simplest explanation. "The corporation has different branches. Bruce just added one we didn't know about, which increases the value by a lot."

"Wow. Okay."

"We'll go over that in more detail later." Alan's attention turned fully on Karen. "I haven't had the pleasure of a formal introduction."

Alan's comment made her blink. Finn cleared his throat. "Karen, this is Alan, our touchstone in the world of mysterious finance and all things from beyond the grave. Alan, this is Karen Coleman."

She held out her hand.

Alan shook it briefly then dipped his chin. "So. You're here, listening to this entire conversation, which I assume means you're involved in more than simply shooting Brandon. Thank you for that, by the way. I've had dreams about shooting the bastard myself."

Karen's lips twitched. "You're welcome?"

The expression in Alan's eyes warned Finn a split second too late to leap in.

"Karen. What are your intentions regarding Finn?"

For fuck's sake.

She opened and shut her mouth a couple of times before narrowing her gaze. "Don't know how that's any of your business."

"Humour me. Would you say you're in a long-term relationship with Mr. Marlette?"

Finn eased forward in his chair. "In the interest of not scaring my woman off just when we've made some progress, yes, we're together. Get on with it."

Alan grinned as he reached into his pocket. "Good thing I came prepared."

He held another white envelope toward Karen

She eyed it as if it were a snake. "Do I even want to know? Dead or not, this mentor of yours seems to enjoy meddling in people's lives."

"It'll be okay. Take the envelope." The reassurance came from Zach. All trace of his grin was gone, just a big-brotherly concern and comfort offered as he tilted his head toward the letter. "If it's something terrible, Finn's got your back. Which means I've got your back as well. Just like you had ours."

He really was the best friend a man could have.

Finn waited in silence as Karen turned her gaze on him. Her mouth quirked. "Never a dull moment, buttercup."

Her smile lasted until she unfolded the message and a slim slip of paper floated toward the floor. She caught it in midair and glanced at the face.

She froze, shock painting her features.

She blinked.

A second later she grabbed for the letter and lifted it, reading rapidly.

The three men sat in silence. Finn wasn't sure if this would be the start of something wonderful or if she would grab her shotgun and use it on Alan.

Karen shook her head. "This doesn't happen to people."

"I assure you, Ms. Coleman, it's real," Alan said. "Do you have any questions?"

"Give me a minute." She poked the letter at Finn. "What the hell?"

Bruce's familiar script covered the page, the sight hitting Finn hard.

The message hit harder.

Sadly, I'm unable to greet you in person. I know you're an amazing woman, though, because Finn would never get involved with anyone who wasn't as smart, talented, and driven as himself.

Which isn't always a good thing. That driven part. It means priorities sometimes get blurred. A good partner in a man's life encourages him to take time to appreciate what's important.

That doesn't mean you get to ignore your dreams while convincing the stubborn ass to smell the roses. So this is yours. No guidelines, no expectations. If you leave tomorrow, this is still yours. Ironclad and irrevocable—Alan will make sure of that.

But I hope that you'll stay, not only for Finn's sake but your own. He's a good man. I want the best for him, and since he picked you as a partner, that's all the recommendation I need.

Welcome to the family,
Bruce

Finn barely finished reading when she laid the cheque across the letter.

He counted zeroes to make sure he wasn't mistaken. That was a hell of a big number.

Karen's breathing was slightly out of kilter. "What's going on?"

It was impossible to sit two feet away from her when all he wanted was her in his arms. Finn gave in to temptation and scooped her back onto his lap, ignoring Zach's chuckle and Alan's outright laugh.

The fact she didn't fight him said more about how unsettled she was than anything.

Finn stroked a hand up her back, petting and soothing even as happiness warmed inside him. His mentor's blessing was a powerful thing, even postscript as it was.

He hurried to answer her question. "What's going on is that it appears you have joined the ranks of Bruce's select protégés. That comes with financial blessings. Congrats."

She lifted a shaky finger to point at the cheque Zach was now examining. "That's for a million dollars, Finn. I can't take that. That's…impossible."

"Are you saying you don't want it?" Alan eyed her sternly.

"I didn't do anything for—" Karen screeched to a stop as she turned to Finn. "Do *you* need the money?"

"Nope," he assured her. "Zach and I are good."

Determination straightened her spine as Karen met Alan's eyes. "I don't want it. It's not mine."

"So you want me to give it to Brandon and—"

A very off-colour curse rang out before she clapped a hand over her mouth. She glared at Alan hard enough it should have lit his hair on fire. "You'd better be kidding."

"Actually, I am." Alan ducked to avoid the Kleenex box

Zach launched at his head. "Just trying to lighten the mood. I mean, it's only money. Give it away if you don't want it."

Her gaze narrowed. "Fine. Do your lawyer thing, then. We'll give it to some charities." Karen wrinkled her nose and turned to Finn. "The animal shelter that Lisa helped set up. It could probably use some money, right?"

"Yup." Finn nodded.

She paused. "And the equine therapy school I was going to attend. They fund scholarships."

The happiness inside was growing. "You can set up a few of those. Alan will help. There are ways to set them up where the income reinvests and keeps producing more money."

A slow nod followed. Karen accepted the cheque back from Zach, shaking her head slightly as she stared at it again in disbelief. "Impossible."

"You keep using that word. I don't think it means what—" Finn found his mouth covered by her hand.

"Hush. *You're* impossible." She blew out a hard breath, as if trying to put out a candle all the way on the other side of the room. But when she raised her gaze to meet Alan's, all confusion was gone. "Thank you. I don't understand what's going on, but I'll accept this money and follow the advice Bruce gave the guys. We'll use it to make our community better, although, *God*, I have no idea how to do this."

Finn pressed his lips to her temple, holding her tightly in his arms where she belonged.

It wasn't about the money they had in their pockets. It was about moving into the future side by side. Building a future right here in Heart Falls.

Her fingers around his tightened. Connected.

Together. *Finally.*

24

With the challenge deadline gone, Finn and Zach both insisted they needed to slow down and get their lives back on an even keel.

"I have a lot of brew-pub beer to try before I get my place up and running next year." Zach eyed the still-incomplete interior of the ranch house they'd relocated to after Alan left. "I probably should pick one of the cabins and finish it before the snow flies so I can live in it comfortably this winter."

"You're not fixing this place up?" Karen asked.

Finn slid in beside her, one strong hand coming to rest on her hip as he twisted her toward the tall windows facing the west. "Zach suggested, and I agreed, that *we* figure out the remodel for this house. Since we're staying in Heart Falls for good, we need a home where we can have family over without bumping into each other. What do you think?"

Another bit of information tossed on top of her already overloaded brain. Yet Finn's grip was firm, but not controlling, and his question was sincere.

She took a deep breath. What would spark joy?

The mountains outside were brightening with the morning sun, late summer green mixing with the golden shades of grasses and crops. Karen pictured living there full time, enjoying the view as the changing seasons brought fall colours before snow would blanket the entire landscape in pristine white.

She turned toward Finn and then eyed Zach, thought of the laughter and discussions that would be held in the evenings by the massive fireplace. Imagined the floors not as plywood, but rich oak. The walls painted with sunlight and pictures of family and friends.

Rooms down the hall with space for family to visit...and children to grow up in.

Happiness welled. "I have so many questions right now, but that one I can answer. I would love to make this our home."

Finn captured her fingers and lifted them to his mouth, kissing her knuckles.

"I'll be back." Zach was already marching out the door, hat firmly in place. "Need to talk to Cody and make some plans. See you guys at lunch."

He winked before firmly shutting the door.

In front of her, Finn still held her hand trapped in his. "I thought he'd never leave."

She chuckled. "He's a good friend. I'm glad he wasn't hurt any worse."

"Me too. Now shut up about Zach." Finn stroked his fingers along her jaw, finishing with his palm cradling her cheek. "I want to build a home with you, and I want it all."

Her throat tightened. "Me too."

"All of it. Every morning, every night. Fights and laughter, family and friends. Kittens in the house, colts in the barn, and children underfoot."

Karen sucked in a breath. "Okay."

He chuckled, leaning in to brush his lips over hers. "You willing to take my name as well?"

"Maybe." She eased her arms around his hips, nestling against him. "You plan to ask? Because if I ask, you'd have to take *my* name, and there's already a lot of Colemans in the world."

Finn paused. "Wait a second." He dipped, scooping up Dandelion Fluff. "No idea how you got over here, but fine..."

He nestled the kitten between them.

"Kittens in the house we've got covered," Karen teased, her heart brimming with joy.

"Marry me, *ma chérie*. I'll do everything I can to make you happy."

She held on tight. "Yes, I'll marry you, and you already do."

The kiss was brief because the furry creature between them wiggled, seeking his freedom.

Before Finn moved away, Karen caught him by the arm. "I want a prenup, though." Surprise flashed on his face as she hurried to explain. "Just in case there's more beyond-the-grave mischief left by your mentor."

Her solid, even-tempered man threw back his head and laughed loud enough the sound bounced off the walls of their future home. When he got it back under control, he kissed her tenderly, a grin on his lips. "Brilliant woman. *Brilliant* idea."

Karen was still smiling from ear to ear that afternoon when they headed over to Silver Stone to catch up with her sisters and let them know the news.

She paused on the stoop outside the kitchen and peeked through the back window. Inside the house, people moved in an easy rhythm, voices raised in laughter. Her sister's faces showed contentment. Children's voices danced along with the low rumble of masculine tones.

A hand slipped over her hip as Finn pressed tight to her

side. Waiting for her to move. Waiting, patiently as always. "Happy?"

She took a deep breath then turned.

Sunlight shone on his face, his eyes bright with love. Finn Marlette was a perfect fit against the background of rolling hills and ranch buildings.

He was the perfect fit for her world.

Karen pressed a hand to his cheek, warmth spreading against her palm. "I've found what sparks joy in my world, and I'm ready to make sure everyone knows. You're not a secret, Finn Marlette. There's too much love inside me for you to ever be a secret again."

Finn leaned in close. "Dammit, woman. Now I've got to kiss you until I don't look one step away from weeping my fool head off."

Amusement rose. "Tears are okay," she reminded him.

"Kisses are better," he insisted.

His demonstration of that fact left her breathless and one hundred percent in agreement.

Secrets were over. Now was the time for joy.

EPILOGUE

R ough Cut pub was that perfect mix of local watering hole and nightclub. With the music turned up to eleven, the full-to-the-rafters crowd seemed determined to enjoy the final night of August with a vengeance.

Over the past five months, Julia had gotten to know a number of people around Heart Falls, including her newfound sisters and some great friends from their girls' night out events. But tonight wasn't about family time.

With two entire days off ahead of her, Julia was ready to kick up her heels and enjoy herself by dancing the night away. No commitments, no relationship building. Just an old old-fashioned dance 'til you drop evening.

She left her most recent partner, grinning as she spotted Brad and Hanna Ford huddled at a high-top table.

They were so cute. It was rare to see her boss and his wife out on the town like this, what with basically being newly-weds *and* having a preteen kid.

Julia swung by the table and placed a hand on Brad's

shoulder. "Hey, boss man. Hanna. Night on the town without the kiddo?"

Hanna offered a smile. "She's at a friend's. We came to dance for a while."

Julia gestured toward the floor. "It's high-speed out there right now."

The night had been busy enough to offer her a wide variety of partners to two-step with, but every now and then, even she had to catch her breath.

Karen and Finn flashed past. He had her tight against him as he spun her quickly. Her head fell back and laughter rang out over the toe-tapping music.

"We're waiting for a little slower song before we join in," Brad confessed, his kind smile taking her in. "You've been working up a sweat."

"It's easier training than hauling hoses up the stairs of doom," Julia told him. "But yeah, I need to catch my breath. I'll see you guys later."

In the corner of the room, Lisa and Josiah were talking quietly while he stared at her like she was the only woman in the world.

Julia's sisters had good solid guys in their lives, and she was glad for them. She had zero desire to follow in their footsteps, though. Not right now, that was for sure.

She headed to the bathroom, pausing to wash her face and hands first. Her cheeks were flushed and beads of sweat clung to the back of her neck, but so far the evening had been a blast.

Pit stop, then a cold drink. Then she'd keeping finding guys to dance with until they shut the place down.

The door to her bathroom stall had barely closed when a rush of voices filled the women's bathroom. Julia ignored the chatter, going about her business—

"I swear it's true. It's disgusting, really. They haven't even been married two months."

This was said at a far, far lower volume. Julia froze.

Another woman spoke up, also barely above a whisper. "He should know better, though. He's been such a good person up until now—coming back to town to care for his dad."

"Guys don't think with anything but their dicks at times."

"Right? I bet everyone will notice before too long. Cheating once is bad enough. Ongoing? Not even Brad can survive that."

Anger flared. Of all the contemptible ideas. For anyone to assume that Brad was cheating on Hanna? Outrageous.

"She seems so nice, but I guess that's how cheaters get away with it." The second woman spoke a little louder, as if feeling more confident.

It had to be a misunderstanding because no way in hell would Brad ever—

"She's only here for a couple more months. That's what I heard."

"She'll come back to visit her sisters, though. It's a terrible thing. I wouldn't want this for anyone, let alone sweet Hanna. Poor thing's gone through so much." Firmer. Getting bolder. "I feel like I should tell that Julia Blushing we don't want her kind around here. She needs to..."

The rush of blood in Julia's ears drowned out the rest of the righteous declaration.

Her? They thought she and Brad were having an *affair?*

Oh. My. God.

She sat on the toilet seat in silence, the room spinning slightly.

By the time she pulled herself together, the bathroom had gone quiet.

No. This was *not* happening. For people to think her and Brad's friendship was anything other than—

Well, if she were absolutely honest it *was* more than

friendship on her part, but not *romantic* interest. And definitely not sexual.

She had to fix this, and now.

Somehow.

Julia snuck out of the washroom and cautiously slipped into the relative darkness of the bar. Sliding along in the shadows until she found a place to observe while she figured out what the hell her next move should be.

How did she prove she and Brad weren't having an affair without ever mentioning the absurd idea? The last things she wanted were to hurt Hanna or ruin Brad's reputation...

Karen and Finn spun past again, the lock between them so tight a crowbar couldn't have pried them apart.

The next moment they were gone, and for a split second a clear path opened all the way across the dance floor to the far side of the room.

There, Zach Sorenson leaned on a pillar, beer in hand and heel tapping as he scanned the room, keeping a watchful eye on his surroundings.

Zach, with his dark good looks and cheeky grin. The man who had made her laugh so hard at a party earlier this year that she'd been tempted to get involved even though she knew from experience short-term relationships weren't a good idea.

Still...

Zach—who was most definitely single and therefore a possible solution to her immediate problem.

If she was already involved with someone, that would reduce the odds she was fooling around with anyone else. Yes?

Julia didn't think twice. Heck, she didn't really even think once. Just let her feet start moving as soon as the idea was partially formed in her brain. If she went too deep into details, somewhere there'd be a flaw, and this moment was for action, not doubts.

Twenty seconds later she was closing in on the man. Eyeing him in the hopes of spotting a clue of how he'd take her demand.

Suggestion?

Nope, she would *demand*. It had to be done for Hanna's sake, and Brad's, and now, before the rumour mill got out of hand and things were unfixable.

She stopped in front of tall, dark, and sexy.

His lazy smile beamed down on her. "Hey, Jules."

"Hey." Julia took a deep breath.

One dark brow rose. "Problem?"

She shook her head. "Nope."

One hand on his arm, Julia leaned in while she went up on her toes, pushing her torso against his so it looked as if she was about to steal a kiss.

His eyes widened.

"Favour, stat. Kiss me," she whispered before he ruined it by pushing her away.

Zach had his hands on her hips now. Eyes narrowing. "You playing a game again, Blushing?"

She laughed softly, forcing a smile because there were people watching. She brushed her cheek past his then spoke as quietly as possible. "I swear I will explain, but you've got to kiss me, *now*. Like I'm your girlfriend. *Please*."

Maybe it was the desperation in her tone, or maybe he just wanted to tease her brain into meltdown mode.

Because the next thing she knew, Zach had wrapped one big hand around her nape. He slid the other around to palm her lower back. A slight bit of pressure tugged her against him, nice and firm, and then he dipped his head in close.

"No idea what you're up to, but I'm game."

His lips hit hers, and the slow, teasing touch she expected flared into a white-hot blaze as he took control.

~

New York Times Bestselling Author Vivian Arend
invites you to Heart Falls. These contemporary ranchers live in
a tiny town in central Alberta, tucked into the rolling foothills.
Enjoy the ride as they each find their happily-ever-afters.

~

The Stones of Heart Falls
A Rancher's Heart
A Rancher's Song
A Rancher's Bride

Holidays in Heart Falls
A Firefighter's Christmas Gift
A Soldier's Christmas Wish
A Hero's Christmas Hope
A Cowboy's Christmas List
A Rancher's Christmas Kiss

The Colemans of Heart Falls
The Cowgirl's Forever Love
The Cowgirl's Secret Love
The Cowgirl's Chosen Love

~

ABOUT THE AUTHOR

With over 2.5 million books sold, Vivian Arend is a *New York Times* and *USA Today* bestselling author of over 60 contemporary and paranormal romance books, including the Six Pack Ranch and Granite Lake Wolves.

Her books are all standalone reads with no cliffhangers. They're humorous yet emotional, with sexy-times and happily-ever-afters. Vivian pretty much thinks she's got the best job in the world, and she's looking forward to giving readers more HEAs. She lives in B.C. Canada with her husband of many years and a fluffy attack Shih-tzu named Luna who ignores everyone except when treats are deployed.

www.vivianarend.com